THE JOURNEY BEGINS . . .

With the first thin line of pink the coyotes hanging on the flanks of the great encampment raised their immemorial salutation to the dawn. Their clamorings were stilled by a new and sterner voice—the notes of the bugle summoning sleepers of the last night to the duties of the first day. Down the line from watch to watch passed the Plains command, "Catch up! Catch up!" It was the morning of the jump-off.

Little fires began at the wagon messes or family bivouacs. Men, boys, barefooted girls went out into the dew-wet grass to round up the transport stock. A vast confusion, a medley of unskilled endeavor marked the hour. But after an hours' wait, adjusted to the situation, the next order passed down the line:

"Roll out! Roll out!"

And now the march to Oregon was at last begun! The first dust cut by an ox hoof was set in motion by the whip crack of a barefooted boy in jeans who had no dream that he one day would rank high in the councils of his state, at the edge of an ocean which no prairie boy had ever envisioned. . . .

THE
COVERED
WAGON

Emerson Hough

A TOM DOHERTY ASSOCIATES BOOK
NEW YORK

This is a work of fiction. All the characters and events portrayed in this book are either products of the author's imagination or are used fictitiously.

THE COVERED WAGON

A Forge Book
Published by Tom Doherty Associates, LLC
175 Fifth Avenue
New York, NY 10010

www.tor.com

Forge® is a registered trademark of Tom Doherty Associates, LLC.

ISBN: 0-812-56688-2

First Forge edition: March 2000

Printed in the United States of America

0 9 8 7 6 5 4 3 2 1

Contents

Chapter I

YOUTH MARCHES

Look at 'em come, Jesse! More and more! Must be forty or fifty families."

Molly Wingate, middle-aged, portly, dark browed and strong, stood at the door of the rude tent which for the time made her home. She was pointing down the road which lay like an écru ribbon thrown down across the prairie grass, bordered beyond by the timber-grown bluffs of the Missouri.

Jesse Wingate allowed his team of harness-marked horses to continue their eager drinking at the watering hole of the little stream near which the camp was pitched until, their thirst quenched, they began burying their muzzles and blowing into the water in sensuous enjoyment. He stood, a strong and tall man of perhaps forty-five years, of keen blue eye and short, close-matted, tawny beard. His garb was the loose dress of the outlying settler of the Western lands three-quarters of a century ago. A farmer he must have been back home.

Could this encampment, on the very front of the American civilization, now be called a home? Beyond the prairie road could be seen a double furrow of jet-black glistening sod, framing the green grass and its spangling flowers, first browsing of the plow on virgin soil. It might have been the opening of a farm. But if so, why the crude bivouac? Why the gear of travelers? Why the massed arklike wagons, the scores of morning fires lifting lazy blue wreaths of smoke against the morning mists?

The truth was that Jesse Wingate, earlier and impatient on the front, out of the very suppression of energy, had been trying his plow in the first white furrows beyond the Missouri in the great year of 1848. Four hundred other near-by plows alike were avid for the soil of Oregon; as witness this long line of newcomers, late at the frontier rendezvous.

"It's the Liberty wagons from down river," said the campmaster at length. "Missouri movers and settlers from lower Illinois. It's time. We can't lie here much longer waiting for Missouri or Illinois, either. The grass is up."

"Well, we'd have to wait for Molly to end her spring term, teaching in Clay School, in Liberty," rejoined his wife, "else why'd we send her there to graduate? Twelve dollars a month, cash money, ain't to be sneezed at."

"No; nor is two thousand miles of trail between here and Oregon, before snow, to be sneezed at, either. If Molly ain't with those wagons I'll send Jed over for her today. If I'm going to be captain I can't hold the people here on the river any longer, with May already begun."

"She'll be here today," asserted his wife. "She said she would. Besides, I think that's her riding a little one side the road now. Not that I know who all is with her. One young man—two. Well"—with maternal pride—"Molly ain't never lacked for beaus!

"But look at the wagons come!" she added. "All the country's going West this spring, it certainly seems like."

It was the spring gathering of the west-bound wagon-trains, stretching from old Independence to Westport Landing, the spot where that very year the new name of Kansas City was heard among the emigrants as the place of the jump-off. It was now an hour by sun, as these Western people would have said, and the low-lying valley mists had not yet fully risen, so that the atmosphere for a great picture did not lack.

It was a great picture, a stirring panorama of an earlier day, which now unfolded. Slow, swaying, stately, the ox teams came on, as though impelled by and not compelling the fleet of white canvas sails. The teams did not hasten, did not abate their speed, but moved in an unagitated advance that gave the massed column something irresistibly epochal in look.

The train, foreshortened to the watchers at the rendezvous, had a well-spaced formation—twenty wagons, thirty, forty, forty-seven—as Jesse Wingate mentally counted them. There were outriders; there were clumps of driven cattle. Along the flanks walked tall men, who flung over the low-headed cattle an admonitory lash whose keen report presently could be heard, still faint and far off. A dull dust cloud arose, softening the outlines of the prairie ships. The broad gestures of arm and trunk, the monotonous soothing of commands to the sophisticated kine as yet remained vague, so that still it was properly a picture done on a vast canvas— that of the frontier in '48; a picture of might, of inevitableness. Even the sober souls of these waiters rose to it, felt some thrill they themselves had never analyzed.

A boy of twenty, tall, blond, tousled, rode up from the grove back of the encampment of the Wingate family.

"You, Jed?" said his father. "Ride on out and see if Molly's there."

"Sure she is!" commented the youth, finding a plug in the pocket of his jeans. "That's her. Two fellers, like usual."

"Sam Woodhull, of course," said the mother, still hand over eye. "He hung around all winter, telling how him and Colonel Doniphan whipped all Mexico and won the war. If Molly ain't in a wagon of her own, it ain't his fault, anyways! I'll rest assured it's account of Molly's going out to Oregon that he's going too! Well!" And again, "Well!"

"Who's the other fellow, though?" demanded Jed. "I can't place him this far."

Jesse Wingate handed over his team to his son and stepped out into the open road, moved his hat in an impatient signal, half of welcome, half of command. It apparently was observed.

To their surprise, it was the unidentified rider who now set spur to his horse and came on at a gallop ahead of the train. He rode carelessly well, a born horseman. In no more than a few minutes he could be seen as rather a gallant figure of the border cavalier—a border just then more martial than it had been before '46 and the days of "Fifty-Four Forty or Fight."

A shrewd man might have guessed this young man—he was no more than twenty-eight—to have got some military air on a border opposite to that of Oregon; the far Southwest, where Taylor and Scott and the less known Doniphan and many another fighting man had been adding certain thousands of leagues to the soil of this republic. He rode a compact, shot-coupled, cat-hammed steed, coal black and with a dashing forelock reaching almost to his red nostrils—a horse never reared on the fat Missouri corn lands. Neither did this heavy embossed saddle with its silver concho decorations then seem familiar so far north; nor yet the thin braided-leather bridle with its hair frontlet band and its mighty bit; nor again the great spurs with jingling rowel bells. This rider's mount and trappings spoke the far and new Southwest, just then coming into our national ken.

The young man himself, however, was upon the face of his appearance nothing of the swashbuckler. True, in his close-cut leather trousers, his neat boots, his tidy gloves, his rather jaunty broad black hat of felted beaver, he made a somewhat raffish figure of a man as he rode up, weight on his under thigh, sidewise, and hand on his horse's quarters, carelessly; but his clean cut, unsmiling features, his direct and grave look out of dark eyes, spoke him a gentleman of his day and place, and no mere spectacular pretender assuming a virtue though he had it not.

He swung easily out of saddle, his right hand on the tall, broad Spanish horn as easily as though rising from a chair at presence of a lady, and removed his beaver to this frontier woman before he accosted her husband. His bridle he flung down over his horse's head, which seemingly anchored the animal, spite of its loud whinnying challenge to these near-by stolid creatures which showed harness rubs and not whitened saddle hairs.

"Good morning, madam," said he in a pleasant, quiet voice. "Good morning, sir. You are Mr. and Mrs. Jesse Wingate, I believe. Your daughter yonder told me so."

"That's my name," said Jesse Wingate, eyeing the newcomer suspiciously, but advancing with ungloved hand. "You're from the Liberty train?"

"Yes, sir. My name is Banion—William Banion. You may not know me. My family were Kentuckians before my father came out to Franklin. I started up in the law at old Liberty town yonder not so long ago, but I've been away a great deal."

"The law, eh?" Jesse Wingate again looked disapproval of the young man's rather pronouncedly neat turnout. "Then you're not going West?"

"Oh, yes, I am, if you please, sir. I've done little else all my life. Two years ago I marched with all the others, with Doniphan, for Mexico. Well, the war's over, and the treaty's likely signed. I thought it high time to march back home. But you know how it is—the long trail's in my blood now. I can't settle down."

Wingate nodded. The young man smilingly went on:

"I want to see how it is in Oregon. What with new titles and the like—and a lot of fighting men cast in together out yonder, too—there ought to be as much law out there as here, don't you think? So I'm going to seek my fortune in the Far West. It's too close and tame in here now. I'm"—he smiled just a bit more obviously and deprecatingly—"I'm leading yonder *caballad* of our neighbors, with a bunch of Illinois and Indiana wagons. They call me Col. William Banion. It is not right—I was no more than Will Banion, major under Doniphan. I am not that now."

A change, a shadow came over his face. He shook it off as though it were tangible.

"So I'm at your service, sir. They tell me you've been elected captain of the Oregon train. I wanted to throw in with you if I might, sir. I know we're late—we should have been in last night. I rode in to explain that. May we pull in just beside you, on this water?"

Molly Wingate, on whom the distinguished address of the stranger, his easy manner and his courtesy had not failed to leave their impression, answered before her husband.

"You certainly can, Major Banion."

"Mister Banion, please."

"Well then, Mister Banion. The water and grass is free. The day's young. Drive in and light down. You said you saw our daughter, Molly—I know you did, for that's her now."

The young man colored under his bronze of tan, suddenly shy.

"I did," said he. "The fact is, I met her earlier this spring at Clay Seminary, where she taught. She told me you-all were moving West this spring—said this was her last day. She asked if she might ride out with our wagons to the rendezvous. Well—"

"That's a fine horse you got there," interrupted young Jed Wingate. "Spanish?"

"Yes, sir."

"Wild?"

"Oh, no, not now; only of rather good spirit. Ride him if you like. Gallop back, if you'd like to try him, and tell my people to come on and park in here. I'd like a word or so with Mr. Wingate."

With a certain difficulty, yet insistent, Jed swung into the deep saddle, sitting the restive, rearing horse well enough withal, and soon was off at a fast pace down the trail. They saw him pull up at the head of the caravan and motion, wide armed, to the riders, the train not halting at all.

He joined the two equestrian figures on ahead, the girl and the young man whom his mother had named as Sam Woodhull. They could see him shaking hands, then doing a curvet or so to show off his newly borrowed mount.

"He takes well to riding, your son," said the newcomer approvingly.

"He's been crazy to get West," assented the father. "Wants to get among the buffalo."

"We all do," said Will Banion. "None left in Kentucky this generation back; none now in Missouri. The Plains!" His eye gleamed.

"That's Sam Woodhull along," resumed Molly Wingate. "He was with Doniphan."

"Yes."

Banion spoke so shortly that the good dame, owner of a sought-for daughter, looked at him keenly.

"He lived at Liberty, too. I've known Molly to write of him."

"Yes?" suddenly and with vigor. "She knows him then?"

"Why, yes."

"So do I," said Banion simply. "He was in our regiment—captain and adjutant, paymaster and quartermaster-chief, too, sometimes. The Army Regulations never meant much with Doniphan's column. We did as we liked—and did the best we could, even with paymasters and quartermasters!"

He colored suddenly, and checked, sensitive to a possible charge of jealousy before this keen-eyed mother of a girl whose beauty had been the talk of the settlement now for more than a year.

The rumors of the charm of Molly Wingate—Little Molly, as her father always called her to distinguish her from her mother—now soon were to have actual and undeniable verification to the eye of any skeptic who mayhap had doubted mere rumors of a woman's beauty. The three advance figures—the girl, Woodhull, her brother Jed—broke away and raced over the remaining few hundred yards, coming up abreast, laughing in the glee of youth exhilarated by the feel of good horseflesh under knee and the breath of a vital morning air.

As they flung off, Will Banion scarce gave a look to his own excited steed. He was first with a hand to Molly Wingate as she sprang lightly down, anticipating her other cavalier, Woodhull, who frowned, none too well pleased, as he dismounted.

Molly Wingate ran up and caught her mother in her strong young arms, kissing her roundly, her eyes shining, her cheeks flushed in the excitement of the hour, the additional excitement of the presence of these young men. She must kiss someone.

Yes, the rumors were true, and more than true. The young school-teacher could well carry her title as the belle of old Liberty town here on the far frontier. A lovely lass of eighteen years or so, she was, blue of eye and of abundant red-brown hair of that tint which ever has turned the eyes and heads of men. Her mouth, smiling to show white, even teeth, was wide enough for comfort in a kiss, and turned up strongly at the corners, so that her face seemed always sunny and carefree, were it not for the recurrent grave, almost somber look of the wide-set eyes in moments of repose.

Above the middle height of woman's stature, she had none of the lank irregularity of the typical frontier woman of the early ague lands; but was round and well developed. Above the open collar of her brown riding costume stood the flawless column of a fair and tall white throat. New ripened into womanhood, wholly fit for love, gay of youth and its racing veins, what wonder Molly Wingate could have chosen not from two but twenty suitors of the best in all that countryside? Her conquests had been many since the time when, as a young girl, and fulfilling her parents' desire to educate their daughter, she had come all the way from the Sangamon country of Illinois to the best school then existent so far west—Clay Seminary, of quaint old Liberty.

The touch of dignity gained of the ancient traditions of the South, never lost in two generations west of the Appalachians, remained about the young girl now, so that she rather might have classed above her parents. They, moving from Kentucky into Indiana, from Indiana into Illinois, and now on to Oregon, never in all their toiling days had forgotten their reverence for the gentlemen and ladies who once were their ancestors east of the Blue Ridge. They valued education—felt that it belonged to them, at least through their children.

Education, betterment, progress, advance—those things perhaps lay in the vague ambitions of twice two hundred men who now lay in camp at the border of our unknown empire. They were all Americans—second, third, fourth generation Americans. Wild, uncouth, rude, unlettered, many or most of them, none the less there stood among them now and again some tall flower of that culture for which they ever hungered; for which they fought; for which they now adventured yet again.

Surely American also were these two young men whose eyes now unconsciously followed Molly Wingate in hot craving even of a morning thus far breakfastless, for the young leader had ordered his wagons on to the rendezvous before crack of day. Of the two, young Woodhull, planter and man of means, mentioned by Molly's mother as open suitor, himself at first sight had not seemed so ill a figure, either. Tall, sinewy, well clad for the place and day, even more foppish than Banion in boot and glove, he would have passed well among the damsels of any courthouse day. The saddle and bridle of his mount also were a trace to the elegant, and the horse itself, a classy chestnut that showed Blue Grass blood, even then had cost a pretty penny somewhere, that was sure.

Sam Woodhull, now moving with a half dozen wagons of his own out to Oregon, was reputed well to do; reputed also to be well skilled at cards, at weapons and at women. Townsmen accorded him first place with Molly Wingate, the beauty from east of the river, until Will Banion came back from the wars. Since then had been another manner of war, that as ancient as male and female.

That Banion had known Woodhull in the field in Mexico he already had let slip. What had been the cause of his sudden pulling up of his starting tongue? Would he have spoken too much of that acquaintance? Perhaps a closer look at the loose lips, the high cheeks, the narrow, close-set eyes of young Woodhull, his rather assertive air, his slight, indefinable swagger, his slouch in standing, might have confirmed some skeptic disposed to analysis who would have guessed him less than strong of soul and character. For the most part, such skeptics lacked.

By this time the last belated unit of the Oregon caravan was at hand. The feature of the dusty drivers could be seen. Unlike Wingate, the newly chosen master of the train, who had horses and mules about him, the young leader, Banion, captained only ox teams. They came now, slow footed, steady, low headed, irresistible, indomitable, the same locomotive power that carried the hordes of Asia into Eastern Europe long ago. And as in the days of that invasion the conquerors carried their households, their flocks and herds with them, so now did these half-savage Saxon folk have with them their all.

Lean boys, brown, barefooted girls flanked the trail with driven stock. Chickens clucked in coops at wagon side. Uncounted children thrust out tousled heads from the openings of the canvas covers. Dogs beneath, jostling the tar buckets, barked in hostile salutation. Women in slatted sunbonnets turned impassive gaze from the high front seats, back of which, swung to the bows by leather loops, hung the inevitable family rifle in each wagon. And now, at the tail gate of every wagon, lashed fast for its last long journey, hung also the family plow.

It was '48, and the grass was up. On to Oregon! The ark of our covenant with progress was passing out. Almost it might have been said to have held every living thing, like that other ark of old.

Banion hastened to one side, where a grassy level beyond the little stream still offered stance. He raised a hand in gesture to the right. A sudden note of command came into his voice, lingering from late military days.

"By the right and left flank—wheel! March!"

With obvious training, the wagons broke apart, alternating right and left, until two long columns were formed. Each of these advanced, curving out, then drawing in, until a long ellipse, closed at front and rear, was formed methodically and without break or flaw. It was the barricade of the Plains, the moving fortresses of our soldiers of fortune, going West, across the Plains, across the Rockies, across the deserts that lay beyond. They did not know all these dangers, but they thus were ready for any that might come.

"Look, mother!" Molly Wingate pointed with kindling eye to the wagon maneuver. "We trained them all day yesterday, and long before. Perfect!"

Her gaze mayhap sought the tall figure of the young commander, chosen by older men above his fellow townsman, Sam Woodhull, as captain of the Liberty train. But he now had other duties in his own wagon group.

Ceased now the straining creak of gear and came rattle of yokes as the pins were loosed. Cattle guards appeared and drove the work animals apart to graze. Women clambered down from wagon seats. Sober-faced children gathered their little arms full of wood for the belated breakfast fires; boys came down for water at the stream.

The west-bound paused at the Missouri, as once they had paused at the Don.

A voice arose, of some young man back among the wagons busy at his work, paraphrasing an ante-bellum air:

> *Oh, then, Susannah,*
> *Don't you cry fer me!*
> *I'm goin' out to Oregon,*
> *With my banjo on my knee!*

Chapter II

THE EDGE OF THE WORLD

M ore than two thousand men, women and children
waited on the Missouri for the green fully to tinge the
grasses of the prairies farther west. The waning town of
Independence had quadrupled its population in thirty days.
Boats discharged their customary western cargo at the newer
landing on the river, not far above that town; but it all was
not enough. Men of upper Missouri and lower Iowa had
driven in herds of oxen, horses, mules; but there were not
enough of these. Rumors came that a hundred wagons would
take the Platte this year via the Council Bluffs, higher up
the Missouri; others would join on from St. Jo and Leavenworth.

March had come, when the wild turkey gobbled and strut-
ted resplendent in the forest lands. April had passed, and the
wild fowl had gone north. May, and the upland plovers now
were nesting all across the prairies. But daily had more wagons come, and neighbors had waited for neighbors, tardy at
the great rendezvous. The encampment, scattered up and
down the river front, had become more and more congested.

Men began to know one another, families became acquainted, the gradual sifting and shifting in social values began. Knots and groups began to talk of some sort of accepted government for the common good.

They now were at the edge of the law. Organized society did not exist this side of the provisional government of Oregon, devised as a *modus vivendi* during the joint occupancy of that vast region with Great Britain—an arrangement terminated not longer than two years before. There must be some sort of law and leadership between the Missouri and the Columbia. Amid much bickering of petty politics, Jesse Wingate had some four days ago been chosen for the thankless task of train captain. Though that office had small authority and less means of enforcing its commands, none the less the train leader must be a man of courage, resource and decision. Those of the earlier arrivals who passed by his well-organized camp of forty-odd wagons from the Sangamon country of Illinois said that Wingate seemed to know the business of the trail. His affairs ran smoothly, he was well equipped and seemed a man of means. Some said he had three thousand in gold at the bottom of his cargo. Moreover—and this appeared important among the Northern element, at that time predominant in the rendezvous—he was not a Calhoun Secesh, or even a Benton Democrat, but an out and out, antislavery, free-soil man. And the provisional constitution of Oregon, devised by thinking men of two great nations, had said that Oregon should be free soil forever.

Already there were mutterings in 1848 of the coming conflict which a certain lank young lawyer of Springfield, in the Sangamon country—Lincoln, his name was—two years ago among his personal friends had predicted as inevitable. In a personnel made up of bold souls from both sides the Ohio, politics could not be avoided even on the trail; nor were these men the sort to avoid politics. Sometimes at their camp fire, after the caravan election, Wingate and his wife, their son Jed, would compare notes, in a day when personal politics and national geography meant more than they do today.

"Listen, son," Wingate one time concluded. "All that talk of a railroad across this country to Oregon is silly, of course. But it's all going to be one country. The talk is that the treaty with Mexico must give us a slice of land from Texas to the Pacific, and a big one; all of it was taken for the sake of slavery. Not so Oregon—that's free forever. This talk of splitting this country, North and South, don't go with me. The Alleghanies didn't divide it. Burr couldn't divide it. The Mississippi hasn't divided it, or the Missouri, so rest assured the Ohio can't. No, nor the Rockies can't! A railroad? No, of course not. But all the same, a practical wagon road from free soil to free soil—I reckon that was my platform, like enough. It made me captain."

"No, 'twasn't that, Jesse," said his wife. "That ain't what put you in for train captain. It was your blamed impatience. Some of them lower Ioway men, them that first nominated you in the train meeting—town meeting—what you call it, they seen where you'd been plowing along here just to keep your hand in. One of them says to me, 'Plowing, hey? Can't wait? Well, that's what we're going out for, ain't it—to plow?' says he. 'That's the clean quill,' says he. So they 'lected you, Jesse. And the Lord ha' mercy on your soul!'"

Now the arrival of so large a new contingent as this of the Liberty train under young Banion made some sort of post-election ratification necessary, so that Wingate felt it incumbent to call the head men of the late comers into consultation if for no better than reasons of courtesy. He dispatched his son Jed to the Banion park to ask the attendance of Banion, Woodhull and such of his associates as he liked to bring, at any suiting hour. Word came back that the Liberty men would join the Wingate conference around eleven of that morning, at which time the hour of the jump-off could be set.

Chapter III

THE RENDEZVOUS

As to the start of the great wagon train, little time, indeed, remained. For days, in some instances for weeks, the units of the train had lain here on the border, and the men were growing restless. Some had come a thousand miles and now were keen to start out for more than two thousand miles additional. The grass was up. The men from Illinois, Indiana, Ohio, Iowa, Missouri, Kentucky, Arkansas fretted on the leash.

All along the crooked river front, on both sides from Independence to the river landing at Westport, the great spring caravan lay encamped, or housed in town. Now, on the last days of the rendezvous, a sort of hysteria seized the multitude. The sound of rifle fire was like that of a battle—every man was sighting-in his rifle. Singing and shouting went on everywhere. Someone fresh from the Mexican War had brought a drum, another a bugle. Without instructions, these began to sound their summons and continued all day long, at such times as the performers could spare from drink.

The Indians of the friendly tribes—Otos, Kaws, Osages—

come in to trade, looked on in wonder at the revelings of the whites. The straggling street of each of the near-by river towns was full of massed wagons. The treble line of white tops, end to end, lay like a vast serpent, curving, ahead to the West. Rivalry for the head of the column began. The sounds of the bugle set a thousand uncoordinated wheels spasmodically in motion. Organization, system were as yet unknown in this rude and dominant democracy. Need was therefore for this final meeting in the interest of law, order and authority. Already some wagons had broken camp and moved on out into the main traveled road, which lay plain enough on westward, among the groves and glades of the valley of the Kaw. Each man wanted to be first to Oregon, no man wished to take the dust of his neighbor's wagon.

Wingate brought up all these matters at the train meeting of some three score men which assembled under the trees of his own encampment at eleven of the last morning. Most of the men he knew. Banion unobtrusively took a seat well to the rear of those who squatted on their heels or lolled full length on the grass.

After the fashion of the immemorial American town meeting, the beginning of all our government, Wingate called the meeting to order and stated its purposes. He then set forth his own ideas of the best manner for handling the trail work.

His plan, as he explained, was one long earlier perfected in the convoys of the old Santa Fé Trail. The wagons were to travel in close order. Four parallel columns, separated by not too great spaces, were to be maintained as much as possible, more especially toward nightfall. Of these, the outer two were to draw in together when camp was made, the other two to angle out, wagon lapping wagon, front and rear, thus making an oblong corral of the wagons, into which, through a gap, the work oxen were to be driven every night after they had fed. The tents and fires were to be outside of the corral unless in case of an Indian alarm, when the corral would represent a fortress.

The transport animals were to be hobbled each night. A guard, posted entirely around the corral and camp, was to be put out each night. Each man and each boy above fourteen was to be subject to guard duty under the ancient common law of the Plains, and from this duty no man might hope excuse unless actually too ill to walk; nor could any man offer to procure any substitute for himself. The watches were to be set as eight, each to stand guard one-fourth part of alternate nights, so that each man would get every other night undisturbed.

There were to be lieutenants, one for each of the four parallel divisions of the train; also eight sergeants of the guard, each of whom was to select and handle the men of the watch under him. No wagon might change its own place in the train after the start, dust or no dust.

When Wingate ended his exposition and looked around for approval it was obvious that many of these regulations met with disfavor at the start. The democracy of the train was one in which each man wanted his own way. Leaning head to head, speaking low, men grumbled at all this fuss and feathers and Army stuff. Some of these were friends and backers in the late election. Nettled by their silence, or by their murmured comments, Wingate arose again.

"Well, you have heard my plan, men," said he. "The Santa Fé men worked it up, and used it for years, as you all know. They always got through. If there's anyone here knows a better way, and one that's got more experience back of it, I'd like to have him get up and say so."

Silence for a time greeted this also. The Northern men, Wingate's partisans, looked uncomfortably one to the other. It was young Woodhull, of the Liberty contingent, who rose at length.

"What Cap'n Wingate has said sounds all right to me," said he. "He's a new friend of mine—I never saw him till two-three hours ago—but I know about him. What he says about the Santa Fé fashion I know for true. As some of you know, I was out that way, up the Arkansas, with Doniphan, for the Stars and Stripes. Talk about wagon travel—you got to have a regular system or you have everything in a mess. This here, now, is a lot like so many volunteers enlisting for war. There's always a sort of preliminary election of officers; sort of shaking down and shaping up. I wasn't here when Cap'n Wingate was elected—our wagons were some late—but speaking for our men, I'd move to ratify his choosing, and that means to ratify his regulations. I'm wondering if I don't get a second for that?"

Some of the bewhiskered men who sat about him stirred, but cast their eyes toward their own captain, young Banion, whose function as their spokesman had thus been usurped by his defeated rival, Woodhull. Perhaps few of them suspected the *argumentum ad hominem*—or rather *ad feminam*—in Woodhull's speech.

Banion alone knew this favor-currying when he saw it, and knew well enough the real reason. It was Molly! Rivals indeed they were, these two, and in more ways than one. But Banion held his peace until one quiet father of a family spoke up.

"I reckon our own train captain, that we elected in case we didn't throw in with the big train, had ought to say what he thinks about it all."

Will Banion now rose composedly and bowed to the leader.

"I'm glad to second Mr. Woodhull's motion to throw our vote and our train for Captain Wingate and the big train," said he. "We'll ratify his captaincy, won't we?"

The nods of his associates now showed assent, and Wingate needed no more confirmation.

"In general, too, I would ratify Captain Wingate's scheme. But might I make a few suggestions?"

"Surely—go on." Wingate half rose.

"Well then, I'd like to point out that we've got twice as far to go as the Santa Fé traders, and over a very different country—more dangerous, less known, harder to travel. We've many times more wagons than any Santa Fé train ever had, and we've hundreds of loose cattle along. That means a sweeping off of the grass at every stop, and grass we've got to have or the train stops.

"Besides our own call on grass, I know there'll be five thousand Mormons at least on the trail ahead of us this spring—they've crossed the river from here to the Bluffs, and they're out on the Platte right now. We take what grass they leave us.

"What I'm trying to get at, captain, is this: We might have to break into smaller detachments now and again. We could not possibly always keep alignment in four columns."

"And then we'd be open to any Indian attack," interrupted Woodhull.

"We might have to fight some of the time, yes," rejoined Banion; "but we'll have to travel all the time, and we'll have to graze our stock all the time. On that one basic condition our safety rests—grass and plenty of it. We're on a long journey.

"You see, gentlemen," he added, smiling, "I was with Doniphan also. We learned a good many things. For instance, I'd rather see each horse on a thirty-foot picket rope, anchored safe each night, than to trust to any hobbles. A homesick horse can travel miles, hobbled, in a night. Horses are a lot of trouble.

"Now, I see that about a fourth of our people, including Captain Wingate, have horses and mules and not ox transport. I wish they all could trade for oxen before they start. Oxen last longer and fare better. They are easier to herd. They can be used for food in the hard first year out in Oregon. The Indians don't steal oxen—they like buffalo better—but they'll take any chance to run off horses or even mules. If they do, that means your women and children are on foot. You know the story of the Donner party, two years ago—on foot, in the snow. They died, and worse than died, just this side of California."

Men of Iowa, of Illinois, Ohio, Indiana, began to nod to one another, approving the words of this young man.

"He talks sense," said a voice aloud.

"Well, I'm talking a whole lot, I know," said Banion gravely, "but this is the time and place for our talking. I'm for throwing in with the Wingate train, as I've said. But will Captain Wingate let me add even just a few words more?

"For instance, I would suggest that we ought to have a record of all our personnel. Each man ought to be required to give his own name and late residence, and the names of all in his party. He should be obliged to show that his wagon is in good condition, with spare bolts, yokes, tires, bows and axles, and extra shoes for the stock. Each wagon ought to be required to carry anyhow half a side of rawhide, and the usual tools of the farm and the trail, as well as proper weapons and abundance of ammunition.

"No man ought to be allowed to start with this caravan with less supplies, for each mouth of his wagon, than one hundred pounds of flour. One hundred and fifty or even two hundred would be much better—there is loss and shrinkage. At least half as much of bacon, twenty pounds of coffee, fifty of sugar would not be too much in my own belief. About double the pro rata of the Santa Fé caravans is little enough, and those whose transport power will let them carry more supplies ought to start full loaded, for no man can tell the actual duration of this journey, or what food may be needed before we get across. One may have to help another."

Even Wingate joined in the outspoken approval of this, and Banion, encouraged, went on:

"Some other things, men, since you have asked each man to speak freely. We're not hunters, but home makers. Each family, I suppose, has a plow and seed for the first crop. We ought, too, to find out all our blacksmiths, for I promise you we'll need them. We ought to have a half dozen forges and as many anvils, and a lot of irons for the wagons.

"I suppose, too, you've located all your doctors; also all your preachers—you needn't camp them all together. Personally I believe in Sunday rest and Sunday services. We're taking church and state and home and law along with us, day by day, men, and we're not just trappers and adventurers. The fur trade's gone.

"I even think we ought to find out our musicians—it's good to have a bugler, if you can. And at night, when the people are tired and disheartened, music is good to help them pull together."

The bearded men who listened nodded yet again.

"About schools, now—the other trains that went out, the Applegates in 1843, the Donners of 1846, each train, I believe, had regular schools along, with hours each day.

"Do you think I'm right about all this? I'm sure I don't want Captain Wingate to be offended. I'm not dividing his power. I'm only trying to stiffen it."

Woodhull arose, a sneer on his face, but a hand pushed him down. A tall Missourian stood before him.

"Right ye air, Will!" said he. "Ye've an old head, an' we kin trust hit. Ef hit wasn't Cap'n Wingate is more older than you, an' already done elected, I'd be for choosin' ye fer cap'n o' this here hull train right now. Seein' hit's the way hit is, I move we vote to do what Will Banion has said is fitten. An' I move we-uns throw in with the big train, with Jess Wingate for cap'n. An' I move we allow one more day to git in supplies an' fixin's, an' trade hosses an' mules an' oxens, an' then we start day atter to-morrow mornin' when the bugle blows. Then hooray fer Oregon!"

There were cheers and a general rising, as though after finished business, which greeted this. Jesse Wingate, somewhat crestfallen and chagrined over the forward ways of this young man, of whom he never had heard till that very morning, put a perfunctory motion or so, asked loyalty and allegiance, and so forth.

But what they remembered was that he appointed as his wagon-column captains Sam Woodhull, of Missouri; Caleb Price, an Ohio man of substance; Simon Hall, an Indiana merchant, and a farmer by name of Kelsey, from Kentucky. To Will Banion the trainmaster assigned the most difficult and thankless task of the train, the captaincy of the cow column; that is to say, the leadership of the boys and men whose families were obliged to drive the loose stock of the train.

There were sullen mutterings over this in the Liberty column. Men whispered they would not follow Woodhull. As for Banion, he made no complaint, but smiled and shook hands with Wingate and all his lieutenants and declared his own loyalty and that of his men; then left for his own little adventure of a half dozen wagons which he was freighting out to Laramie—bacon, flour and sugar, for the most part; each wagon driven by a neighbor or a neighbor's son.

Among these already arose open murmurs of discontent over the way their own contingent had been treated. Banion had to mend a potential split before the first wheel had rolled westward up the Kaw.

The men of the meeting passed back among their neighbors and families, and spoke with more seriousness than hitherto. The rifle firing ended, the hilarity lessened that afternoon. In the old times the keel-boatmen bound west started out singing. The packtrain men of the fur trade went shouting and shooting, and the confident hilarity of the Santa Fé wagon caravans was a proverb. But now, here in the great Oregon train, matters were quite otherwise. There were women and children along. An unsmiling gravity marked them all. When the dusky velvet of the prairie night settled on almost the last day of the rendezvous it brought a general feeling of anxiety, dread, uneasiness, fear. Now, indeed, and at last, all these realized what was the thing that they had undertaken.

To add yet more to the natural apprehensions of men and women embarking on so stupendous an adventure, all manner of rumors now continually passed from one company to another. It was said that five thousand Mormons, armed to the teeth, had crossed the river at St. Joseph and were lying in wait on the Platte, determined to take revenge for the persecutions they had suffered in Missouri and Illinois. Another story said that the Kaw Indians, hitherto friendly, had banded together for robbery and were only waiting for the train to appear. A still more popular story had it that a party of several Englishmen had hurried ahead on the trail to excite all the savages to waylay and destroy the caravans, thus to wreak the vengeance of England upon the Yankees for the loss of Oregon. Much unrest arose over reports, hard to trace, to the effect that it was all a mistake about Oregon; that in reality it was a truly horrible country, unfit for human occupancy, and sure to prove the grave of any lucky enough to survive the horrors of the trail, which never yet had been truthfully reported. Some returned travelers from the West beyond the Rockies, who were hanging about the landing at the river, made it all worse by relating what purported to be actual experiences.

"If you ever get through to Oregon," they said, "you'll be ten years older than you are now. Your hair will be white, but not by age."

The Great Dipper showed clear and close that night, as if one might almost pick off by hand the familiar stars of the traveler's constellation. Overhead countless brilliant points of lesser light enameled the night mantle, matching the many camp fires of the great gathering. The wind blew soft and low. Night on the prairie is always solemn, and tonight the tense anxiety, the strained anticipation of more than two thousand souls invoked a brooding melancholy which it seemed even the stars must feel.

A dog, ominous, lifted his voice in a long, mournful howl which made mothers put out their hands to their babes. In answer a coyote in the grass raised a high, quavering cry, wild and desolate, the voice of the Far West.

Chapter IV

FEVER OF NEW FORTUNES

The notes of a bugle, high and clear, sang reveille at
dawn. Now came hurried activities of those who had
delayed. The streets of the two frontier settlements were
packed with ox teams, horses, wagons, cattle driven through.
The frontier stores were stripped of their last supplies. One
more day, and then on to Oregon!

Wingate broke his own camp early in the morning and
moved out to the open country west of the landing, making
a last bivouac at what would be the head of the train. He
had asked his four lieutenants to join him there. Hall, Price,
and Kelsey headed in with straggling wagons to form the
nucleuses of their columns; but the morning wore on and
the Missourians, now under Woodhull, had not yet broken
park. Wingate waited moodily.

Now at the edge of affairs human apprehensions began to
assert themselves, especially among the womenfolk. Even
stout Molly Wingate gave way to doubt and fears. Her husband caught her, apron to eyes, sitting on the wagon tongue
at ten in the morning, with her pots and pans unpacked.

"What?" he exclaimed. "You're not weakening? Haven't you as much courage as those Mormon women on ahead? Some of them pushing carts, I've heard."

"They've done it for religion, Jess. Oregon ain't no religion for me."

"Yet it has music for a man's ears, Molly."

"Hush! I've heard it all for the last two years. What happened to the Donners two years back? And four years ago it was the Applegates left home in old Missouri to move to Oregon. Who will ever know where their bones are laid? Look at our land we left—rich—black and rich as any in the world. What corn, what wheat—why, everything grew well in Illinois!"

"Yes, and cholera below us wiping out the people, and the trouble over slave-holding working up the river more and more, and the sun blazing in the summer, while in the wintertime we froze!"

"Well, as for food, we never saw any part of Kentucky with half so much grass. We had no turkeys at all there, and where we left you could kill one any gobbling time. The pigeons roosted not four miles from us. In the woods along the river even a woman could kill coons and squirrels, all we'd need—no need for us to eat rabbits like the Mormons. Our chicken yard was fifty miles across. The young ones'd be flying by roasting-ear time—and in fall the sloughs was black with ducks and geese. Enough and to spare we had; and our land opening; and Molly teaching the school, with twelve dollars a month cash for it, and Ted learning his blacksmith trade before he was eighteen. How could we ask more? What better will we do in Oregon?"

"You always throw the wet blanket on Oregon, Molly."

"It is so far!"

"How do we know it is far? We know men and women have crossed, and we know the land is rich. Wheat grows fifty bushels to the acre, the trees are big as the spires on meeting houses, the fish run by millions in the streams. Yet the winters have little snow. A man can live there and not slave out a life.

"Besides"—and the frontier now spoke in him—"this

country is too old, too long settled. My father killed his elk
and his buffalo, too, in Kentucky; but that was before my
day. I want the buffalo. I crave to see the Plains, Molly.
What real American does not?"

Mrs. Wingate threw her apron over her face.

"The Oregon fever has witched you, Jesse!" she exclaimed between dry sobs.

Wingate was silent for a time.

"Corn ought to grow in Oregon," he said at last.

"Yes, but does it?"

"I never heard it didn't. The soil is rich, and you can file
on six hundred and forty acres. There's your donation claim,
four times bigger than any land you can file on here. We
sold out at ten dollars an acre—more'n our land really was
worth, or ever is going to be worth. It's just the speculators
says any different. Let 'em have it, and us move on. That's
the way money's made, and always has been made, all
across the United States."

"Huh! You talk like a land speculator your own self!"

"Well, if it ain't the movers make a country, what does?
If we don't settle Oregon, how long'll we hold it? The
preachers went through to Oregon with horses. Like as not
even the Applegates got their wagons across. Like enough
they got through. I want to see the country before it gets
too late for a good chance, Molly. First thing you know
buffalo'll be getting scarce out West, too, like deer was getting scarcer on the Sangamon. We ought to give our children
as good a chance as we had ourselves."

"As good a chance! Haven't they had as good a chance
as we ever had? Didn't our land more'n thribble, from a
dollar and a quarter? It may thribble again, time they're old
as we are now."

"That's a long time to wait."

"It's a long time to live a life-time, but everybody's got
to live it."

She stood, looking at him.

"Look at all the good land right in here! Here we got
walnut and hickory and oak—worlds of it. We got sassafras
and pawpaw and hazel brush. We get all the hickory nuts

and pecans we like any fall. The wild plums is better'n any in Kentucky; and as for grapes, they're big as your thumb, and thousands, on the river. Wait till you see the plum and grape jell I could make this fall!"

"Women—always thinking of jell!"

"But we got every herb here we need—boneset and sassafras and Injun physic and bark for the fever. There ain't nothing you can name we ain't got right here, or on the Sangamon, yet you talk of taking care of our children. Huh! We've moved five times since we was married. Now just as we got into a good country, where a woman could dry corn and put up jell, and where a man could raise some hogs, why, you wanted to move again—plumb out to Oregon! I tell you, Jesse Wingate, hogs is a blame sight better to tie to than buffalo! You talk like you had to settle Oregon!"

"Well, haven't I got to? Somehow it seems a man ain't making up his own mind when he moves West. Pap moved twice in Kentucky, once in Tennessee, and then over to Missouri, after you and me was married and moved up into Indiana, before we moved over into Illinois. He said to me—and I know it for the truth—he couldn't hardly tell who it was or what it was hitched up the team. But first thing he knew, there the old wagon stood, front of the house, cover all on, plow hanging on behind, tar bucket under the wagon, and dog and all. All he had to do, Pap said, was just to climb up on the front seat and speak to the team. My maw, she climb up on the seat with him. Then they moved—on West. You know, Molly. My maw, she climb up on the front seat—"

His wife suddenly turned to him, the tears still in her eyes.

"Yes, and Jesse Wingate, and you know it, your wife's as good a woman as your maw! When the wagon was a-standing, cover on, and you on the front seat, I climb up by you, Jess, same as I always have and always will. Haven't I always? You know that. But it's harder on women, moving is. They care more for a house that's rain tight in a storm."

"I know you did, Molly," said her husband soberly.

"I suppose I can pack my jells in a box and put in the wagon, anyways." She was drying her eyes.

"Why, yes, I reckon so. And then a few sacks of dried corn will go mighty well on the road."

"One thing"—she turned on him in wifely fury—"you shan't keep me from taking my bureau and my six chairs all the way across! No, nor my garden seeds, all I saved. No, nor yet my rose roots that I'm taking along. We got to have a home, Jess—we got to have a home! There's Jed and Molly coming on."

"Where's Molly now?" suddenly asked her husband. "She'd ought to be helping you right now."

"Oh, back at the camp, I s'pose—her and Jed, too. I told her to pick a mess of dandelion greens and bring over. Larking around with them young fellows, like enough. Huh! She'll have less time. If Jed has to ride herd, Molly's got to take care of that team of big mules, and drive 'em all day in the light wagon too. I reckon if she does that, and teaches night school right along, she won't be feeling so gay."

"They tell me folks has got married going across," she added, "not to mention buried. One book we had said, up on the Platte, two years back, there was a wedding and a birth and a burying in one train, all inside of one hour, and all inside of one mile. That's Oregon!"

"Well, I reckon it's life, ain't it?" rejoined her husband. "One thing, I'm not keen to have Molly pay too much notice to that young fellow Banion—him they said was a leader of the Liberty wagons. Huh, he ain't leader now!"

"You like Sam Woodhull better for Molly, Jess?"

"Some ways. He falls in along with my ideas. He ain't so apt to make trouble on the road. He sided in with me right along at the last meeting."

"He done that? Well, his father was a sheriff once, and his uncle, Judge Henry D. Showalter, he got into Congress. Politics! But some folks said the Banions was the best family. Kentucky, they was. Well, comes to siding in, Jess, I reckon it's Molly herself'll count more in that than either o' them or either o' us. She's eighteen past. Another year and she'll be an old maid. If there's a wedding going across—"

"There won't be," said her husband shortly. "If there is it won't be her and no William Banion, I'm saying that."

Chapter V

THE BLACK SPANIARD

Meantime the younger persons referred to in the frank discussion of Wingate and his wife were ocupying themselves in their own fashion their last day in camp. Molly, her basket full of dandelion leaves, was reluctant to leave the shade of the grove by the stream, and Jed had business with the team of great mules that Molly was to drive on the trail.

As for the Liberty train, its oval remained unbroken, the men and women sitting in the shade of the wagons. Their outfitting had been done so carefully that little now remained for attention on the last day, but the substantial men of the contingent seemed far from eager to be on their way. Groups here and there spoke in monosyllables, sullenly. They wanted to join the great train, had voted to do so; but the cavalier deposing of their chosen man Banion—who before them all at the meeting had shown himself fit to lead—and the cool appointment of Woodhull in his place had on reflection seemed to them quite too high-handed a proposition. They said so now.

"Where's Woodhull now?" demanded the bearded man who had championed Banion. "I see Will out rounding up his cows, but Sam Woodhull ain't turned a hand to hooking up to pull in west o' town with the others."

"That's easy," smiled another. "Sam Woodhull is where he's always going to be—hanging around the Wingate girl. He's over at their camp now."

"Well, I dunno's I blame him so much for that, neither. And he kin stay there fer all o' me. Fer one, I won't foller no Woodhull, least o' all Sam Woodhull, soldier or no soldier. I'll pull out when I git ready, and tomorrow mornin' is soon enough fer me. We kin jine on then, if so's we like."

Someone turned on his elbow, nodded over shoulder. They heard hoof beats. Banion came up, fresh from his new work on the herd. He asked for Woodhull, and learning his whereabouts trotted across the intervening glade.

"That's shore a hoss he rides," said one man.

"An' a shore man a-ridin' of him," nodded another. "He may ride front o' the train an' not back o' hit, even yet."

Molly Wingate sat on the grass in the little grove, curling a chain of dandelion stems. Near by Sam Woodhull, in his best, lay on the sward regarding her avidly, a dull fire in his dark eyes. He was so enamored of the girl as to be almost unfit for aught else. For weeks he had kept close to her. Not that Molly seemed over-much to notice or encourage him. Only, woman fashion, she ill liked to send away any attentive male. Just now she was uneasy. She guessed that if it were not for the presence of her brother Jed near by this man would declare himself unmistakably.

If the safety of numbers made her main concern, perhaps that was what made Molly Wingate's eye light up when she heard the hoofs of Will Banion's horse splashing in the little stream. She sprang to her feet, waving a hand gayly.

"Oh, so there you are!" she exclaimed. "I was wondering if you'd be over before Jed and I left for the prairie. Father and Mother have moved on out west of town. We're all ready for the jump-off. Are you?"

"Yes, tomorrow by sun," said Banion, swinging out of

saddle and forgetting any errand he might have had. "Then it's on to Oregon!"

He nodded to Woodhull, who little more than noticed him. Molly advanced to where Banion's horse stood, nodding and pawing restively as was his wont. She stroked his nose, patted his sweat-soaked neck.

"What a pretty horse you have, Major," she said. "What's his name?"

"I call him Pronto," smiled Banion. "That means sudden."

"He fits the name. May I ride him?"

"What? You ride him?"

"Yes, surely. I'd love to. I can ride anything. That funny saddle would do—see how big and high the horn is, good as the fork of a lady's saddle."

"Yes, but the stirrup!"

"I'd put my foot in between the flaps above the stirrup. Help me up, sir?"

"I'd rather not."

Molly pouted.

"Stingy!"

"But no woman ever rode that horse—not many men but me. I don't know what he'd do."

"Only one way to find out."

Jed, approaching, joined the conversation.

"I rid him," said he. "He's a goer all right, but he ain't mean."

"I don't know whether he would be bad or not with a lady," Banion still argued. "These Spanish horses are always wild. They never do get over it. You've got to be a rider."

"You think I'm not a rider? I'll ride him now to show you! I'm not afraid of horses."

"That's right," broke in Sam Woodhull. "But, Miss Molly, I wouldn't tackle that horse if I was you. Take mine."

"But I will! I've not been horseback for a month. We've all got to ride or drive or walk a thousand miles. I can ride him, man saddle and all. Help me up, sir?"

Banion walked to the horse, which flung a head against him, rubbing a soft muzzle up and down.

"He seems gentle," said he. "I've pretty well topped him off this morning. If you're sure—"

"Help me up, one of you?"

It was Woodhull who sprang to her, caught her up under the arms and lifted her fully gracious weight to the saddle. Her left foot by fortune found the cleft in the stirrup fender, her right leg swung around the tall horn, hastily concealed by a clutch at her skirt even as she grasped the heavy knotted reins. It was then too late. She must ride.

Banion caught at a cheek strap as he saw Woodhull's act, and the horse was the safer for an instant. But in terror or anger at his unusual burden, with flapping skirt and no grip on his flanks, the animal reared and broke away from them all. An instant and he was plunging across the stream for the open glade, his head low.

He did not yet essay the short, stiff-legged action of the typical bucker, but made long, reaching, lowheaded plunges, seeking his own freedom in that way, perhaps half in some equine wonder of his own. None the less the wrenching of the girl's back, the leverage on her flexed knee, unprotected, were unmistakable.

The horse reared again and yet again, high, striking out as she checked him. He was getting in a fury now, for his rider still was in place. Then with one savage sidewise shake of his head after another he plunged this way and that, rail-fencing it for the open prairie. It looked like a bolt, which with a horse of his spirit and stamina meant but one thing, no matter how long delayed.

It all happened in a flash. Banion caught at the rein too late, ran after—too slow, of course. The girl was silent, shaken, but still riding. No footman could aid her now.

With a leap, Banion was in the saddle of Woodhull's horse, which had been left at hand, its bridle down. He drove in the spurs and headed across the flat at the top speed of the fast and racy chestnut—no match, perhaps, for the black Spaniard, were the latter once extended, but favored now by the angle of the two.

Molly had not uttered a word or cry, either to her mount or in appeal for aid. In sooth she was too frightened to do so. But she heard the rush of hoofs and the high call of Banion's voice back of her:

"Ho, Pronto! Pronto! *Vien' aqui!*"

Something of a marvel it was, and showing companionship of man and horse on the trail; but suddenly the mad black ceased his plunging. Turning, he trotted whinnying as though for aid, obedient to his master's command, "Come here!" An instant and Banion had the cheek strap. Another and he was off, with Molly Wingate, in a white dead faint, in his arms.

By now others had seen the affair from their places in the wagon park. Men and women came hurrying. Banion laid the girl down, sought to raise her head, drove back the two horses, ran with his hat to the stream for water. By that time Woodhull had joined him, in advance of the people from the park.

"What do you mean, you damned fool, you, by riding my horse off without my consent!" he broke out. "If she ain't dead—that damned wild horse—you had the gall—"

Will Banion's self-restraint at last was gone. He made one answer, voicing all his acquaintance with Sam Woodhull, all his opinion of him, all his future attitude in regard to him.

He dropped his hat to the ground, caught off one wet glove, and with a long back-handed sweep struck the cuff of it full and hard across Sam Woodhull's face.

Chapter VI

Issue Joined

There were dragoon revolvers in the holsters at Wood-hull's saddle. He made a rush for a weapon—indeed, the crack of the blow had been so sharp that the nearest men thought a shot had been fired—but swift as was his leap, it was not swift enough. The long, lean hand of the bearded Missourian gripped his wrist even as he caught at a pistol grip. He turned a livid face to gaze into a cold and small blue eye.

"No, ye don't, Sam!" said the other, who was first of those who came up running.

Even as a lank woman stooped to raise the head of Molly Wingate the sinewy arm back of the hand whirled Woodhull around so that he faced Banion, who had not made a move.

"Will ain't got no weepon, an' ye know it," went on the same cool voice. "What ye mean—a murder, besides that?"

He nodded toward the girl. By now the crowd surged between the two men, voices rose.

"He struck me!" broke out Woodhull. "Let me go! He struck me!"

"I know he did," said the intervener. "I heard it. I don't know why. But whether it was over the girl or not, we ain't goin' to see this other feller shot down till we know more about hit. Ye can meet—"

"Of course, any time."

Banion was drawing on his glove. The woman had lifted Molly, straightened her clothing.

"All blood!" said one. "That saddle horn! What made her ride that critter?"

The Spanish horse stood facing them now, ears forward, his eyes showing through his forelock not so much in anger as in curiosity. The men hustled the two antagonists apart.

"Listen, Sam," went on the tall Missourian, still with his grip on Woodhull's wrist. "We'll see ye both fair. Ye've got to fight now, in course—that's the law, an' I ain't learned it in the fur trade o' the Rockies fer nothin', ner have you people here in the settlements. But I'll tell ye one thing, Sam Woodhull, ef ye make one move afore we-uns tell ye how an' when to make hit, I'll drop ye, shore's my name's Bill Jackson. Ye got to wait, both on ye. We're startin' out, an' we kain't start out like a mob. Take yer time."

"Any time, any way," said Banion simply. "No man can abuse me."

"How'd you gentlemen prefer fer to fight?" inquired the man who had described himself as Bill Jackson, one of the fur brigaders of the Rocky Mountain Company; a man with a reputation of his own in Plains and mountain adventures of hunting, trading and scouting. "Hit's yore ch'ice o' weapons, I reckon, Will. I reckon he challenged you-all."

"I don't care. He'd have no chance on an even break with me, with any sort of weapon, and he knows that."

Jackson cast free his man and ruminated over a chew of plug.

"Hit's over a gal," said he at length, judicially. "Hit ain't usual; but seein' as a gal don't pick atween men because one's a quicker shot than another, but because he's maybe stronger, or something like that, why, how'd knuckle and skull suit you two roosters, best man win and us to see hit fair? Hit's one of ye fer the gal, like enough. But not right now. Wait till we're on the trail and clean o' the law. I heern there's a sheriff round yere some'rs."

"I'll fight him any way he likes, or any way you say," said Banion. "It's not my seeking. I only slapped him because he abused me for doing what he ought to have done. Yes, I rode his horse. If I hadn't that girl would have been killed. It's not his fault she wasn't. I didn't want her to ride that horse."

"I don't reckon hit's so much a matter about a hoss as hit is about a gal," remarked Bill Jackson sagely. "Ye'll hatter fight. Well then, seein' as hit's about a gal, knuckle an' skull, is that right?"

He cast a glance around this group of other fighting men of a border day. They nodded gravely, but with glittering eyes.

"Well then, *gentlemen*"—and now he stood free of Woodhull—"ye both give word ye'll make no break till we tell ye? I'll say, two-three days out?"

"Suits me," said Woodhull savagely. "I'll break his neck for him."

"Any time that suits the gentleman to break my neck will please me," said Will Banion indifferently. "Say when, friends. Just now I've got to look after my cows. It seems to me our wagon master might very well look after his wagons."

"That sounds!" commented Jackson. "That sounds! Sam, git on about yer business, er ye kain't travel in the Liberty train nohow! An' don't ye make no break, in the dark especial, fer we kin track ye anywhere's. Ye'll fight fair fer once—an' ye'll fight!"

By now the group massed about these scenes had begun to relax, to spread. Women had Molly in hand as her eyes opened. Jed came up a run with the mule team and the light wagon from the grove, and they got the girl into the seat with him, neither of them fully cognizant of what had gone on in the group of tight-mouthed men who now broke apart and sauntered silently back, each to his own wagon.

Chapter VII

THE JUMP-OFF

With the first thin line of pink the coyotes hanging on the flanks of the great encampment raised their immemorial salutation to the dawn. Their clamorings were stilled by a new and sterner voice—the notes of the bugle summoning sleepers of the last night to the duties of the first day. Down the line from watch to watch passed the Plains command, "Catch up! Catch up!" It was morning of the jump-off.

Little fires began at the wagon messes or family bivouacs. Men, boys, barefooted girls went out into the dew-wet grass to round up the transport stock. A vast confusion, a medley of unskilled endeavor marked the hour. But after an hour's wait, adjusted to the situation, the next order passed down the line:

"Roll out! Roll out!"

And now the march to Oregon was at last begun! The first dust cut by an ox hoof was set in motion by the whip crack of a barefooted boy in jeans who had no dream that he one day would rank high in the councils of his state, at the edge of an ocean which no prairie boy ever had envisioned.

The compass finger of the trail, leading out from the timber groves, pointed into a sea of green along the valley of the Kaw. The grass, not yet tall enough fully to ripple as it would a half month later, stood waving over the blackburned ground which the semi-civilized Indians had left the fall before. Flowers dotted it, sometimes white like bits of old ivory on the vast rug of spindrift—the pink verbena, the wild indigo, the larkspur and the wild geranium—all woven into a wondrous spangled carpet. At times also appeared the shy buds of the sweet wild rose, loveliest flower of the prairie. Tall rosinweeds began to thrust up rankly, banks of sunflowers prepared to fling their yellow banners miles wide. The opulent, inviting land lay in a ceaseless succession of easy undulations, stretching away illimitably to far horizons, in such exchanging pictures of grace and charm as raised the admiration of even these simple folk to a pitch bordering upon exaltation.

Here lay the West, barbaric, abounding, beautiful. Surely it could mean no harm to any man.

The men lacked experience in column travel, the animals were unruly. The train formation—clumsily trying to conform to the orders of Wingate to travel in four parallel columns—soon lost order. At times the wagons halted to re-form. The leaders galloped back and forth, exhorting, adjuring and restoring little by little a certain system. But they dealt with independent men. On ahead the landscape seemed so wholly free of danger that to most of these the road to the Far West offered no more than a pleasure jaunt. Wingate and his immediate aids were well worn when at mid afternoon they halted, fifteen miles out from Westport.

"What in hell you pulling up so soon for?" demanded Sam Woodhull surlily, riding up from his own column, far at the rear, and accosting the train leader. "We can go five miles further, anyhow, and maybe ten. We'll never get across in this way."

"This is the very way we will get across," rejoined Wingate. "While I'm captain I'll say when to start and stop. But

I've been counting on you, Woodhull, to throw in with me and help me get things shook down."

"Well, hit looks to me ye're purty brash as usual," commented another voice. Bill Jackson came and stood at the captain's side. He had not been far from Woodhull all day long. "Ye're a nacherl damned fool, Sam Woodhull," said he. "Who 'lected ye fer train captain, an' when was it did? If ye don't like the way this train's run go on ahead an' make a train o' yer own, ef that's way ye feel. Pull on out tonight. What ye say, Cap?"

"I can't really keep any man from going back or going ahead," replied Wingate. "But I've counted on Woodhull to hold those Liberty wagons together. Any, plainsman knows that a little party takes big risks."

"Since when did you come a plainsman?" scoffed the malcontent, for once forgetting his policy of favor currying with Wingate in his own surly discontent. He had not been able to speak to Molly all day.

"Well, if he ain't a plainsman yit he will be, and I'm one right now, Sam Woodhull." Jackson stood squarely in front of his superior. "I say he's talkin' sense to a man that ain't got no sense. I was with Doniphan too. We found ways, huh?"

His straight gaze outfronted the other, who turned and rode back. But that very night eight men, covertly instigated or encouraged by Woodhull, their leader, came to the headquarters fire with a joint complaint. They demanded places at the head of the column, else would mutiny and go on ahead together. They said good mule teams ought not to take the dust of ox wagons.

"What do you say, men?" asked the train captain of his aids helplessly. "I'm in favor of letting them go front."

The others nodded silently, looking at one another significantly. Already cliques and factions were beginning.

Woodhull, however, had too much at stake to risk any open friction with the captain of the train. His own seat at the officers' fire was dear to him, for it brought him close to the Wingate wagons, and in sight—if nothing else—of Molly Wingate. That young lady did not speak to him all day, but drew close the tilt of her own wagon early after the evening meal and denied herself to all.

As for Banion, he was miles back, in camp with his own wagons, which Woodhull had abandoned, and on duty that night with the cattle guard—a herdsman and not a leader of men now. He himself was moody enough when he tied his cape behind his saddle and rode his black horse out into the shadows. He had no knowledge of the fact that the old mountain man, Jackson, wrapped in his blanket, that night instituted a solitary watch all his own.

The hundreds of camp fires of the scattered train, stretched out over five miles of grove and glade at the end of the first undisciplined day, lowered, glowed and faded. They were one day out to Oregon, and weary withal. Soon the individual encampments were silent save for the champ or cough of tethered animals, or the whining howl of coyotes, prowling in. At the Missouri encampment, last of the train, and that heading the great cattle drove, the hardy frontier settlers, as was their wont, soon followed the sun to rest.

The night wore on, incredibly slow to the novice watch for the first time now drafted under the prairie law. The sky was faint pink and the shadows lighter when suddenly the dark was streaked by a flash of fire and the silence broken by the crack of a border rifle. Then again and again came the heavier bark of a dragoon revolver, of the sort just then becoming known along the Western marches.

The camp went into confusion. Will Banion, just riding in to take his own belated turn in his blankets, almost ran over the tall form of Bill Jackson, rifle in hand.

"What was it, man?" demanded Banion. "You shooting at a mule?"

"No, a man," whispered the other. "He ran this way. Reckon I must have missed. It's hard to draw down inter a hindsight in the dark, an' I jest chanced hit with the pistol. He was runnin' hard."

"Who was he—some thief?"

"Like enough. He was crawlin' up towards yore wagon. I halted him an' he run."

"You don't know who he was?"

"No. I'll see his tracks, come day. Go on to bed. I'll set out a whiles, boy."

When dawn came, before he had broken his long vigil, Jackson was bending over footmarks in the moister portions of the soil.

"Tall man, young an' tracked clean," he muttered to himself. "Fancy boots, with rather little heels. Shame I done missed him!"

But he said nothing to Banion or anyone else. It was the twentieth time Bill Jackson, one of Sublette's men and a nephew of one of his partners, had crossed the Plains, and the lone hand pleased him best. He instituted his own government for the most part, and had thrown in with this train because that best suited his book, since the old pack trains of the fur trade were now no more. For himself, he planned settlement in Eastern Oregon, a country he once had glimpsed in long-gone beaver days, a dozen years ago. The Eastern settlements had held him long enough, the Army life had been too dull, even with Doniphan.

"I must be gittin' old," he muttered to himself as he turned to a breakfast fire. "Missed—at seventy yard!"

Chapter VIII

MAN AGAINST MAN

There were more than two thousand souls in the great caravan which reached over miles of springy turf and fat creek lands. There were more than a thousand children, more than a hundred babes in arm, more than fifty marriageable maids pursued by avid swains. There were bold souls and weak, strong teams and weak, heavy loads and light loads, neighbor groups and coteries of kindred blood or kindred spirits.

The rank and file had reasons enough for shifting. There were a score of Helens driving wagons—reasons in plenty for the futility of all attempts to enforce an arbitrary rule of march. Human equations, human elements would shake themselves down into place, willy-nilly. The great caravan therefore was scantily less than a rabble for the first three or four days out. The four columns were abandoned the first half day. The loosely knit organization rolled on in a broken-crested wave, ten, fifteen, twenty miles a day, the horse-and-mule men now at the front. Far to the rear, heading only the cow column, came the lank men of Liberty, trudging alongside their swaying ox teams, with many a monotonous "Gee-whoa-haw! Git along thar, ye Buck an' Star!" So soon they passed the fork where the road to Oregon left the trail to Santa Fé; topped the divide that held them back from the greater valley of the Kaw.

Noon of the fifth day brought them to the swollen flood of the latter stream, at the crossing known as Papin's Ferry. Here the semicivilized Indians and traders had a single rude ferryboat, a scow operated in part by setting poles, in part by the power of the stream against a cable. The noncommittal Indians would give no counsel as to fording. They had ferry hire to gain. Word passed that there were other fords a few miles higher up. A general indecision existed, and now the train began to pile up on the south bank of the river.

Late in the afternoon the scout, Jackson, came riding back to the herd where Banion was at work, jerking up his horse in no pleased frame of mind.

"Will," säid he, "leave the boys ride now an' come on up ahead. We need ye."

"What's up?" demanded Banion. "Anything worse?"

"Yes. The old fool's had a row over the ferryboat. Hit'd take two weeks to git us all over that way, anyhow. He's declared fer fordin' the hull outfit, lock, stock an' barrel. To save a few dollars, he's a goin' to lose a lot o' loads an' drownd a lot o' womern an' babies—that's what he's goin' to do. Some o' us called a halt an' stood out fer a council. We want you to come on up.

"Woodhull's there," he added. "He sides with the old man, o' course. He rid on the same seat with that gal all day till now. Lord knows what he done or said. Ain't hit nigh about time now, Major?"

"It's nigh about time," said Will Banion quietly.

They rode side by side, past more than a mile of the covered wagons, now almost end to end, the columns continually closing up. At the bank of the river, at the ferry head, they found a group of fifty men. The ranks opened as Banion and Jackson approached, but Banion made no attempt to join a council to which he had not been bidden.

A half dozen civilized Indians of the Kaws, owners or operators of the ferry, sat in a stolid line across the head of the scow at its landing stage, looking neither to the right nor the left and awaiting the white men's pleasure. Banion rode down to them.

"How deep?" he asked.

They understood but would not answer.

"Out of the way!" he cried, and rode straight at them. They scattered. He spurred his horse, the black Spaniard, over the stage and on the deck of the scow, drove him its full length, snorting; set the spurs hard at the farther end and plunged deliberately off into the swift, muddy stream.

The horse sank out of sight below the roily surface. They saw the rider go down to his armpits; saw him swing off saddle, upstream. The gallant horse headed for the center of the heavy current, but his master soon turned him downstream and inshore. A hundred yards down they landed on a bar and scrambled up the bank.

Banion rode to the circle and sat dripping. He had brought not speech but action, not theory but facts, and he had not spoken a word.

His eyes covered the council rapidly, resting on the figure of Sam Woodhull, squatting on his heels. As though to answer the challenge of his gaze, the latter rose.

"Gentlemen," said he, "I'm not, myself, governed by any mere spirit of bravado. It's swimming water, yes—any fool knows that, outside of yon one. What I do say is that we can't afford to waste time here fooling with that boat. We've got to swim it. I agree with you, Wingate. This river's been forded by the trains for years, and I don't see as we need be any more chicken-hearted than those others that went through last year and earlier. This is the old fur-trader crossing, the Mormons crossed here, and so can we."

Silence met his words. The older men looked at the swollen stream, turned to the horseman who had proved it.

"What does Major Banion say?" spoke up a voice.

"Nothing!" was Banion's reply. "I'm not in your council, am I?"

"You are, as much as any man here," spoke up Caleb

Price, and Hall and Kelsey added yea to that. "Get down. Come in."

Banion threw his rein to Jackson and stepped into the ring, bowing to Jesse Wingate, who sat as presiding officer.

"Of course we want to hear what Mr. Banion has to say," said he. "He's proved part of the question right now. I've always heard it's fording, part way, at Papin's Ferry. It don't look it now."

"The river's high, Mr. Wingate," said Banion. "If you ask me, I'd rather ferry than ford. I'd send the women and children over by this boat. We can make some more out of the wagon boxes. If they leak we can cover them with hides. The sawmill at the mission has some lumber. Let's knock together another boat or two. I'd rather be safe than sorry, gentlemen; and believe me, she's heavy water yonder."

"I've never seed the Kaw so full," asserted Jackson, "an' I've crossed her twenty times in spring flood. Do what ye like, you-all—ole Missoury's goin' to take her slow an' keerful."

"Half of you Liberty men are a bunch of damned cowards!" sneered Woodhull.

There was silence. An icy voice broke it.

"I take it, that means me?" said Will Banion.

"It does mean you, if you want to take it that way," rejoined his enemy. "I don't believe in one or two timid men holding up a whole train."

"Never mind about holding up the train—we're not stopping any man from crossing right now. What I have in mind now is to ask you, do you classify me as a coward just because I counsel prudence here?"

"You're the one is holding back."

"Answer me! Do you call that to me?"

"I do answer you, and I do call it to you then!" flared Woodhull.

"I tell you, you're a liar, and you know it, Sam Woodhull! And if it pleases your friends and mine, I'd like to have the order now made on unfinished business."

Not all present knew what this meant, for only a few knew of the affair at the rendezvous, the Missourians having held their counsel in the broken and extended train, where men might travel for days and not meet. But Woodhull knew, and sprang to his feet, hand on revolver. Banion's hand was likewise employed at his wet saddle holster, to which he sprang, and perhaps then one man would have been killed but for Bill Jackson, who spurred between.

"Make one move an' I drop ye!" he called to Woodhull. "Ye've give yer promise."

"All right then, I'll keep it," growled Woodhull.

"Ye'd better! Now listen! Do ye see that tall cottingwood tree a half mile down—the one with the flat umbreller top, like a cypress? Ye kin? Well, in half a hour be thar with three o' yore friends, no more. I'll be thar with my man an' three o' his, no more, an' I'll be one o' them three. I allow our meanin' is to see hit fa'r. An' I allow that what has been unfinished business ain't goin' to be unfinished come sundown.

"Does this suit ye, Will?"

"It's our promise. Officers didn't usually fight that way, but you said it must be so, and we both agreed. I agree now."

"You other folks all stay back," said Bill Jackson grimly. "This here is a little matter that us Missourians is goin' to settle in our own way an' in our own camp. Hit ain't none o' you-uns' business. Hit's plenty o' ourn."

Men started to their feet over all the river front. The Indians rose, walked down the bank covertly.

"Fight!"

The word passed quickly. It was a day of personal encounters. This was an assemblage in large part of fighting men. But some sense of decency led the partisans to hurry away, out of sight and hearing of the womenfolk.

The bell-top cottonwood stood in a little space which had been a dueling ground for thirty years. The grass was firm and even for a distance of fifty yards in any direction, and the light at that hour favored neither man.

For Banion, who was prompt, Jackson brought with him two men. One of them was a planter by name of Dillon, the other none less than stout Caleb Price, one of Wingate's chosen captains.

"I'll not see this made a thing of politics," said he. "I'm Northern, but I like the way that young man has acted. He hasn't had a fair deal from the officers of this train. He's going to have a fair deal now."

"We allow he will," said Dillon grimly.

He was fully armed, and so were all the seconds. For Woodhull showed the Kentuckian, Kelsey, young Jed Wingate—the latter by Woodhull's own urgent request— and the other train captain, Hall. So in its way the personal quarrel of these two hotheads did in a way involve the entire train.

"Strip yore man," commanded the tall mountaineer. "We're ready. It's go till one hollers enough; fa'r stand up, heel an' toe, no buttin' er gougin'. Fust man ter break them rules gits shot. Is that yore understandin', gentle*men*.

"How we get it, yes," assented Kelsey.

"See you enforce it then, fer we're a-goin' to," concluded Jackson.

He stepped back. From the opposite sides the two antagonists stepped forward. There was no ring, there was no timekeeper, no single umpire. There were no rounds, no duration set. It was man to man, for cause the most ancient and most bitter of all causes—sex.

Chapter IX

THE BRUTE

B etween the two stalwart men who fronted one another, stripped to trousers and shoes, there was not so much to choose. Woodhull perhaps had the better of it by a few pounds in weight, and forsooth looked less slouchy out of his clothes than in them. His was the long and sinewy type of muscle. He was in hard condition.

Banion, two years younger than his rival, himself was round and slender, thin of flank, a trace squarer and fuller of shoulder. His arms showed easily rippling bands of muscles, his body was hard in the natural vigor of youth and life in the open air. His eye was fixed all the time on his man. He did not speak or turn aside, but walked on in.

There were no preliminaries, there was no delay. In a flash the Saxon ordeal of combat was joined. The two fighters met in a rush.

At the center of the fighting space they hung, body to body, in a whirling *melèe*. Neither had much skill in real boxing, and such fashion of fight was unknown in that region, the offensive being the main thing and defense remaining incidental. The thud of fist on face, the discoloration that rose under the savage blows, the blood that oozed and scattered, proved that the fighting blood of both these mad creatures was up, so that they felt no pain, even as they knew no fear.

In their first fly, as witnesses would have termed it, there was no advantage to either, and both came out well marked. In the combat of the time and place there were no rules, no periods, no resting times. Once they were dispatched to it, the fight was the affair of the fighters, with no more than a very limited number of restrictions as to fouls.

They met and broke, bloody, gasping, once, twice, a dozen times. Banion was fighting slowly, carefully.

"I'll make it free, if you dare!" panted Woodhull at length.

They broke apart once more by mutual need of breath. He meant he would bar nothing; he would go back to the days of Boone and Kenton and Girty, when hair, eye, any part of the body was fair aim.

"You can't dare me!" rejoined Will Banion. "It's as my seconds say."

Young Jed Wingate, suddenly pale, stood by and raised no protest. Kelsey's face was stony calm. The small eye of Hall narrowed, but he too held to the etiquette of non-interference in this matter of man and man, though what had passed here was a deadly thing. Mutilation, death might now ensue, and not mere defeat. But they all waited for the other side.

"Air ye game to hit, Will?" demanded Jackson at length.

"I don't fear him, anyway he comes," replied Will Banion. "I don't like it, but all of this was forced on me."

"The hell it was!" exclaimed Kelsey. "I heard ye call my man a liar."

"An' he called my man a coward!" cut in Jackson.

"He is a coward," sneered Woodhull, panting, "or he'd not flicker now. He's afraid I'll take his eye out, damn him!"

Will Banion turned to his friends.

"Are we gentlemen at all?" said he. "Shall we go back a hundred years?"

"If your man's afraid, we claim the fight!" exclaimed Kelsey. "Breast yore bird!"

"So be it then!" said Will Banion. "Don't mind me, Jackson! I don't fear him and I think I can beat him. It's free! I bar nothing, nor can he! Get back!"

Woodhull rushed first in the next assault, confident of his skill in rough-and-tumble. He felt at his throat the horizontal arm of his enemy. He caught away the wrist in his own hand, but sustained a heavy blow at the side of his head. The defense of his adversary angered him to blind rage. He forgot everything but contact, rushed, closed and caught his antagonist in the brawny grip of his arms. The battle at once resolved itself into the wrestling and battering match of the frontier. And it was free! Each might kill or maim if so he could.

The wrestling grips of the frontiersmen were few and primitive, efficient when applied by masters; and no schoolboy but studied all the holds as matter of religion, in a time when physical prowess was the most admirable quality a man might have.

Each fighter tried the forward jerk and trip which sometimes would do with an opponent not much skilled; but this primer work got results for neither. Banion evaded and swung into a hip lock, so swift that Woodhull left the ground. But his instinct gave him hold with one hand at his enemy's collar. He spread wide his feet and cast his weight aside, so that he came standing, after all. He well knew that a man must keep his feet. Woe to him who fell when it all was free! His own riposte was a snakelike glide close into his antagonist's arms, a swift thrust of his leg between the other's—the grapevine, which sometimes served if done swiftly.

It was done swiftly, but it did not serve. The other spread his legs, leaned against him, and in a flash came back in the dreaded crotch lock of the frontier, which some men boasted no one could escape at their hands. Woodhull was flung fair, but he broke wide and rose and rushed back and joined again, grappling; so that they stood once more body to body, panting, red, savage as any animals that fight, and more cruel. The seconds all were on their feet, scarce breathing.

They pushed in sheer test, and each found the other's stark strength. Yet Banion's breath still came even, his eye betokened no anxiety of the issue. Both were bloody now, clothing and all. Then in a flash the scales turned against the challenger *a l'outrance*.

Banion caught his antagonist by the wrist, and swift as a flash stooped, turning his own back and drawing the arm of his enemy over his own shoulder, slightly turned, so that the elbow joint was in peril and so that the pain must be intense. It was one of the jiu jitsu holds, discovered independently perhaps at that instant; certainly a new hold for the wrestling school of the frontier.

Woodhull's seconds saw the look of pain come on his face, saw him wince, saw him writhe, saw him rise on his toes. Then, with a sudden squatting heave, Banion cast him full length in front of him, upon his back! Before he had time to move he was upon him, pinning him down. A growl came from six observers.

In an ordinary fall a man might have turned, might have escaped. But Woodhull had planned his own undoing when he had called it free. Eyeless men, usually old men, in this day brought up talk of the ancient and horrible warfare of a past generation, when destruction of the adversary was the one purpose and any means called fair when it was free.

But the seconds of both men raised no hand when they saw the balls of Will Banion's thumbs pressed against the upper orbit edge of his enemy's eyes.

"Do you say enough?" panted the victor.

A groan from the helpless man beneath.

"Am I the best man? Can I whip you?" demanded the voice above him, in the formula prescribed.

"Go on—do it! Pull out his eye!" commanded Bill Jackson savagely. "He called it free to you! But don't wait!"

But the victor sprang free, stood, dashed the blood from his own eyes, wavered on his feet.

The hands of his fallen foe were across his eyes. But even as his men ran in, stooped and drew them away the conqueror exclaimed:

"I'll not! I tell you I won't maim you, free or no free! Get up!"

So Woodhull knew his eyes were spared, whatever might be the pain of the sore nerves along the socket bone.

He rose to his knees, to his feet, his face ghastly in his own sudden sense of defeat, the worse for his victor's magnanimity, if such it might be called. Humiliation was worse than pain. He staggered, sobbing.

"I won't take nothing for a gift from you!"

But now the men stood between them, like and like. Young Jed Wingate pushed back his man.

"It's done!" said he. "You shan't fight no more with the man that let you up. You're whipped, and by your own word it'd have been worse!"

He himself handed Will Banion his coat.

"Go get a pail of water," he said to Kelsey, and the latter departed.

Banion stepped apart, battered and pale beneath his own wounds.

"I didn't want to fight him this way," said he. "I left him his eyes so he can see me again. If so he wants, I'll meet him any way. I hope he won't rue back."

"You fool!" said old Bill Jackson, drawing Banion to one side. "Do ye know what ye're a-sayin'? Whiles he was a-layin' thar I seen the bottoms o' his boots. Right fancy they was, with smallish heels! That skunk'll kill ye in the dark, Will. Ye'd orto hev put out'n both his two eyes!"

A sudden sound made them all turn. Came crackling of down brush, the scream of a woman's voice. At the side of the great tree stood a figure that had no right there. They turned mute.

It was Molly Wingate who faced them all now, turning from one bloody, naked figure to the other. She saw Sam Woodhull standing, his hands still at his face; caught some sense out of Jackson's words, overheard as she came into the clearing.

"You!" she blazed at Will Banion. "You'd put out a man's eyes! You brute!"

Chapter X

OLE MISSOURY

Molly Wingate looked from one to the other of the group of silent, shamefaced men. Puzzled, she turned again to the victor in the savage combat.

"You!"

Will Banion caught up his clothing, turned away.

"You are right!" said he. "I have been a brute! Good-by!"

An instant later Molly found herself alone with the exception of her brother.

"You, Jed, what was this?" she demanded.

Jed took a deep and heartfelt chew of plug.

"Well, it was a little argument between them two," he said finally. "Like enough a little jealousy, like, you know—over place in the train, or something. This here was for men. You'd no business here."

"But it was a shame!"

"I reckon so."

"Who started this?"

"Both of them. All we was here for was to see fair. Men got to fight sometimes."

"But not like animals, not worse than savages!"

"Well, it was right savage, some of the time, Sis."

"They said—about eyes—oh!"

The girl shivered, her hands at her own eyes.

"Yes, they called it free. Anybody else, Sam Woodhull'd be sorry enough right now. T'other man throwed him clean and had him down, but he let him up. He didn't never hurt Sam's eyes, only pinched his head a little. He had a right, but didn't. It had to be settled and it was settled, fair and more'n fair, by him."

"But, Jed"—the eternal female now—"then, which one really whipped?"

"Will Banion did, ain't I told you? You insulted him, and he's gone. Having come in here where you wasn't no ways wanted, I reckon the best thing you can do is to go back to your own wagon and stay there. What with riding horses you hadn't ought, and seeing fights when you don't know a damned thing about nothing, I reckon you've made trouble about enough. Come on!"

"Price," said Bill Jackon to the grave and silent man who walked with him toward the wagon train beyond the duelling ground, "this settles hit. Us Missoury wagons won't go on under no sech man as Sam Woodhull. We didn't no ways eleck him—he was app'inted. Mostly, elected is better'n app'inted. An' I seen afore now, no man can hold his place on the trail unless'n he's fitten. We'll eleck Will Banion our cap'n, an' you fellers kin go to hell. What us fellers started out to do was to go to Oregon."

"But that'll mean the train's split!"

"Shore hit will! Hit is split right now. But thar's enough o' the Liberty wagons to go through without no help. We kin whup all the rest o' this train, give we need ter, let alone a few Injuns now an' then.

"Tonight," he concluded, "we'll head up the river, an' leave you fellers the boat an' all o' Papin's Ferry to git acrost the way you want. Thar hain't no manner o' man, outfit, river er redskin that Ole Missoury kain't lick, take 'em as they come, them to name the holts an' the rules. We done showed you-all that. We're goin' to show you some more. So good-by." He held out his hand. "Ye helped see f'ar, an' ye're a f'ar man, an' we'll miss ye. Ef ye git in need o' help come to us. Ole Missoury won't need no help."

"Well, Woodhull's one of you Missourians," remarked Price.

"Yes, but he'ain't bred true. Major Banion is. Hit was me that made him fight knuckle an' skull an' not with weepons. He didn't want to, but I had a reason. I'm content an' soothe jest the way she lies. Ef Will never sees the gal agin she ain't wuth the seein'.

"Ye'll find Col. William Banion at the head o' his own train. He's fitten, an' he's fout an' proved hit."

Chapter XI

WHEN ALL THE WORLD WAS YOUNG

Molly Wingate kneeled by her cooking fire the following morning, her husband meantime awaiting the morning meal impatiently. All along the medley of crowded wagons rose confused sounds of activity at a hundred similar firesides.

"Where's Little Molly?" demanded Wingate. "We got to be up and coming."

"Her and Jed is off after the cattle. Well, you heard the news last night. You've got to get someone else to run the herd. If each family drives its own loose stock everything'll be all mixed up. The Liberty outfit pulled on by at dawn. Well, anyways they left us the sawmill and the boat.

"Sam Woodhull, he's anxious to get on ahead of the Missourians," she added. "He says he'll take the boat anyhow, and not pay them Kaws any such hold-up price like they ask."

"All I got to say is, I wish we were across," grumbled Wingate, stooping to the bacon spider.

"Huh! So do I—me and my bureau and my hens. Yes, after you've fussed around a while you men'll maybe come to the same conclusion your head cow guard had; you'll be making more boats and doing less swimming. I'm sorry he quit us."

"It's the girl," said her husband sententiously.

"Yes. But"—smiling grimly—"one furse don't make a parting."

"She's same as promised Sam Woodhull, Molly, and you know that."

"Before he got whipped by Colonel Banion."

"Colonel! Fine business for an officer! Woodhull told me he tripped and this other man was on top of him and nigh gouged out his two eyes. And he told me other things too. Banion's a traitor, to split the train. We can spare all such."

"Can we?" rejoined his wife. "I sort of thought—"

"Never mind what you thought. He's one of the unruly, servigerous sort; can't take orders, and a trouble maker always. We'll show that outfit. I've ordered three more scows built and the seams calked in the wagon boxes."

Surely enough, the Banion plan of crossing, after all, was carried out, and although the river dropped a foot meantime, the attempt to ford *en masse* was abandoned. Little by little the wagon parks gathered on the north bank, each family assorting its own goods and joining in the general *sauve qui peut*.

Nothing was seen of the Missouri column, but rumor said they were ferrying slowly, with one boat and their doubled wagon boxes, over which they had nailed hides. Woodhull was keen to get on north ahead of this body. He had personal reasons for that. None too well pleased at the smiles with which his explanations of his bruised face were received, he made a sudden resolution to take a band of his own immediate neighbors and adherents and get on ahead of the Missourians. He based his decision, as he announced it, on the necessity of a scouting party to locate grass and water.

Most of the men who joined him were single men, of the more restless sort. There were no family wagons with them. They declared their intention of traveling fast and light until they got among the buffalo. This party left in advance of the main caravan, which had not yet completed the crossing of the Kaw.

"Roll out! Ro-o-o-ll out!" came the mournful command at last, once more down the line.

It fell on the ears of some who were unwilling to obey. The caravan was disintegrating at the start. The gloom cast by the long delay at the ford had now resolved itself in certain instances into fear amounting half to panic. Some companies of neighbors said the entire train should wait for the military escort; others declared they would not go further west, but would turn back and settle here, where the soil was so good. Still others said they all should lie here, with good grass and water, until further word came from the Platte Valley train and until they had more fully decided what to do. In spite of all the officers could do, the general advance was strung out over two or three miles. The rapid loss in order, these premature divisions of the train, augured ill enough.

The natural discomforts of the trail now also began to have their effect. A plague of green-headed flies and flying ants assailed them by day, and at night the mosquitoes made an affliction well-nigh insufferable. The women and children could not sleep, the horses groaned all night under the clouds of tormentors which gathered on them. Early as it was, the sun at times blazed with intolerable fervor, or again the heat broke in savage storms of thunder, hail and rain. All the elements, all the circumstances seemed in league to warn them back before it was too late, for indeed they were not yet more than on the threshold of the Plains.

The spring rains left the ground soft in places, so that in creek valleys stretches of corduroy sometimes had to be laid down. The high waters made even the lesser fords difficult and dangerous, and all knew that between them and the Platte ran several strong and capricious rivers, making in general to the southeast and necessarily transected by the great road to Oregon.

They still were in the eastern part of what is now the state of Kansas, one of the most beautiful and exuberantly rich portions of the country, as all early travelers declared. The land lay in a succession of timber-lined valleys and open prairie ridges. Groves of walnut, oak, hickory, elm, ash at first were frequent, slowly changing, farther west, to larger proportions of poplar, willow and cottonwood. The white dogwood passed to make room for scattering thickets of wild plum. Wild tulips, yellow or of broken colors; the campanula, the wild honeysuckle, lupines—not yet quite in bloom—the sweetbrier and increasing quantities of the wild rose gave life to the always changing scene. Wild game of every sort was unspeakably abundant—deer and turkey in every bottom, thousands of grouse on the hills, vast flocks of snipe and plover, even numbers of the green parrakeets then so numerous along that latitude. The streams abounded in game fish. All Nature was easy and generous.

Men and women grumbled at leaving so rich and beautiful a land lying waste. None had seen a country more supremely attractive. Emotions of tenderness, of sadness, also came to many. Nostalgia was not yet shaken off. This strained condition of nerves, combined with the trail hardships, produced the physical irritation which is inevitable in all amateur pioneer work. Confusions, discordances, arising over the most trifling circumstances, grew into petulance, incivility, wrangling and intrigue, as happened in so many other earlier caravans. In the Babel-like excitement of the morning catchup, amid the bellowing and running of the cattle evading the yoke, more selfishness, less friendly accommodation now appeared, and men met without speaking, even this early on the road.

The idea of four parallel columns had long since been discarded. They broke formation, and at times the long caravan, covering the depressions and eminences of the prairie, wound along in mile-long detachments, each of which hourly grew more surly and more independent. Overdriven oxen now began to drop. By the time the prairies proper were reached more than a score of oxen had died. They were repeating trail history as recorded by the travelers of that day.

Personal and family problems also made divisions more natural. Many suffered from ague; fevers were very common. An old woman past seventy died one night and was buried by the wayside the next day. Ten days after the start twins were born to parents moving out to Oregon. There were numbers of young children, many of them in arms, who became ill. For one or other cause, wagons continually were dropping out. It was difficult for some wagons to keep up, the unseasoned oxen showing distress under loads too heavy for their draft. It was by no means a solid and compact army, after all, this west-bound wave of the first men with plows. All these things sat heavily on the soul of Jesse Wingate, who daily grew more morose and grim.

As the train advanced bands of antelope began to appear. The striped prairie gophers gave place to the villages of countless barking prairie dogs, curious to the eyes of the newcomers. At night the howling and snarling of gray wolves now made regular additions to the coyote chorus and the voices of the owls and whippoorwills. Little by little, day by day, civilization was passing, the need for organization daily became more urgent. Yet the original caravan had split practically into three divisions within a hundred and fifty miles from the jump-off, although the bulk of the train hung to Wingate's company and began to shake down, at least into a sort of tolerance.

Granted good weather, as other travelers had written, it was indeed impossible to evade the sense of exhilaration in the bold, free life. At evening encampment the scene was one worthy of any artist of all the world. The oblong of the wagon park, the white tents, the many fires, made a spectacle of marvelous charm and power. Perhaps within sight, at one time, under guard for the evening feed on the fresh young grass, there would be two thousand head of cattle. In the wagon village men, women and children would be engaged as though at home. There was little idleness in the train, and indeed there was much gravity and devoutness in the personnel. At one fireside the young men might be roaring "Old Grimes is dead, that good old man," or "Oh, then, Susannah"; but quite as likely close at hand some family group would be heard in sacred hymns. A strange envisagement it all made, in a strange environment, a new atmosphere, here on the threshold of the wilderness.[1]

[1] To get the local descriptions, the color, atmosphere, "feel" of a day and a country so long gone by, any writer of today must go to writers of another day. The Author would acknowledge free use of the works of Palmer, Bryant, Kelly and others who give us journals of the great transcontinental trail.

Chapter XII

THE DEAD MEN'S TALE

The wilderness, close at hand, soon was to make itself felt. Wingate's outriders moved out before noon of one day, intending to locate camp at the ford of the Big Vermilion. Four miles in advance they unexpectedly met the scout of the Missouri column, Bill Jackson, who had passed the Wingate train by a cut-off of his own on a solitary ride ahead for sake of information. He was at a gallop now, and what he said sent them all back at full speed to the head of the Wingate column.

Jackson riding ahead, came up with his hand raised for a halt.

"My God, Cap'n, stop the train!" he called. "Hit won't do for the womern and children to see what's on ahead yan!"

"What's up—where?" demanded Wingate.

"On three mile, on the water where they camped night afore last. Thar they air ten men, an' the rest's gone. Woodhull's wagons, but he ain't thar. Wagons burned, mules standing with arrers in them, rest all dead but a few. Hit's the Pawnees!"

The column leaders all galloped forward, seeing first what later most of the entire train saw—the abominable phenomena of Indian warfare on the Plains.

Scattered over a quarter of a mile, where the wagons had stood not grouped and perhaps not guarded, lay heaps of wreckage beside heaps of ashes. One by one the corpses were picked out, here, there, over more than a mile of ground. They had fought, yes, but fought each his own losing individual battle after what had been a night surprise.

The swollen and blackened features of the dead men stared up, mutilated as savages alone mark the fallen. Two were staked out, hand and foot, and ashes lay near them, upon them. Arrows stood up between the ribs of the dead men, driven through and down into the ground. A dozen mules, as Jackson had said, drooped with low heads and hanging ears, arrow shafts standing out of their paunches, waiting for death to end their agony.

"Finish them, Jackson."

Wingate handed the hunter his own revolver, signaling for Kelsey and Hall to do the same. The methodical cracking of the hand arms began to end the suffering of the animals.

They searched for scraps of clothing to cover the faces of the dead, the bodies of some dead. They motioned the women and children back when the head of the train came up. Jackson beckoned the leaders to the side of one wagon, partially burned.

"Look," said he, pointing.

A long stick, once a whipstock, rose from the front of the wagon bed. It had been sharpened and thrust under the wrist skin of a human hand—a dried hand, not of a white man, but a red. A half-corroded bracelet of copper still clung to the wrist.

"If I read signs right, that's why!" commented Bill Jackson.

"But how do you explain it?" queried Hall. "Why should they do that? And how could they, in so close a fight?"

"They couldn't," said Jackson. "That hand's a day an' a half older than these killings. Hit's Sam Woodhull's wagon. Well, the Pawnees like enough counted coup on the man that swung that hand up for a sign, even if hit wasn't one o' their own people."

"Listen, men," he concluded, "hit was Woodhull's fault. We met some friendlies—Kaws—from the mission, an' they was mournin'. A half dozen o' them follered Woodhull out above the ferry when he pulled out. They told him he hadn't paid them for their boat, asked him for more presents. He got mad, so they say, an' shot down one o' them an' stuck up his hand—fer a warnin', so he said.

"The Kaws didn't do this killin'. This band of Pawnees was away down below their range. The Kaws said they was comin' fer a peace council, to git the Kaws an' Otoes to raise against us whites, comin' out so many, with plows and womernfolks—they savvy.

Well, the Kaws has showed the Pawnees. The Pawnees has showed us."

"Yes," said the deep voice of Caleb Price, property owner and head of a family; "they've showed us that Sam Woodhull was not fit to trust. There's one man that is."

"Do you want him along with your wagons?" demanded Jackson. He turned to Wingate.

"Well," said the train captain after a time, "we are striking the Indian country now."

"Shall I bring up our wagons an' jine ye all here at the ford this evenin'?"

"I can't keep you from coming on up the road if you want to. I'll not ask you."

"All right! We'll not park with ye then. But we'll be on the same water. Hit's my own fault we split. We wouldn't take orders from Sam Woodhull, an' we never will."

He nodded to the blackened ruins, to the grim dead hand pointing to the sky, left where it was by the superstitious blood avengers.

Wingate turned away and led the wagon train a half mile up the stream, pitching camp above the ford where the massacre had occurred. The duties of the clergy and the appointed sextons were completed. Silence and sadness fell on the encampment.

Jackson, the scout of the Missouri column, still lingered

for some sort of word with Molly Wingate. Some odds and ends of brush lay about. Of the latter Molly began casting a handful on the fire and covering it against the wind with her shawl, which at times she quickly removed. As a result the confined smoke arose at more or less well defined intervals, in separate puffs or clouds.

"Ef ye want to know how to give the smoke signal right an' proper, Miss Molly," said he at length, quietly, "I'll larn ye how."

The girl looked up at him.

"Well, I don't know much about it."

"This way: Hit takes two to do hit best. You catch holt two corners o' the shawl now. Hist it on a stick in the middle. Draw it down all over the fire. Let her simmer under some green stuff. Now! Lift her clean off, sideways, so's not ter break the smoke ball. See 'em go up? That's how."

He looked at the girl keenly under his bushy gray brows.

"That's the Injun signal fer 'Enemy in the country.' S'pose you ever wanted to signal, say to white folks, 'Friend in the country,' you might remember—three short puffs an' one long one. That might bring up a friend. Sech a signal can be seed a long ways."

Molly flushed to the eyes.

"What do you mean?"

"Nothin' at all, any more'n you do."

Jackson rose and left her.

Chapter XIII

WILD FIRE

The afternoon wore on, much occupied with duties connected with the sad scenes of the tragedy. No word came of Woodhull, or of two others who could not be identified as among the victims at the death camp. No word, either, came from the Missourians, and so cowed or dulled were most of the men of the caravan that they did not venture far, even to undertake trailing out after the survivors of the massacre. In sheer indecision the great aggregation of wagons, piled up along the stream, lay apathetic, and no order came for the advance.

Jed and his cow guards were obliged to drive the cattle back into the ridges for better grazing, for the valley and adjacent country, which had not been burned over by the Indians the preceding fall, held a lower matting of heavy dry grass through which the green grass of springtime appeared only in sparser and more smothered growth. As many of the cattle and horses even now showed evil results from injudicious driving on the trail, it was at length decided to make a full day's stop so that they might feed up.

Molly Wingate, now assured that the Pawnees no longer were in the vicinity, ventured out for pasturage with her team of mules, which she had kept tethered close to her own wagon. She now rapidly was becoming a good frontierswoman and thoughtful of her locomotive power. Taking the direction of the cattle herd, she drove from camp a mile or two, resolving to hobble and watch her mules while they grazed close to the cattle guards.

She was alone. Around her, untouched by any civilization, lay a wild, free world. The ceaseless wind of the prairie swept old and new grass into a continuous undulating surface, silver crested, a wave always passing, never past. The sky was unspeakably fresh and blue, with its light clouds, darker edged toward the far horizon of the unbounded, unbroken expanse of alternating levels and low hills. Across the broken ridges passed the teeming bird life of the land. The Eskimo plover in vast bands circled and sought their nesting places. Came also the sweep of cinnamon wings as the giant sickle-billed curlews wheeled in vast aerial phalanx, with their eager cries, "Curlee! Curlee! Curlee!"—the wildest cry of the old prairies. Again, from some unknown, undiscoverable place, came the liquid, baffling, mysterious note of the nesting upland plover, sweet and clean as pure white honey.

Now and again a band of antelope swept ghostlike across a ridge. A great gray wolf stood contemptuously near on a hillock, gazing speculatively at the strange new creature, the white woman, new come in his lands. It was the wilderness, rude, bold, yet sweet.

Who shall say what thoughts the flowered wilderness of spring carried to the soul of a young woman beautiful and ripe for love, her heart as sweet and melting as that of the hidden plover telling her mate of happiness? Surely a strange spell, born of youth and all this free world of things beginning, fell on the soul of Molly Wingate. She sat and dreamed, her hands idle, her arms empty, her beating pulses full, her heart full of a maid's imaginings.

How long she sat alone, miles apart, an unnoticed figure, she herself could not have said—surely the sun was past zenith—when, moved by some vague feeling of her own, she noticed the uneasiness of her feeding charges.

The mules, hobbled and side-lined as Jed had shown her, turned face to the wind, down the valley, standing for a time studious and uncertain rather than alarmed. Then, their great ears pointed, they became uneasy; stirred, stamped, came back again to their position, gazing steadily in the one direction.

The ancient desert instinct of the wild ass, brought down through thwarted generations, never had been lost to them. They had foreknowledge of danger long before horses or human beings could suspect it.

Danger? What was it? Something, surely. Molly sprang to her feet. A band of antelope, running, had paused a hundred yards away, gazing back. Danger—yes; but what?

The girl ran to the crest of the nearest hillock and looked back. Even as she did so, it seemed that she caught touch of the great wave of apprehension spreading swiftly over the land.

Far off, low lying like a pale blue cloud, was a faint line of something that seemed to alter in look, to move to rise and fall, to advance—down the wind. She never had seen it, but knew what it must be—the prairie fire! The lack of fall burning had left it fuel even now.

Vast numbers of prairie grouse came by, hurtling through the silence, alighting, strutting with high heads, fearlessly close. Gray creatures came hopping, halting or running fully extended—the prairie hares, fleeing far ahead. Band after band of antelope came on, running easily, but looking back. A heavy line of large birds, black to the eye, beat on laboriously, alighted, and ran onward with incredible speed—the wild turkeys, fleeing the terror. Came also broken bands of white-tailed deer, easy, elastic, bounding irregularly, looking back at the miles-wide cloud, which now and then spun up, black as ink toward the sky, but always flattened and came onward with the wind.

Danger? Yes! Worse than Indians, for yonder were the cattle; there lay the parked train, two hundred wagons, with the household goods that meant their life savings and their future hope in far-off Oregon. Women were there, and children—women with babes that could not walk. True, the water lay close, but it was narrow and deep and offered no salvation against the terror now coming on the wings of the wind.

That the prairie fire would find in this strip fuel to carry it even at this green season of the grass the wily Pawnees had known. This was cheaper than assault by arms. They would wither and scatter the white nation here! Worse than plumed warriors was yonder broken undulating line of the prairie fire.

Instinct told the white girl, gave her the same terror as that which inspired all these fleeing creatures. But what could she do? This was an elemental, gigantic wrath, and she but a frightened girl. She guessed rather than reasoned what it would mean when yonder line came closer, when it would sweep down, roaring, over the wagon train.

The mules began to bray, to plunge, too wise to undertake flight. She would at least save them. She would mount one and ride with the alarm for the camp.

The wise animals let her come close, did not plunge, knew that she meant help, allowed her trembling hands to loose one end of the hobble straps, but no more. As soon as each mule got its feet it whirled and was away. No chance to hold one of them now, and if she had mounted a hobbled animal it had meant nothing. But she saw them go toward the stream, toward the camp. She must run that way herself.

It was so far! There was a faint smell of smoke and a mysterious low humming in the air. Was it too late?

A swift, absurd, wholly useless memory came to her from the preceding day. Yes, it would be no more than a prayer, but she would send it out blindly into the air. . . . Some instinct—yes, quite likely.

Molly ran to her abandoned wagonette, pushed in under the white tilt where her pallet bed lay rolled, her little personal plunder stored about. Fumbling, she found her sulphur matches. She would build her signal fire. It was, at least, all that she could do. It might at least alarm the camp.

Trembling, she looked about her, tore her hands breaking

off little faggots of tall dry weed stems, a very few bits of
wild thorn and fragments of a plum thicket in the nearest
shallow coulee. She ran to her hillock, stooped and broke a
dozen matches, knowing too little of fire-making in the
wind. But at last she caught a wisp of dry grass, a few dry
stems—others, the bits of wild plum branches. She shielded
her tiny blaze with her frock, looking back over her shoulder, where the black curtain was rising taller. Now and then,
even in the blaze of full day, a red, dull gleam rose and
passed swiftly. The entire country was afire. Fuel? Yes; and
a wind.

The humming in the air grew, the scent of fire came
plainly. The plover rose around their nests and circled, crying piteously. The scattered hares became a great body of
moving gray, like camouflage blots on the still undulating
waves of green and silver, passing but not yet past—soon
now to pass.

The girl, her hands arrested, her arms out, in her terror,
stood trying to remember. Yes, it was three short puffs and
a long pillar. She caught her shawl from her shoulder,
stooped, spread it with both hands, drove in her stiffest
bough for a partial support, cast in under the edge, timidly,
green grass enough to make smoke, she hoped.

An instant and she sprang up, drawing the shawl swiftly
aside, the next moment jealously cutting through the smoke
with a side sweep of the covering.

It worked! The cut-off column rose, bent over in a little
detached cloud. Again, with a quick flirt, eager eyed, and
again the detached irregular ball! A third time—Molly rose,
and now cast on dry grass and green grass till a tall and
moving pillar of cloud by day arose.

At least she had made her prayer. She could do no more.
With vague craving for any manner of refuge, she crawled
to her wagon seat and covered her eyes. She knew that the
wagon train was warned—they now would need but little
warning, for the menace was written all across the world.

She sat she knew not how long, but until she became
conscious of a roaring in the air. The line of fire had come
astonishingly soon, she reasoned. But she forgot that. All

the vanguard and the full army of wild creatures had passed by now. She alone, the white woman, most helpless of the great creatures, stood before the terror.

She sprang out of the wagon and looked about her. The smoke crest, black, red-shot, was coming close. The grass here would carry it. Perhaps yonder on the flint ridge where the cover was short—why had she not thought of that long ago? It was half a mile, and no sure haven then.

She ran, her shawl drawn about her head—ran with long, free stride, her limbs envigored by fear, her full-bosomed body heaving chokingly. The smoke was now in the air, and up the unshorn valley came the fire remorselessly, licking up the under lying layer of sun-cured grass which a winter's snow had matted down.

She could never reach the ridge now. Her over-burdened lungs functioned but little. The world went black, with many points of red. Everywhere was the odor and feel of smoke. She fell and gasped, and knew little, cared little what might come. The elemental terror at last had caught its prey—soft, young, beautiful prey, this huddled form, a bit of brown and gray, edged with white of wind-blown skirt. It would be a sweet morsel for the flames.

Along the knife-edged flint ridge which Molly had tried to reach there came the pounding of hoofs, heavier than any of these that had passed. The cattle were stampeding directly down wind and before the fire. Dully, Molly heard the lowing, heard the far shouts of human voices. Then, it seemed to her, she heard a rush of other hoofs coming toward her. Yes, something was pounding down the slope toward her wagon, toward her. Buffalo, she thought, not knowing the buffalo were gone from that region.

But it was not the buffalo, nor yet the frightened herd, nor yet her mules. Out of the smoke curtain broke a rider, his horse flat; a black horse with flying frontlet—she knew what horse. She knew what man rode him, too, black with smoke as he was now. He swept close to the wagon and was off. Something flickered there, with smoke above it, beyond the wagon by some yards. Then he was in saddle and racing again, his eyes and teeth white in the black mask of his face.

She heard no call and no command. But an arm reached down to hers, swept up—and she was going onward, the horn of a saddle under her, her body held to that of the rider, swung sidewise. The horse was guided not down but across the wind.

Twice and three times, silent, he flung her off and was down, kindling his little back fires—the only defense against a wildfire. He breathed thickly, making sounds of rage.

"Will they never start?" he broke out at last. "The fools—the fools!"

But by now it was too late. A sudden accession in the force of the wind increased the speed of the fire. The little line near Molly's wagon spared it, but caught strength. Could she have seen through the veils of smoke she would have seen a half dozen fires this side the line of the great fire. But fire is fire.

Again he was in saddle and had her against his thigh, his body, flung any way so she came with the horse. And now the horse swerved, till he drove in the steel again and again, heading him not away from the fire but straight into it!

Molly felt a rush of hot air; surging, actual flame singed the ends of her hair. She felt his hand again and again sweep over her skirts, wiping out the fire as it caught. It was blackly hot, stifling—and then it was past!

Before her lay a wide black world. Her wagon stood, even its white top spared by miracle of the back fire. But beyond came one more line of smoke and flame. The black horse neighed now in the agony of his hot hoofs. His rider swung him to a lower level, where under the tough cover had lain moist ground, on which uncovered water now glistened. He flung her into the mire of it, pulled up his horse there and himself lay down, full length, his blackened face in the moist mud above which still smoked stubbles of the flame-shorn grass. He had not spoken to her, nor she to him. His eyes rested on the singed ends of her blown hair, her charred garments, in a frowning sympathy which found no speech. At length he brought the reins of his horse to her, flirting up the singed ends of the long mane, further proof of their narrow escape.

"I must try once more," he said. "The main fire might catch the wagon."

He made off afoot. She saw him start a dozen nucleuses of fires; saw them advance till they halted at the edge of the burned ground, beyond the wagon, so that it stood safe in a vast black island. He came to her, drove his scorched boots deep as he could into the mud and sat looking up the valley toward the emigrant train. An additional curtain of smoke showed that the men there now were setting out back fires of their own. He heard her voice at last:

"It is the second time you have saved me—saved my life, I think. Why did you come?"

He turned to her as she sat in the edge of the wallow, her face streaked with smoke, her garments half burned off her limbs. She now saw his hands, which he was thrusting out on the mud to cool them, and sympathy was in her gaze also.

"I don't know why I came," said he. "Didn't you signal for me? Jackson told me you could."

"No, I had no hope. I meant no one. It was only a prayer."

"It carried ten miles. We were all back-firing. It caught in the sloughs—all the strips of old grass. I thought of your camp, of you. At least your signal told me where to ride."

At length he waved his hand.

"They're safe over there," said he. "Think of the children!"

"Yes, and you gave me my one chance. Why?"

"I don't know. I suppose it was because I am a brute!" The bitterness of his voice was plain.

"Come, we must go to the wagons," said Molly at length, and would have risen.

"No, not yet. The burned ground must cool before we can walk on it. I would not even take my horse out on it again." He lifted a foot of the black Spaniard, whose muzzle quivered whimperingly. "All right, old boy!" he said, and stroked the head thrust down to him. "It might have been worse."

His voice was so gentle that Molly Wingate felt a vague

sort of jealousy. He might have taken her scorched hand in his, might at least have had some thought for her welfare. He did speak at last as to that.

"What's in your wagon?" he asked. "We had better go there to wait. Have you anything along—oil, flour, anything to use on burns? You're burned. It hurts me to see a woman suffer."

"Are not you burned too?"

"Yes."

"It pains you?"

"Oh, yes, of course."

He rose and led the way over the damper ground to the wagon, which stood smoke-stained but not charred, thanks to his own resourcefulness.

Molly climbed up to the seat, and rummaging about found a jar of butter, a handful of flour.

"Come up on the seat," said she. "This is better medicine than nothing."

He climbed up and sat beside her. She frowned again as she now saw how badly scorched his hands were, his neck, his face. His eyebrows, caught by one wisp of flame, were rolled up at the ends, whitened. One cheek was a dull red.

Gently, without asking his consent, she began to coat his burned skin as best she might with her makeshift of alleviation. His hand trembled under hers.

"Now," she said, "hold still. I must fix your hand some more."

She still bent over, gently, delicately touching his flesh with hers. And then all in one mad, unpremeditated instant it was done!

His hand caught hers, regardless of the pain to either. His arm went about her, his lips would have sought hers.

It was done! Now he might repent.

A mad way of wooing, inopportune, fatal as any method he possibly could have found, moreover a cruel, unseemly thing to do, here and with her situated thus. But it was done.

Till now he had never given her grounds for more than guessing. Yet now here was this!

He came to his senses as she thrust him away; saw her cheeks whiten, her eyes grow wide.

"Oh!" she said. "Oh! Oh! Oh!"

"Oh!" whispered Will Banion to himself, hoarsely.

He held his two scorched hands each side her face as she drew back, sought to look into her eyes, so that she might believe either his hope, his despair or his contrition.

But she turned her eyes away. Only he could hear her outraged protest—"Oh! Oh! Oh!"

Chapter XIV

THE KISS

It was the wind!" Will Banion exclaimed. "It was the sky, the earth! It was the fire! I don't know what it was! I swear it was not I who did it! Don't forgive me, but don't blame me. Molly! Molly!

"It had to be sometime," he went on, since she still drew away from him. "What chance have I had to ask you before now? It's little I have to offer but my love."

"What do you mean? It will never be at any time!" said Molly Wingate slowly, her hand touching his no more.

"What do you yourself mean?" He turned to her in agony of soul. "You will not let me repent? You will not give me some sort of chance?"

"No," she said coldly. "You have had chance enough to be a gentleman—as much as you had when you were in Mexico with other women. But Major William Banion falsified the regimental accounts. I know that too. I didn't—I couldn't believe it—till now."

He remained dumb under this. She went on mercilessly.

"Oh, yes, Captain Woodhull told us. Yes, he showed us

the very vouchers. My father believed it of you, but I didn't. Now I do. Oh, fine! And you an officer of our Army!"

She blazed out at him now, her temper rising.

"Chance? What more chance did you need? No wonder you couldn't love a girl—any other way than this. It would have to be sometime, you say. What do you mean? That I'd ever marry a thief?"

Still he could not speak. The fire marks showed livid against a paling cheek.

"Yes, I know you saved me—twice, this time at much risk," resumed the girl. "Did you want pay so soon? You'd—you'd—"

"Oh! Oh! Oh!"

It was his voice that now broke in. He could not speak at all beyond the exclamation under torture.

"I didn't believe that story about you," she added after a long time. "But you are not what you looked, not what I thought you were. So what you say must be sometime is never going to be at all."

"Did he tell you that about me?" demanded Will Banion savagely. "Woodhull—did he say that?"

"I have told you, yes. My father knew. No wonder he didn't trust you. How could he?"

She moved now as though to leave the wagon, but he raised a hand.

"Wait!" said he. "Look yonder! You'd not have time now to reach camp."

In the high country a great prairie fire usually or quite often was followed by a heavy rainstorm. What Banion now indicated was the approach of yet another of the epic phenomena of the prairies, as rapid, as colossal and as merciless as the fire itself.

On the western horizon a low dark bank of clouds lay for miles, piled, serrated, steadily rising opposite to the course of the wind that had driven the fire. Along it more and more visibly played almost incessant sheet lightning, broken with ripping zigzag flames. A hush had fallen close at hand, for now even the frightened breeze of evening had fled. Now and then, at first doubtful, then unmistakable and continu-

ous, came the mutter and rumble and at length the steady
roll of thunder.

They lay full in the course of one of the tremendous
storms of the high country, and as the cloud bank rose and
came on swiftly, spreading its flanking wings so that nothing
might escape, the spectacle was terrifying almost as much
as that of the fire, for, unprotected, as they were, they could
make no counter battle against the storm.

The air grew supercharged with electricity. It dripped, literally, from the barrel of Banion's pistol when he took it
from its holster to carry it to the wagon. He fastened the
reins of his horse to a wheel and hastened with other work.
A pair of trail ropes lay in the wagon. He netted them over
the wagon top and lashed the ends to the wheels to make
the top securer, working rapidly, eyes on the advancing
storm.

There came a puff, then a gust of wind. The sky blackened. The storm caught the wagon train first. There was no
interval at all between the rip of the lightning and the crash
of thunder as it rolled down on the clustered wagons. The
electricity at times came not in a sheet or a ragged bolt, but
in a ball of fire, low down, close to the ground, exploding
with giant detonations.

Then came the rain, with a blanketing rush of level wind,
sweeping away the last vestige of the wastrel fires of the
emigrant encampment. An instant and every human being
in the train, most of them ill defended by their clothing, was
drenched by the icy flood. One moment and the battering of
hail made climax of it all. The groaning animals plunged
and fell at their picket ropes, or broke and fled into the open.
The remaining cattle caught terror, and since there was no
corral, most of the cows and oxen stampeded down the
wind.

The canvas of the covered wagons made ill defense. Many
of them were stripped off, others leaked like sieves. Mothers
sat huddled in their calicoes, bending over their tow-shirted
young, some of them babes in arms. The single jeans garments of the boys gave them no comfort. Under the wagons
and carts, wrapped in blankets or patched quilts whose col-

ors dripped, they crawled and sat as the air grew strangely chill. Only wreckage remained when they saw the storm muttering its way across the prairies, having done what it could in its elemental wrath to bar the road to the white man.

As for Banion and Molly, they sat it out in the light wagon, the girl wrapped in blankets, Banion much of the time out in the storm, swinging on the ropes to keep the wagon from overturning. He had no apparent fear. His calm assuaged her own new terrors. In spite of her bitter arraignment, she was glad that he was here, though he hardly spoke to her at all.

"Look!" he exclaimed at last, drawing back the flap of the wagon cover. "Look at the rainbow!"

Over the cloud banks of the rain-wet sky there indeed now was flung the bow of promise. But this titanic land did all things gigantically. This was no mere prismatic arch bridging the clouds. The colors all were there, yes, and of an unspeakable brilliance and individual distinctness in the scale; but they lay like a vast painted mist, a mural of some celestial artist flung *en masse* against the curtain of the night. The entire clouded sky, miles on untold miles, was afire. All the opals of the universe were melted and cast into a tremendous picture painted by the Great Spirit of the Plains.

"Oh, wonderful!" exclaimed the girl. "It might be the celestial city in the desert, promised by the Mormon prophet!"

"It may be so to them. May it be so to us. Blessed be the name of the Lord God of Hosts!" said Will Banion.

She looked at him suddenly, strangely. What sort of man was he, after all, so full of strange contradictions—a savage, a criminal, yet reverent and devout?

"Come," he said, "we can get back now, and you must go. They will think you are lost."

He stepped to the saddle of his shivering horse and drew off the poncho, which he had spread above the animal instead of using it himself. He was wet to the bone. With apology he cast the waterproof over Molly's shoulders, since she now had discarded her blankets. He led the way, his horse following them.

They walked in silence in the deep twilight which began to creep across the blackened land. All through the storm he had scarcely spoken to her, and he spoke but rarely now. He was no more than guide. But as she approached safety, Molly Wingate began to reflect how much she really owed this man. He had been a pillar of strength, elementally fit to combat all the elements, else she had perished.

"Wait!"

She had halted at the point of the last hill which lay between them and the wagons. They could hear the wailing of the children close at hand. He turned inquiringly. She handed back the poncho.

"I am all right now. You're wet, you're tired, you're burned to pieces. Won't you come on in?"

"Not tonight!"

But still she hesitated. In her mind there were going on certain processes she could not have predicted an hour earlier.

"I ought to thank you," she said. "I do thank you."

His utter silence made it hard for her. He could see her hesitation, which made it hard for him, coveting sight of her always, loath to leave her.

Now a sudden wave of something, a directness and frankness born in some way in this new world apart from civilization, like a wind-blown flame, irresponsible and irresistible, swept over Molly Wingate's soul as swiftly, as unpremeditatedly as it had over his. She was a young woman fit for love, disposed for love, at the age for love. Now, to her horror, the clasp of this man's arm, even when repelled in memory, returned, remained in memory! She was frightened that it still remained—frightened at her own great curiousness.

"About—that"—he knew what she meant—"I don't want you to think anything but the truth of me. If you have deceived people, I don't want to deceive you."

"What do you mean?" He was a man of not very many words.

"About—that!"

"You said it could never be."

"No. If it could, I would not be stopping here now to say so much."

He stepped closer, frowning.

"What is it you are saying then—that a man's a worse brute when he goes mad, as I did?"

"I expect not," said Molly Wingate queerly. "It is very far, out here. It's some other world, I believe. And I suppose men have kissed girls. I suppose no girl ever was married who was not ever kissed."

"What are you saying?"

"I said I wanted you to know the truth about a woman—about me. That's just because it's not ever going to be between us. It can't be, because of that other matter in Mexico. If it had not been for that, I suppose after a time I wouldn't have minded what you did back there. I might have kissed you. It must be terrible to feel as you feel now, so ashamed. But after all—"

"It was criminal!" he broke out. "But even criminals are loved by women. They follow them to jail, to the gallows. They don't mind what the man is—they love him, they forgive him. They stand by him to the very end!"

"Yes, I suppose many a girl loves a man she knows she never can marry. Usually she marries someone else. But kissing! That's terrible!"

"Yes. But you will not let me make it splendid and not terrible. You say it never can be—that means we've got to part. Well, how can I forget?"

"I don't suppose you can. I don't suppose that—that I can!"

"What are you going to say? Don't! Oh, please don't!"

But she still went on, strangely, not in the least understanding her own swift change of mood, her own intent with him, *vis-à-vis*, here in the wilderness.

"While we were walking down here just now," said she, "somehow it all began to seem not so wrong. It only seemed to stay wrong for you to have deceived me about yourself— what you really were—when you were in the Army. I could maybe forgive you up to that far, for you did—for men are—well, men. But about that other—you knew all the time we couldn't—couldn't ever—I'd never marry a thief."

The great and wistful regret of her voice was a thing not to be escaped. She stood, a very splendid figure, clean and marvelous of heart as she was begrimed and bedraggled of body now, her great vital force not abated by what she had gone through. She spread her hands just apart and looked at him in what she herself felt was to be the last meeting of their lives; in which she could afford to reveal all her soul for once to a man, and then go about a woman's business of living a life fed on the husks of love given her by some other man.

He knew that he had seen one more miracle. But, chastened now, he could, he must, keep down his own eager arms. He heard her speak once more, her voice like some melancholy bell of vespers of a golden evening.

"Oh, Will Banion, how could you take away a girl's heart and leave her miserable all her life?"

The cry literally broke from her. It seemed in her own ears the sudden voice of some other woman speaking— some unaccountable, strange woman whom she never had seen or known in all her life.

"Your—heart?" he whispered, now close to her in the dusk. "You were not—you did not—you—"

But he choked. She nodded, not brazenly or crudely or coarsely, not even bravely, but in utter simplicity. For the time she was wholly free of woman coquetry. It was as though the elements had left her also elemental. Her words now were of the earth, the air, the fire, the floods of life.

"Yes," she said, "I will tell you now, because of what you have done for me. If you gave me life, why shouldn't I give you love—if so I could?"

"Love? Give me love?"

"Yes! I believe I was going to love you, until now, although I had promised him—you know—Captain Woodhull. Oh, you see, I understand a little of what it was to you—what made you—" She spoke disconnectedly. "I believe—I believe I'd not have cared. I believe I could follow a man to the gallows. Now I will not, because you didn't tell me you were a thief. I can't trust you. But I'll kiss you once for good-by. I'm sorry. I'm so sorry."

Being a man, he never fathomed her mind at all. But being a man, slowly, gently, he took her in his arms, drew her tight. Long, long it was till their lips met—and long then. But he heard her whisper "Good-by," saw her frank tears, felt her slowly, a little by a little, draw away from him.

"Good-by," she said. "Good-by. I would not dare, any more, ever again. Oh, Will Banion, why did you take away my heart? I had but one!"

"It is mine!" he cried savagely. "No other man in all the world shall ever have it! Molly!"

But she now was gone.

He did not know how long he stood alone, his head bowed on his saddle. The raucous howl of a great gray wolf near by spelled out the lonesome tragedy of his future life for him.

Quaint and sweet philosopher, and bold as she but now had been in one great and final imparting of her real self, Molly Wingate was only a wet, weary and bedraggled maid when at length she entered the desolate encampment which stood for home. She found her mother sitting on a box under a crude awning, and cast herself on her knees, her head on that ample bosom that she had known as haven in her childhood. She wept now like a little child.

"It's bad!" said stout Mrs. Wingate, not knowing. "But you're back and alive. It looks like we're wrecked and everything lost, and we come nigh about getting all burned up, but you're back alive to your ma! Now, now!"

That night Molly turned on a sodden pallet which she had made down beside her mother in the great wagon. But she slept ill. Over and over to her lips rose the same question:

"Oh, Will Banion, Will Banion, why did you take away my heart?"

Chapter XV

THE DIVISION

The great wagon train of 1848 lay banked along the Vermilion in utter and abject confusion. Organization there now was none. But for Banion's work with the back fires the entire train would have been wiped out. The effects of the storm were not so capable of evasion. Sodden, wretched, miserable, chilled, their goods impaired, their cattle stampeded, all sense of gregarious self-reliance gone, two hundred wagons were no more than two hundred individual units of discontent and despair. So far as could be prophesied on facts apparent, the journey out to Oregon had ended in disaster almost before it was well begun.

Bearded men at smoking fires looked at one another in silence, or would not look at all. Elan, morale, *esprit de corps* were gone utterly.

Stout Caleb Price walked down the wagon lines, passing fourscore men shaking in their native agues, not yet conquered. Women, pale, gaunt, grim, looked at him from limp sunbonnets whose stays had been half dissolved. Children whimpered. Even the dogs, curled nose to tail under the wagons, growled surlily. But Caleb Price found at last the wagon of the bugler who had been at the wars and shook him out.

"Sound, man!" said Caleb Price. "Play up Oh, Susannah! Then sound the Assembly. We've got to have a meeting."

They did have a meeting. Jesse Wingate scented mutiny and remained away.

"There's no use talking, men," said Caleb Price, "no use trying to fool ourselves. We're almost done, the way things are. I like Jess Wingate as well as any man I ever knew, but Jess Wingate's not the man. What shall we do?"

He turned to Hall, but Hall shook his head; to Kelsey, but Kelsey only laughed.

"I could get a dozen wagons through, maybe," said he. "Here's two hundred. Woodhull's the man, but Woodhull's gone—lost, I reckon, or maybe killed and lying out somewhere on these prairies. You take it, Cale."

Price considered for a time.

"No," said he at length. "It's no time for one of us to take on what may be done better by someone else, because our women and children are at stake. The very best man's none too good for this job, and the more experience he has the better. The man who thinks fastest and clearest at the right time is the man we want, and the man we'd follow—the only man. Who'll he be?"

"Oh, I'll admit Banion had the best idea of crossing the Kaw," said Kelsey. "He got his own people over, too, somehow."

"Yes, and they're together now ten miles below us. And Molly Wingate—she was caught out with her team by the fire—says it was Banion who started the back-fire. That saved his train and ours. Ideas that come too late are no good. We need some man with the right ideas at the right time."

"You think it's Banion?" Hall spoke.

"I do think it's Banion. I don't see how it can be anyone else."

"Woodhull'd never stand for it."

"He isn't here."

"Wingate won't."

"He'll have to."

The chief of mutineers, a grave and bearded man, waited for a time.

"This is a meeting of the train," said he. "In our government the majority rules. Is there any motion on this?"

Silence. Then rose Hall of Ohio, slowly, a solid man, with three wagons of his own.

"I've been against the Missouri outfit," said he. "They're a wild bunch, with no order or discipline to them. They're not all free-soilers, even if they're going out to Oregon. But if one man can handle them, he can handle us. An Army man with a Western experience—who'll it be unless it is their man? So. Mister Chairman, I move for a committee of three, yourself to be one, to ride down and ask the Missourians to join on again, all under Major Banion."

"I'll have to second that," said a voice. Price saw a dozen nods. "You've heard it, men," said he. "All in favor rise up."

They stood, with not many exceptions—rough-clad, hardheaded men of the nation's vanguard. Price looked them over soberly.

"You see the vote, men," said he. "I wish Jess had come, but he didn't. Who'll be the man to ride down? Wingate?"

"He wouldn't go," said Kelsey. "He's got something against Banion; says he's not right on his war record—something—"

"He's right on his train record this far," commented Price. "We're not electing a Sabbath-school superintendent now, but a train captain who'll make these wagons cover twelve miles a day, average.

"Hall, you and Kelsey saddle up and ride down with me. We'll see what we can do. One thing sure, something has got to be done, or we might as well turn back. For one, I'm not used to that."

They did saddle and ride—to find the Missouri column coming up with intention of pitching below, at the very scene of the massacre, which was on the usual Big Vermilion ford, steep-banked on either side, but with hard bottom.

Ahead of the train rode two men at a walk, the scout Jackson, and the man they sought. They spied him as the man on the black Spanish horse, found him a pale and tired young man, who apparently had slept as ill as they themselves. But in straight and manful fashion they told him their errand.

The pale face of Will Banion flushed, even with the livid scorch marks got in the prairie fire the day before. He considered.

"Gentlemen," he said after a time, "you don't know what you are asking of me. It would be painful for me to take that work on now."

"It's painful for us to see our property lost and our families set afoot," rejoined Caleb Price. "It's not pleasant for me to do this. But it's no question, Major Banion, what you or I find painful or pleasant. The question is on the women and children. You know that very well."

"I do know it—yes. But you have other men. Where's Woodhull?"

"We don't know. We think the Pawnees got him among the others."

"Jackson"—Banion turned to his companion—"we've got to make a look-around for him. He's probably across the river somewhere."

"Like enough," rejoined the scout. "But the first thing is for all us folks to git acrost the river too. Let him go to hell."

"We want you, Major," said Hall quietly, and even Kelsey nodded.

"What shall I do, Jackson?" demanded Banion.

"Fly inter hit, Will," replied that worthy. "Least-ways, take hit on long enough so's to git them acrost an' help git their cattle together. Ye couldn't git Wingate to work under ye no ways. But mebbe-so we can show 'em fer a day er so how Old Missoury gits acrost a country. Uh-huh?"

Again Banion considered, pondering many things of which none of these knew anything at all. At length he drew aside with the men of the main train.

"Park our wagons here, Bill," he said. "See that they are

well parked, too. Get out your guards. I'll go up and see what we can do. We'll all cross here. Have your men get all the trail ropes out and lay in a lot of dry cottonwood logs. We'll have to raft some of the stuff over. See if there's any wild grapevines along the bottoms. They'll help hold the logs. So long."

He turned, and with the instinct of authority rode just a half length ahead of the others on the return.

Jesse Wingate, a sullen and discredited Achilles, held to his tent, and Molly did as much, her stout-hearted and just-minded mother being the main source of Wingate news. Banion kept as far away from them as possible, but had Jed sent for.

"Jed," said he, "first thing, you get your boys together and go after the cattle. Most of them went downstream with the wind. The hobbled stuff didn't come back down the trail and must be below there too. The cows wouldn't swim the big river on a run. If there's rough country, with any shelter, they'd like enough begin to mill—it might be five miles, ten—I can't guess. You go find out.

"Now, you others, first thing, get your families all out in the sun. Spread out the bedclothes and get them dried. Build fires and cook your best right away—have the people eat. Get that bugle going and play something fast—Sweet Hour of Prayer is for evening, not now. Give 'em Reveille, and then the cavalry charge. Play Susannah.

"I'm going to ride the edge of the burning to look for loose stock. You others get a meal into these people— coffee, quinine, more coffee. Then hook up all the teams you can and move down to the ford. We'll be on the Platte and among the buffalo in a week or ten days. Nothing can stop us. All you need is just a little more coffee and a little more system, and then a good deal more of both.

"Now's a fine time for this train to shake into place," he added. "You, Price, take your men and go down the lines. Tell your kinfolk and families and friends and neighbors to make bands and hang together. Let 'em draw cuts for place if they like, but stick where they go. We can't tell how the grass will be on ahead, and we may have to break the train into sections on the Platte; but we'll break it ourselves, and not see it fall apart or fight apart. So?"

He wheeled and went away at a trot. All he had given them was the one thing they lacked.

The Wingate wagons came in groups and halted at the river bank, where the work of rafting and wagon boating went methodically forward. Scores of individual craft, tipsy and risky, two or three logs lashed together, angled across and landed far below. Horsemen swam across with lines and larger rafts were steadied fore and aft with ropes snubbed around tree trunks on either bank. Once started, the resourceful pioneer found a dozen ways to skin his cat, as one man phrased it, and presently the falling waters permitted swimming and fording the stock. It all seemed ridiculously simple and ridiculously cheerful.

Toward evening a great jangling of bells and shouting of young captains announced the coming of a great band of the stampeded livestock—cattle, mules and horses mixed. Afar came the voice of Jed Wingate singing, "Oh, then Susannah," and urging Susannah to have no concern.

But Banion, aloof and morose, made his bed that night apart even from his own train. He had not seen Wingate— did not see him till the next day, noon, when he rode up and saluted the former leader, who sat on his own wagon seat and not in saddle.

"My people are all across, Mr. Wingate," he said, "and the last of your wagons will be over by dark and straightened out. I'm parked a mile ahead."

"You are parked? I thought you were elected—by my late friends—to lead this whole train."

He spoke bitterly and with a certain contempt that made Banion color.

"No. We can travel apart, though close. Do you want to go ahead, or shall I?"

"As you like. The country's free."

"It's not free for some things, Mr. Wingate," rejoined the younger man hotly. "You can lead or not, as you like; but I'll not train up with a man who thinks of me as you do. After this think what you like, but don't speak any more."

"What do you mean by that?"

"You know very well. You've believed another man's word about my personal character. It's gone far enough and too far."

"The other man is not here. He can't face you."

"No, not now. But if he's on earth he'll face me sometime."

Unable to control himself further, Banion wheeled and galloped away to his own train.

"You ask if we're to join in with the Yankees," he flared out to Jackson. "No! We'll camp apart and train apart. I won't go on with them."

"Well," said the scout, "I didn't never think we would, er believe ye could; not till they git in trouble agin—er till a certain light wagon an' mules throws in with us, huh?"

"You'll say no more of that, Jackson! But one thing: you and I have got to ride and see if we can get any trace of Woodhull."

"Like looking for a needle in a haystack, an' a damn bad needle at that," was the old man's comment.

Chapter XVI

THE PLAINS

On to the Platte! The buffalo!" New cheer seemed to come to the hearts of the emigrants now, and they forgot bickering. The main train ground grimly ahead, getting back, if not all its egotism, at least more and more of its self-reliance. By courtesy, Wingate still rode ahead, though orders came now from a joint council of his leaders, since Banion would not take charge.

The great road to Oregon was even now not a trail but a road, deep cut into the soil, though no wheeled traffic had marked it until within the past five years. A score of paralled paths it might be at times, of tentative location along a hillside or a marshy level; but it was for the most part a deep-cut, unmistakable road from which it had been impossible to wander. At times it lay worn into the sod a half foot, a foot in depth. Sometimes it followed the ancient buffalo trails to water—the first roads of the Far West, quickly seized on by hunters and engineers—or again it transected these, hanging to the ridges after frontier road fashion, heading out for the proved fords of the greater streams. Always the wheel marks of those who had gone ahead in previous years, the continuing thread of the trail itself, worn in by trader and trapper and Mormon and Oregon or California man, gave hope and cheer to these who followed with the plow.

Stretching out, closing up, almost inch by inch, like some giant measuring worm in its slow progress, the train held on through a vast and stately landscape, which some travelers had called the Eden of America, such effect was given by the series of altering scenes. Small imagination, indeed, was needed to picture here a long-established civilization, although there was not a habitation. They were beyond organized society and beyond the law.

Game became more abundant, wild turkeys still appeared in the timbered creek bottoms. Many elk were seen, more deer and very many antelope, packed in northward by the fires. A number of panthers and giant gray wolves beyond counting kept the hunters always excited. The wild abundance of an unexhausted Nature offered at every hand. The sufficiency of life brought daily growth in the self-reliance which had left them for a time.

The wide timberlands, the broken low hills of the green prairie at length began to give place to a steadily rising inclined plane. The soil became less black and heavy, with more sandy ridges. The oak and hickory, stout trees of their forefathers, passed, and the cottonwoods appeared. After they had crossed the ford of the Big Blue—a hundred yards of racing water—they passed what is now the line between Kansas and Nebraska, and followed up the Little Blue, beyond whose ford the trail left these quieter river valleys and headed out over a high table-land in a keen straight flight over the great valley of the Platte, the highway to the Rockies.

Now the soil was sandier; the grass changed yet again. They had rolled under wheel by now more than one hundred different varieties of wild grasses. The vegetation began to show the growing altitude. The cactus was seen now and then. On the far horizon the wavering mysteries of the mirage appeared, marvelous in deceptiveness, mystical, alluring, the very spirits of the Far West, appearing to move before their eyes in giant pantomime. They were passing from the Prairies to the Plains.

Shouts and cheers arose as the word passed back that the sand hills known as the Coasts of the Platte were in sight. Some mothers told their children they were now almost to Oregon. The whips cracked more loudly, the tired teams, tongues lolling, quickened their pace as they struck the down-grade gap leading through the sand ridges.

Two thousand Americans, some of them illiterate and ignorant, all of them strong, taking with them law, order, society, the church, the school, anew were staging the great drama of human life, act and scene and episode, as though upon some great moving platform drawn by invisible cables beyond the vast proscenium of the hills.

Chapter XVII

THE GREAT ENCAMPMENT

As the long columns of the great wagon train broke through the screening sand hills there was disclosed a vast and splendid panorama. The valley of the Platte lay miles wide, green in the full covering of spring. A crooked and broken thread of timber growth appeared, marking the moister soil and outlining the general course of the shallow stream, whose giant cottonwoods were dwarfed now by the distances. In between, and for miles up and down the flat expanse, there rose the blue smokes of countless camp fires, each showing the location of some whitetopped ship of the Plains. Black specks, grouped here and there, proved the presence of the livestock under herd.

Over all shone a pleasant sun. Now and again the dark shadow of a moving cloud passed over the flat valley, softening its high lights for the time. At times, as the sun shone full and strong, the faint loom of the mirage added the last touch of mysticism, the figures of the wagons rising high, multiplied many-fold, with giant creatures passing between, so that the whole seemed, indeed, some wild phantasmagoria of the desert.

"Look!" exclaimed Wingate, pulling up his horse. "Look, Caleb, the Northern train is in and waiting for us! A hundred wagons! They're camped over the whole bend."

The sight of this vast re-enforcement brought heart to every man, woman and child in all the advancing train. Now, indeed, Oregon was sure. There would be, all told, four hundred—five hundred—above six hundred wagons. Nothing could withstand them. They were the same as arrived!

As the great trains blended before the final emparkment men and women who had never met before shook hands, talked excitedly, embraced, even wept, such was their joy in meeting their own kind. Soon the vast valley at the foot of the Grand Island of the Platte—ninety miles in length it then was—became one vast bivouac whose parallel had not been seen in all the world.

Even so, the Missouri column held back, an hour or two later on the trail. Banion, silent and morose, still rode ahead, but all the flavor of his adventure out to Oregon had left him—indeed, the very savor of life itself. He looked at his arms, empty; touched his lips, where once her kiss had been, so infinitely and ineradicably sweet. Why should he go on to Oregon now?

As they came down through the gap in the Coasts, looking out over the Grand Island and the great encampment, Jackson pulled up his horse.

"Look! Someone comin' out!"

Banion sat his horse awaiting the arrival of the rider, who soon cut down the intervening distance until he could well be noted. A tall, spare man he was, middleaged, of long lank hair and gray stubbled beard, and eyes overhung by bushy brows. He rode an Indian pad saddle, without stirrups, and was clad in the old costume of the hunter of the Far West—fringed shirt and leggings of buckskin. Moccasins made his footcovering, though he wore a low, wide hat. As he came on at speed, guiding his wiry mount with a braided rope looped around the lower jaw, he easily might have been mistaken for a savage himself had he not come alone and from such company as that ahead. He jerked up his horse

close at hand and sat looking at the newcomers, with no
salutation beyond a short "How!"

Banion met him.

"We're the Westport train. Do you come from the Bluffs?
Are you for Oregon?"

"Yes. I seen ye comin'. Thought I'd projeck some. Who's
that back of ye?" He extended an imperative skinny finger
toward Jackson. "If it hain't Bill Jackson hit's his ghost!"

"The same to you, Jim. How!"

The two shook hands without dismounting. Jackson
turned grinning to Banion.

"Major," said he, "this is Jim Bridger, the oldest scout in
the Rockies, an' that knows more West than ary man this
side the Missouri. I never thought to see him again, sartain
not this far east."

"Ner me," retorted the other, shaking hands with one man
after another.

"Jim Bridger? That's a name we know," said Banion.
"I've heard of you back in Kentucky."

"Whar I come from, gentlemen—whar I come from
more'n forty year ago, near's I can figger. Leastways I was
borned in Virginny an' must of crossed Kentucky sometime.
I kain't tell right how old I am, but I rek'lect perfect when
they turned the water inter the Missoury River." He looked
at them solemnly.

"I come back East to the new place, Kansas City. It didn't
cut no mustard, an' I drifted to the Bluffs. This train was
pullin' west, an' I hired on for guide. I've got a few wagons
o' my own—iron, flour an' bacon for my post beyant the
Rockies—ef we don't all git our ha'r lifted afore then!

"We're in between the Sioux and the Pawnees now," he
went on. "They're huntin' the bufflers not ten mile ahead.
But when I tell these pilgrims, they laugh at me. The hull
Sioux nation is on the spring hunt right now. I'll not have
it said Jim Bridger led a wagon train into a massacree. If
ye'll let me, I'm for leavin' 'em an' trainin' with you-all,
especial since you got anyhow one good man along. I've
knowed Bill Jackson many a year at the Rendyvous afore
the fur trade petered. Damn the pilgrims! The hull world's

broke loose this spring. There's five thousand Mormons on ahead, praisin' God every jump an' eatin' the grass below the roots. Womern an' children—so many of 'em, so many! I kain't talk about hit! Women don't belong out here! An' now here you come bringin' a thousand more!

"There's a woman an' a baby layin' dead in our camp now," he concluded. "Died last night. The pilgrims is tryin' to make coffins fer 'em out'n cottonwood logs."

"Lucky for all!" Jackson interrupted the garrulity of the other. "We buried men in blankets on the Vermilion a few days back. The Pawnees got a small camp o' our own folks."

"Yes, I know all about that."

"What's that?" cut in Banion. "How do you know?"

"Well, we've got the survivors—three o' them, countin' Woodhull, their captain."

"How did they get here?"

"They came in with a small outfit o' Mormons that was north o' the Vermilion. They'd come out on the St. Jo road. They told me—"

"Is Woodhull here—can you find him?"

"Shore! Ye want to see him?"

"Yes."

"He told me all about hit—"

"We know all about it, perhaps better than you do—after he's told you all about it."

Bridger looked at him, curious.

"Well, anyhow, hit's over," said he. "One of the men had a Pawnee arrer in his laig. Reckon hit hurt. I know, fer I carried a Blackfoot arrerhead under my shoulder blade fer sever'l years.

"But come on down and help me make these pilgrims set guards. Do-ee mind, now, the hull Sioux nation's just in ahead o' us, other side the river! Yet these people didn't want to ford to the south side the Platte; they wanted to stick north o' the river. Ef we had, we'd have our ha'r dryin' by now. I tell ye, the tribes is out to stop the wagon trains this spring. They say too many womern and children is comin', an' that shows we want to take their land away fer keeps.

"From now on to Oregon—look out! The Cayuses
cleaned out the Whitman mission last spring in Oregon.
Even the Shoshones is dancin'. The Crows is out, the Cheyennes is marchin', the Bannocks is east o' the Pass, an' ye
kain't tell when ter expeck the Blackfoots an' Grow Vaws.
Never was gladder to see a man than I am to see Bill Jackson."

"Stretch out!"

Banion gave the order. The Missouri wagons came on,
filed through the gap in order and with military exactness
wheeled into a perfect park at one side the main caravan.

As the outer columns swung in, the inner spread out till
the lapped wagons made a great oblong, Bridger watching
them. Quickly the animals were outspanned, the picket ropes
put down and the loose horses driven off to feed while the
cattle were close herded. He nodded his approval.

"Who's yer train boss, Bill?" he demanded. "That's good
work."

"Major Banion, of Doniphan's column in the war."

"Will he fight?"

"Try him!"

News travels fast along a wagon train. Word passed now
that there was a big Sioux village not far ahead, on the other
side of the river, and that the caravan should be ready for a
night attack. Men and women from the earlier train came
into the Westport camp and the leaders formulated plans.
More than four hundred families ate in sight of one another
fires that evening.

Again on the still air of the Plains that night rose the bugle
summons, by now become familiar. In groups the wagon
folk began to assemble at the council fire. They got instructions which left them serious. The camp fell into semi-
silence. Each family returned to its own wagon. Out in the
dark, flung around in a wide circle, a double watch stood
guard. Wingate and his aids, Banion, Jackson, Bridger, the
pick of the hardier men, went out for all the night. It was
to Banion, Bridger and Jackson that most attention now was
paid. Banion could not yet locate Woodhull in the train.

The scouts crept out ahead of the last picket line, for

though an attack in mass probably would not come before
dawn, if the Sioux really should cross the river, some horse
stealing or an attempted stampede might be expected before
midnight or soon after.

The night wore on. The fires of willow twigs and *bois
des vaches* fell into pale coals, into ashes. The chill of the
Plains came, so that the sleepers in the great wagon corral
drew their blankets closer about them as they lay.

It was approaching midnight when the silence was ripped
apart by the keen crack of a rifle—another and yet another.

Then, in a ripple of red detonation, the rifle fire ran along
the upper front of the entire encampment.

"Turn out! Turn out, men!" called the high, clear voice
of Banion, riding back. "Barricade! Fill in the wheels!"

Chapter XVIII

ARROW AND PLOW

The night attack on the great emigrant encampment was a thing which had been preparing for years. The increasing number of the white men, the lessening numbers of the buffalo, meant inevitable combat with all the tribes sooner or later.

Now the spring hunt of the northern Plains tribes was on. Five hundred lodges of the Sioux stood in one village on the north side of the Platte. The scaffolds were red with meat, everywhere the women were dressing hides and the camp was full of happiness. For a month the great Sioux nation had prospered, according to its lights. Two hundred stolen horses were under the wild herdsmen, and any who liked the meat of the spotted buffalo might kill it close to camp from the scores taken out of the first caravans up the Platte that year—the Mormons and other early trailers whom the Sioux despised because their horses were so few.

But the Sioux, fat with *boudins* and *dépouille* and marrowbones, had waited long for the great Western train which should have appeared on the north side of the Platte, the emigrant road from the Council Bluffs. For some days now they had known the reason, as Jim Bridger had explained— the wagons had forded the river below the Big Island. The white men's medicine was strong.

The Sioux did not know of the great rendezvous at the forks of the Great Medicine Road. Their watchmen, stationed daily at the eminences along the river bluffs of the north shore, brought back scoffing word of the carelessness of the whites. When they got ready they, too, would ford the river and take them in. They had not heeded the warning sent down the trail that no more whites should come into this country of the tribes. It was to be war.

And now the smoke signals said yet more whites were coming in from the south! The head men rode out to meet their watchmen. News came back that the entire white nation now had come into the valley from the south and joined the first train.

Here then was the chance to kill off the entire white nation, their women and their children, so there would be none left to come from toward the rising sun! Yes, this would end the race of the whites without doubt or question, because they all were here. After killing these it would be easy to send word west to the Arapahoes and Gros Ventres and Cheyennes, the Crows, the Blackfeet, the Shoshones, the Utes, to follow west on the Medicine Road and wipe out all who had gone on West that year and the year before. Then the Plains and the mountains would all belong to the red men again.

The chiefs knew that the hour just before dawn is when an enemy's heart is like water, when his eyes are heavy, so they did not order the advance at once. But a band of the young men who always fought together, one of the inner secret societies or clans of the tribe, could not wait so long. First come, first served. Daylight would be time to look over the children and to keep those not desired for killing, and to select and distribute the young women of the white nation. But the night would be best for taking the elk-dogs and the spotted buffalo.

Accordingly a band from this clan swam and forded the

wide river, crossed the island, and in the early evening came downstream back of a shielding fringe of cottonwoods. Their scouts saw with amazement the village of tepees that moved on wheels. They heard the bugle, saw the white nation gather at the medicine fire, heard them chant their great medicine song; then saw them disperse; saw the fires fall low.

They laughed. The white nation was strong, but they did not put out guards at night! For a week the Sioux had watched them, and they knew about that. It would be easy to run off all the herd and to kill a few whites even now, beginning the sport before the big battle of tomorrow, which was to wipe out the white nation altogether.

But when at length, as the handle of the Great Dipper reached the point agreed, the line of the Sioux clansmen crawled away from the fringe of trees and out into the cover of a little slough that made toward the village of tepees on wheels, a quarter of a mile in front of the village men arose out of the ground and shot into them. Five of their warriors fell. Tall men in the dark came out and counted coup on them, took off their war bonnets; took off even more below the bonnets. And there was a warrior who rode this way and that, on a great black horse, and who had a strange war cry not heard before, and who seemed to have no fear. So said the clan leader when he told the story of the repulse.

Taken aback, the attacking party found cover. But the Sioux would charge three times. So they scattered and crawled in again over a half circle. They found the wall of tepees solid; found that the white nation knew more of war than they had thought. They sped arrow after arrow, ball after ball, against the circle of the white tepees, but they did not break, and inside no one moved or cried out in terror; whereas outside, in the grass, men rose up and fired into them and did not run back, but came forward. Some had short rifles in their hands that did not need to be loaded, but kept on shooting. And none of the white nation ran away. And the elk-dogs with long ears, and the spotted buffalo, were no longer outside the village in the grass, but inside the village. What men could fight a nation whose warriors were so unfair as all this came to?

The tribesmen drew back to the cottonwoods a half mile.

"My heart is weak," said their clan leader. "I believe they are going to shoot us all. They have killed twenty of us now, and we have not taken a scalp."

"I was close," said a young boy whom they called Bull Gets Up or The Sitting Bull. "I was close, and I heard the spotted buffalo running about inside the village; I heard the children. Tomorrow we can run them away."

"But tonight what man knows the gate into their village? They have got a new chief today. They are many as the grass leaves. Their medicine is strong. I believe they are going to kill us all if we stay here." Thus the partisan.

So they did not stay there, but went away. And at dawn Banion and Bridger and Jackson and each of the column captains—others also—came into the corral carrying war bonnets, shields and bows; and some had things which had been once below war bonnets. The young men of this clan always fought on foot or on horse in full regalia of their secret order, day or night. The emigrants had plenty of this savage war gear now.

"We've beat them off," said Bridger, "an' maybe they won't ring us now. Get the cookin' done, Cap'n Banion, an' let's roll out. But for your wagon park they'd have cleaned us."

The whites had by no means escaped scathless. A dozen arrows stood sunk into the sides of the wagons inside the park, hundreds had thudded into the outer sides, nearest the enemy. One shaft was driven into the hard wood of a plow beam. Eight oxen staggered, legs wide apart, shafts fast in their bodies; four lay dead; two horses also; as many mules.

This was not all. As the fighting men approached the wagons they saw a group of stern-faced women weeping around something which lay covered by a blanket on the ground. Molly Wingate stooped, drew it back to show them. Even Bridger winced.

An arrow, driven by a buffalo bow, had glanced on the spokes of a wheel, risen in its flight and sped entirely across the inclosure of the corral. It had slipped through the canvas cover of a wagon on the opposite side as so much paper and caught fair a woman who was lying there, a nursing baby in her arms, shielding it, as she thought, with her body. But the missile had cut through one of her arms, pierced the head of the child and sunk into the bosom of the mother deep enough to kill her also. The two lay now, the shaft transfixing both; and they were buried there; and they lie there still, somewhere near the Grand Island, in one of a thousand unknown and unmarked graves along the Great Medicine Road. Under the ashes of a fire they left this grave, and drove six hundred wagons over it, and the Indians never knew.

The leaders stood beside the dead woman, hats in hand. This was part of the price of empire—the life of a young woman, a bride of a year.

The wagons all broke camp and went on in a vast caravan, the Missourians now at the front. Noon, and the train did not halt. Banion urged the teamsters. Bridger and Jackson were watching the many signal smokes.

"I'm afeard o' the next bend," said Jackson at length.

The fear was justified. Early in the afternoon they saw the outriders turn and come back to the train at full run. Behind them, riding out from the concealment of a clump of cottonwoods on the near side of the scattering river channels, there appeared rank after rank of the Sioux, more than two thousand warriors bedecked in all the savage finery of their war dress. They were after their revenge. They had left their village and, paralleling the white men's advance, had forded on ahead.

They came out now, five hundred, eight hundred, a thousand, two thousand strong, and the ground shook under the thunder of the hoofs. They were after their revenge, eager to inflict the final blow upon the white nation.

The spot was not ill chosen for their tactics. The alkali plain of the valley swung wide and flat, and the trail crossed it midway, far back from the water and not quite to the flanking sand hills. While a few dashed at the cattle, waving their blankets, the main body, with workman-like precision, strung out and swung wide, circling the train and riding in to arrow range.

The quick orders of Banion and his scouts were obeyed as fully as time allowed. At a gallop, horse and ox transport alike were driven into a hurried park and some at least of the herd animals inclosed. The riflemen flanked the train on the danger side and fired continually at the long string of running horses, whose riders had flung themselves off-side so that only a heel showed above a pony's back, a face under his neck. Even at this range a half dozen ponies stumbled, figures crawled off for cover. The emigrants were stark men with rifles. But the circle went on until, at the running range selected, the crude wagon park was entirely surrounded by a thin racing ring of steel and fire stretched out over two or three miles.

The Sioux had guns also, and though they rested most on the bow, their chance rifle fire was dangerous. As for the arrows, even from this disadvantageous station these peerless bowmen sent them up in a high arc so that they fell inside the inclosure and took their toll. Three men, two women lay wounded at the first ride, and the animals were plunging.

The war chief led his warriors in the circle once more, chanting his own song to the continuous chorus of savage ululations. The entire fighting force of the Sioux village was in the circle.

The ring ran closer. The Sioux were inside seventy-five yards, the dust streaming, the hideously painted faces of the riders showing through, red, saffron, yellow, as one after another warrior twanged a bow under his horse's neck as he ran.

But this was easy range for the steady rifles of men who kneeled and fired with careful aim. Even the six-shooters, then new to the Sioux, could work. Pony after pony fell, until the line showed gaps; whereas as now the wagon corral showed no gap at all, while through the wheels, and over the tongue spaces, from every crevice of the gray towering wall came the fire of more and more men. The medicine of the white men was strong.

Three times the ring passed, and that was all. The third circuit was wide and ragged. The riders dared not come close enough to carry off their dead and wounded. Then the attack dwindled, the savages scattering and breaking back to the cover of the stream.

"Now, men, come on!" called out Banion. "Ride them down! Give them a trimming they'll remember! Come on, boys!"

Within a half hour fifty more Sioux were down, dead or very soon to die. Of the living not one remained in sight.

"They wanted hit, an' they got hit!" exclaimed Bridger, when at length he rode back, four war bonnets across his saddle and scalps at his cantle. He raised his voice in a fierce yell of triumph, not much other than savage himself, dismounted and disdainfully cast his trophies across a wagon tongue.

"I've et horse an' mule an' dog," said he, "an' wolf, wil' cat an' skunk, an' perrairy dog an' snake an' most ever'thing else that wears a hide, but I never could eat Sioux. But to-morrer we'll have ribs in camp. I've seed the buffler, an' we own this side the river now."

Molly Wingate sat on a bed roll near by, knitting as calmly as though at home, but filled with wrath.

"Them nasty, dirty critters!" she exclaimed. "I wish't the boys had killed them all. Even in daylight they don't stand up and fight fair like men. I lost a whole churnin' yesterday. Besides, they killed my best cow this mornin', that's what they done. And lookit this thing!"

She held up an Indian arrow, its strap-iron head bent over at right angles. "They shot this into our plow beam. Looks like they got a spite at our plow."

"Ma'am, they have got a spite at hit," said the old scout, seating himself on the ground near by. "They're scared o' hit. I've seed a bunch o' Sioux out at Laramie with a plow some Mormon left around when he died. They'd walk around and around that thing by the hour, talkin' low to theirselves. They couldn't figger hit out no ways a-tall.

"That season they sent a runner down to the Pawnees to make a peace talk, an' to find out what this yere thing was the whites had brung out. Pawnees sent to the Otoes, an' the Otoes told them. They said hit was the white man's big medicine, an' that hit buried all the buffler under the ground wherever hit come, so no buffler ever could git out again. Nacherl, when the runners come back an' told what that thing really was, all the Injuns, every tribe, said if the white man was goin' to bury the buffler the white man had got to stay back.

Us trappers an' traders got along purty well with the Injuns—they could get things they wanted at the posts or the Rendyvous, an' that was all right. They had pelts to sell. But now these movers didn't buy nothin' an' didn't sell nothin'. They just went on through, a-carryin' this thing for buryin' the buffler. From now on the Injuns is goin' to fight the whites. Ye kain't blame 'em, ma'am; they only see their finish.

"Five years ago nigh a thousand whites drops down in Oregon. Next year come fifteen hundred, an' in '45 twicet that many, an' so it has went, doublin' an' doublin'. Six or seven thousand whites go up the Platte this season, an' a right smart sprinklin' o' them'll git through to Oregon. Them 'at does'll carry plows.

"Ma'am, if the brave that sunk a arrer in yore plow beam didn't kill yore plow hit warn't because he didn't want to. Hit's the truth—the plow does bury the buffler, an' fer keeps! Ye kain't kill a plow, ner neither kin yer scare hit away. Hit's the holdin'est thing ther is, ma'am—hit never does let go."

"How long'll we wait here?" the older woman demanded.

"Anyhow fer two-three days, ma'am. Thar's a lot has got to sort out stuff an' throw hit away here. One man has drug a pair o' millstones all the way to here from Ohio. He allowed to get rich startin' a gris'mill out in Oregon. An' then ther's chairs an' tables, an' God knows what—"

"Well, anyhow," broke in Mrs. Wingate truculently, "no difference what you men say, I ain't going to leave my bureau, nor my table, nor my chairs! I'm going to keep my two churns and my feather bed too. We've had butter all the way so far, and I mean to have it all the way—and eggs.

I mean to sleep at nights, too, if the pesky muskeeters'll let me. They most have et me up. And I'd give a dollar for a drink of real water now. It's all right to settle this water overnight, but that don't take the sody out of it.

"Besides," she went on, "I got four quarts o' seed wheat in one of them bureau drawers, and six cuttings of my best rose-bush I'm taking out to plant in Oregon. And I got three pairs of Jed's socks in another bureau drawer. It's flat on its back, bottom of the load. I ain't going to dig it out for no man."

"Well, hang on to them socks, ma'am. I've wintered many a time without none—only grass in my moccasins. There's outfits in this train that's low on flour an' side meat right now, let alone socks. We got to cure some meat. There's a million buffler just south in the breaks wantin' to move on north, but scared of us an' the Injuns. We'd orto make a good hunt inside o' ten mile to-morrer. We'll git enough meat to take us a week to jerk hit all, or else Jim Bridger's a liar—which no one never has said yit, ma'am."

"Flowers?" he added. "You takin' flowers acrost? Flowers—do they go with the plow, too, as well as weeds? Well, well! Wimminfolks shore air a strange race o' people, hain't that the truth? Buryin' the buffler an' plantin' flowers on his grave!

"But speakin' o' buryin' things," he suddenly resumed, "an' speakin' o' plows, 'minds me o' what's delayin' us all right now. Hit's a fool thing, too—buryin' Injuns!"

"As which, Mr. Bridger? What you mean?" inquired Molly Wingate, looking over her spectacles.

"This new man, Banion, that come in with the Missouri wagons—he taken hit on hisself to say, atter the fight was over, we orto stop an' bury all them Injuns! Well, I been on the Plains an' in the Rockies all my life, an' I never yit, before now, seed a Injun buried. Hit's onnatcherl. But this here man he, now, orders a ditch plowed an' them Injuns hauled in an' planted. Hit's wastin' time. That's what's keepin' him an' yore folks an' sever'l others. Yore husband an' yore son is both out yan with him. Hit beats hell, ma'am, these new-fangled ways!"

"So that's where they are? I wanted them to fetch me something to make a fire."

"I kain't do that, ma'am. Mostly my squaws—"

"Your what? Do you mean to tell me you got squaws, you old heathen?"

"Not many, ma'am—only two. Times is hard sence beaver went down. I kain't tell ye how hard this here depressin' has set on us folks out here."

"Two squaws! My laws! Two—what's their names?" This last with feminine curiosity.

"Well now, ma'am, I call one on 'em Blast Yore Hide— she's a Ute. The other is younger an' pertier. She's a Shoshone. I call her Dang Yore Eyes. Both them women is powerful fond o' me, ma'am. They both are right proud o' their names, too, because they air white names, ye see. Now when time comes fer a fire, Blast Yore Hide an' Dang Yore Eyes, they fight hit out between 'em which gits the wood. I don't study none over that, ma'am."

Molly Wingate rose so ruffled that, like an angered hen, she seemed twice her size.

"You old heathen!" she exclaimed. "You old murderin' lazy heathen man! How dare you talk like that to me?"

"As what, ma'am? I hain't said nothin' out'n the way, have I? O' course, ef ye don't want to git the fire stuff, thar's yer darter—she's young an' strong. Yes, an perty as a pitcher besides, though like enough triflin', like her maw. Where's she at now?"

"None of your business where."

"I could find her."

"Oh, you could! How?"

"I'd find that young feller Sam Woodhull that come in from below, renegardin' away from his train with that party o' Mormons—him that had his camp jumped by the Pawnees. I got a eye fer a womern, ma'am, but so's he—more'n fer Injuns, I'd say. I seed him with yore darter right constant, but I seemed to miss him in the ride. Whar was he at?"

"I don't know as it's none of your business, anyways."

"No? Well, I was just wonderin', ma'am, because I heerd Cap'n Banion ast that same question o' yore husband, Cap'n

Wingate, an' Cap'n Wingate done said jest what ye said yerself—that hit wasn't none o' his business. Which makes things look shore hopeful an' pleasant in this yere train o' pilgrims, this bright and pleasant summer day, huh?"

Grinning amicably, the incorrigible old mountaineer rose and went his way, and left the irate goodwife to gather her apron full of plains fuel for herself.

Chapter XIX

BANION OF DONIPHAN'S

Molly Wingate was grumbing over her fire when at length her husband and son returned to their wagon. Jed was vastly proud over a bullet crease he had got in a shoulder. After his mother's alarm had taken the form of first aid, he was all for showing his battle scars to a certain damsel in Caleb Price's wagon. Wingate remained dour and silent as was now his wont, and cursing his luck that he had had no horse to carry him up in the late pursuit of the Sioux. He also was bitter over the delay in making a burial trench.

"Some ways, Jess," commented his spouse, "I'd a'most guess you ain't got much use for Will Banion."

"Why should I have? Hasn't he done all he could to shoulder me out of my place as captain of this train? And wasn't I elected at Westport before we started?"

"Mostly, a man has to stay elected, Jess."

"Well, I'm going to! I had it out with that young man right now. I told him I knew why he wanted in our train—it was Molly."

"What did he say?"

"What could he say? He admitted it. And he had the gall to say I'd see it his way some day. Huh! That's a long day off, before I do. Well, at least he said he was going back to his own men, and they'd fall behind again. That suits me."

"Did he say anything about finding Sam Woodhull?"

"Yes. He said that would take its time, too."

"Didn't say he wouldn't?"

"No, I don't know as he did."

"Didn't act scared of it?"

"He didn't say much about it."

"Sam does."

"I reckon—and why shouldn't he? He'll play evens some day, of course. But now, Molly," he went on, with heat, "what's the use talking? We both know that Molly's made up her mind. She loves Sam and don't love this other man any more than I do. He's only a drift-about back from the war, and wandering out to Oregon. He'll maybe not have a cent when he gets there. He's got one horse and his clothes, and one or two wagons, maybe not paid for. Sam's got five wagons of goods to start a store with, and three thousand gold—so he says—as much as we have. The families are equal, and that's always a good thing. This man Banion can't offer Molly nothing, but Sam Woodhull can give her her place right from the start, out in Oregon. We got to think of all them things.

"And I've got to think of a lot of other things, too. It's our girl. It's all right to say a man can go out to Oregon and live down his past, but it's a lot better not to have no past to live down. You know what Major Banion done, and how he left the Army—even if it wasn't why, it was how, and that's bad enough. Sam Woodhull has told us both all about Banion's record. If he'd steal in Mexico he'd steal in Oregon."

"You didn't ever get so far along as to talk about that!"

"We certainly did—right now, him and me, not half an hour ago, while we was riding back."

"I shouldn't have thought he'd of stood it," said his wife, "him sort of fiery-like."

"Well, it did gravel him. He got white, but wouldn't talk.

Asked if Sam Woodhull had the proof, and I told him he
had. That was when he said he'd go back to his own wagons.
I could see he was avoiding Sam. But I don't see how, away
out here, and no law nor nothing, we're ever going to keep
the two apart."

"They wasn't."

"No. They did have it out, like schoolboys behind a barn.
Do you suppose that'll ever do for a man of spirit like Sam
Woodhull? No, there's other ways. And as I said, it's a far
ways from the law out here, and getting farther every day,
and wilder and wilder every day. It's only putting it off,
Molly, but on the whole I was glad when Banion said he'd
give up looking for Sam Woodhull this morning and go on
back to his own men."

"Did he say he'd give it up?"

"Yes, he did. He said if I'd wait I'd see different. Said
he could wait—said he was good at waiting."

"But he didn't say he'd give it up?"

"I don't know as he did in so many words."

"He won't," said Molly Wingate.

Chapter XX

THE BUFFALO

The emigrants had now arrived at the eastern edge of the great region of free and abundant meat. They now might count on at least six or seven hundred miles of buffalo to subsist them on their way to Oregon. The cry of "Buffalo! Buffalo!" went joyously down the lines of wagons, and every man who could muster a horse and a gun made ready for that chase which above all others meant most, whether in excitement or in profit.

Of these hundreds of hunters, few had any experience on the Plains. It was arranged by the head men that the hunt should be strung out over several miles, the Missourians farthest down the river, the others to the westward, so that all might expect a fairer chance in an enterprise of so much general importance.

Banion and Jackson, in accordance with the former's promise to Wingate, had retired to their own train shortly after the fight with the Sioux. The Wingate train leaders therefore looked to Bridger as their safest counsel in the matter of getting meat. That worthy headed a band of the best equipped men and played his own part in full character. A wild figure he made as he rode, hatless, naked to the waist, his legs in Indian leggings and his feet in moccasins. His mount, a compact cayuse from west of the Rockies, bore no saddle beyond a folded blanket cinched on with a rawhide band.

For weapons Bridger carried no firearms at all, but bore a short buffalo bow of the Pawnees—double-curved, sinew-backed, made of the resilient *bois d'arc*, beloved bow wood of all the Plains tribes. A thick sheaf of arrows, newly sharpened, swung in the beaver quiver at his back. Lean, swart, lank of hair, he had small look of the white man left about him as he rode now, guiding his horse with a jaw rope of twisted hair and playing his bow with a half dozen arrows held along it with the fingers of his left hand.

"For buffler the bow's the best," said he. "I'll show ye before long."

They had not too far to go. At that time the short-grass country of the Platte Valley was the great center of the bison herds. The wallows lay in thousands, the white alkali showing in circles which almost touched edge to edge. The influx of emigrants had for the time driven the herds back from their ancient fords and watering places, to which their deep-cut trails led down, worn ineradicably into the soil. It was along one of the great buffalo trails that they now rode, breasting the line of hills that edged the Platte to the south.

When they topped the flanking ridge a marvelous example of wild abundance greeted them. Bands of elk, yet more numerous bands of antelope, countless curious gray wolves, more than one grizzly bear made away before them, although by orders left unpursued. Of the feathered game they had now forgot all thought. The buffalo alone was of interest. The wild guide rode silent, save for a low Indian chant he hummed, his voice at times rising high, as though importunate.

"Ye got to pray to the Great Speret when-all ye hunt, men," he explained. "An' ye got to have someone that can call the buffler, as the Injuns calls that when they hunt on foot. I kin call 'em, too, good as ary Injun. Why shouldn't I?

"Thar now!" he exclaimed within the next quarter of an hour. "What did Jim Bridger tell ye? Lookee yonder! Do-ee say Jim Bridger can't make buffler medicine? Do-ee see 'em over yan ridge—thousands?"

The others felt their nerves jump as they topped the ridge and saw fully the vast concourse of giant black-topped, beard-fronted creatures which covered the plateau in a body a mile and more across—a sight which never failed to thrill any who saw it.

It was a rolling carpet of brown, like the prairie's endless wave of green. Dust clouds of combat rose here and there. A low muttering rumble of hoarse dull bellowing came audible even at that distance. The spectacle was to the novice not only thrilling—it was terrifying.

The general movement of the great pack was toward the valley; closest to them a smaller body of some hundreds that stood, stupidly staring, not yet getting the wind of their assailants.

Suddenly rose the high-pitched yell of the scout, sounding the charge. Snorting, swerving, the horses of the others followed his, terror smitten but driven in by men most of whom at least knew how to ride.

Smoothly as a bird in flight, Bridger's trained buffalo horse closed the gap between him and a plunging bunch of the buffalo. The white savage proved himself peer of any savage of the world. His teeth bared as he threw his body into the bow with a short, savage jab of the left arm as he loosed the sinew cord. One after another feather showed, clinging to a heaving flank; one after another muzzle dripped red with the white foam of running; then one after another great animal began to slow; to stand braced, legs apart; soon to begin slowly kneeling down. The living swept ahead, the dying lay in the wake.

The insatiate killer clung on, riding deep into the surging sea of rolling humps. At times, in savage sureness and cruelty, he did not ride abreast and drive the arrow into the lungs, but shot from the rear, quartering, into the thin hide back of the ribs, so that the shaft ranged forward into the intestines of the victim. If it did not bury, but hung free as the animal kicked at it convulsively, he rode up, and with his hand pushed the shaft deeper, feeling for the life, as the Indians called it, with short jabs of the imbedded missile. Master of an old trade he was, and stimulated by the proofs of his skill, his followers emulated him with their own weapons. The report of firearms, muffled by the rolling thunder of hoofs, was almost continuous so long as the horses could keep touch with the herd.

Bridger paused only when his arrows were out, and grumbled to himself that he had no more, so could count only a dozen fallen buffalo for his product. That others, wounded, carried off arrows, he called bad luck and bad shooting. When he trotted back on his reeking horse, his quiver dancing empty, he saw other black spots than his own on the short grass. His followers had picked up the art not so ill. There was meat in sight now, certainly—as well as a half dozen unhorsed riders and three or four wounded buffalo disposed to fight.

The old hunter showed his men how to butcher the buffalo, pulling them on their bellies, if they had not died thus, and splitting the hide down the back, to make a receptacle for the meat as it was dissected; showed them how to take out the tongue beneath the jaw, after slitting open the lower jaw. He besought them not to throw away the back fat, the hump, the boss ribs or the intestinal *boudins*; in short, gave them their essential buffalo-hunting lessons. Then he turned for camp, he himself having no relish for squaw's work, as he called it, and well assured the wagons would now have abundance.

Banion and Jackson, with their followers, held their hunt some miles below the scene of Bridger's chase, and had no greater difficulty in getting among the herds.

"How're ye ridin', Will?" asked Jackson before they mounted for the start from camp.

Banion slapped the black stallion on the neck.

"Not his first hunt!" said he.

"I don't mean yore hoss, but yore shootin' irons. Whar's yore guns?"

"I'll risk it with the dragoon revolvers," replied Banion, indicating his holsters. "Not the first time for them, either."

"No? Well, maybe-so they'll do; but fer me, I want a hunk o' lead. Fer approachin' a buffler, still-huntin', the rifle's good, fer ye got time an' kin hold close. Plenty o' our men'll hunt thataway today, an' git meat; but fer me, give me a hunk o' lead. See here now, I got only a shotgun, cap an' ball, fourteen gauge, she is, an' many a hide she's stretched. I kerry my bullets in my mouth an' don't use no patchin'— ye hain't got time, when ye're runnin' in the herd. I let go a charge o' powder out'n my horn, clos't as I kin guess hit, spit in a bullet, and roll her home on top the powder with a jar o' the butt on top my saddle horn. That sots her down, an' she holds good enough to stay in till I ram the muzzle inter ha'r an' let go. She's the same as meat on the fire."

"Well," laughed Banion, "you've another case of *de gustibus*, I suppose."

"You're another, an' I call it back!" exclaimed the old man so truculently that his friend hastened to explain.

"Well, I speak Blackfoot, Crow, Bannack, Grow Vaw, Snake an' Ute," grumbled the scout, "but I never run acrost no Latins out here. I allowed maybe-so ye was allowin' I couldn't kill buffler with Ole Sal. That's what I keep her fer—just buffler. I'll show ye afore long."

And even as Bridger had promised for his favorite weapon, he did prove beyond cavil the efficiency of Old Sal. Time after time the roar or the double roar of his fusee was heard, audible even over the thunder of the hoofs; and quite usually the hunk of lead, driven into heart or lights, low down, soon brought down the game, stumbling in its stride. The old halfbreed style of loading, too, was rapid enough to give Jackson as many buffalo as Bridger's bow had claimed before his horse fell back and the dust cloud lessened in the distance.

The great speed and bottom of Banion's horse, as well as the beast's savage courage and hunting instinct, kept him in longer touch with the running game. Banion was in no haste.

From the sound of firing he knew his men would have meat. Once in the surge of the running herd, the rolling backs, low heads and lolling tongues, shaggy frontlets and gleaming eyes all about him, he dropped the reins on Pronto's neck and began his own work carefully, riding close and holding low, always ready for the sudden swerve of the horse away from the shot to avoid the usual rush of the buffalo when struck. Since he took few chances, his shot rarely failed. In a mile or so, using pains, he had exhausted all but two shots, one in each weapon, and of course no man could load the old cap-and-ball revolver while in the middle of a buffalo run. Now, out of sheer pride in his own skill with small arms, he resolved upon attempting a feat of which he once had heard but never had seen.

Jackson, at a considerable distance to the rear, saw his leader riding back of two bulls which he had cut off and which were making frantic efforts to overtake the herd. After a time they drew close together, running parallel and at top speed. At the distance, what Jackson saw was a swift rush of the black horse between the two bulls. For an instant the three seemed to run neck and neck. Then the rider's arms seemed extended, each on its side. Two puffs of blue smoke stained the gray dust. The black horse sprang straight ahead, not swerving to either side. Two stumbling forms slowed, staggered and presently fell. Then the dust passed, and he saw the rider trot back, glancing here and there over the broad rolling plain at the work of himself and his men.

"I seed ye do hit, boy!" exclaimed the grizzled old hunter when they met. "I seed ye plain, an' ef I hadn't, an' ye'd said ye'd did hit, I'd of said ye was a liar."

"Oh, the double?" Banion colored, not ill pleased at praise from Sir Hubert, praise indeed. "Well, I'd heard it could be done."

"Once is enough. Let 'em call ye a liar atter this! Ef ary one o' them bulls had hit ye ye'd have had no hoss; an' ary one was due to hit ye, or drive ye against the other, an' then he would. That's a trap I hain't ridin' inter noways, not me!"

He looked at his own battered piece a trifle ruefully.

"Well, Ole Sal," said he, " 'pears like you an' me ain't

newfangled enough for these times, not none! When I git to Oregon, ef I ever do, I'm a goin' to stay thar. Times back, five year ago, no one dreamed o' wagons, let alone plows. Fust thing, they'll be makin' plows with wheels, an' rifles that's six-shooters too!"

He laughed loud and long at his own conceit.

"Well, anyways," said he, "we got meat. We've licked one red nation an' got enough meat to feed the white nation, all in a couple o' days. Not so bad—not so bad."

And that night, in the two separate encampments, the white nation, in bivouac, on its battle ground, sat around the fires of *bois des vaches* till near morning, roasting boss ribs, breaking marrowbones, laughing, singing, boasting, shaking high their weapons of war, men making love to their women—the Americans, most terrible and most successful of all savages in history.

But from one encampment two faces were missing until late—Banion and Jackson of the Missourians. Sam Woodhull, erstwhile column captain of the great train, of late more properly to be called unattached, also was absent. It was supposed by their friends that these men might be out late, superintending the butchering, or that at worst they were benighted far out and would find their way to camp the next morning.

Neither of these guesses was correct. Any guess, to be correct, must have included in one solution the missing men of both encampments, who had hunted miles apart.

Chapter XXI

THE QUICKSANDS

As Banion and Jackson ended their part in the buffalo running and gave instructions to the wagon men who followed to care for the meat, they found themselves at a distance of several miles from their starting point. They were deep into a high rolling plateau where the going was more difficult than in the level sunken valley of the Platte. Concluding that it would be easier to ride the two sides of the triangle than the one over which they had come out, they headed for the valley at a sharp angle. As they rode, the keen eye of Jackson caught sight of a black object apparently struggling on the ground at the bottom of a little swale which made down in a long ribbon of green.

"Look-ee yan!" he exclaimed. "Some feller's lost his buffler, I expect. Let's ride down an' put him out'n his misery afore the wolves does."

They swung off and rode for a time toward the strange object. Banion pulled up.

"That's no buffalo! That's a man and his horse! He's bogged down!"

"You're right, Will, an' bogged bad! I've knew that light-green slough grass to cover the wurst sort o' quicksand. She runs black sand under the mud, God knows how deep. Ye kain't run a buffler inter hit—he knows. Come on!"

They spurred down a half mile of gentle slope, hard and firm under foot, and halted at the edge of one of the strange man-traps which sometimes were found in the undrained Plains—a slough of tall, coarse, waving grass which undoubtedly got its moisture from some lower stratum.

In places a small expanse of glistening black mud appeared, although for the most part the mask of innocent-looking grass covered all signs of danger. It was, in effect, the dreaded quicksand, the octopus of the Plains, which covered from view more than one victim and left no discoverable trace.

The rider had attempted to cross a narrow neck of the slough. His mount had begun to sink and flounder, had been urged forward until the danger was obvious. Then, too late, the rider had flung off and turned back, sinking until his feet and legs were gripped by the layer of deep soft sand below. It was one of the rarest but most terrible accidents of the savage wilderness.

Blackened by the mud which lay on the surface, his hat half buried, his arms beating convulsively as he threw himself forward again and again, the victim must in all likelihood soon have exhausted himself. The chill of night on the high Plains soon would have done the rest, and by good fortune he might have died before meeting his entombment. His horse ere this had accepted fate, and ceasing to struggle lay almost buried, his head and neck supported by a trembling bit of floating grass roots.

"Steady, friend!" called out Banion as he ran to the edge. "Don't fight it! Spread out your arms and lie still! We'll get you out!"

"Quick! My lariat, Jackson, and yours!" he added.

The scout was already freeing the saddle ropes. The two horses stood, reins down, snorting at the terror before them, whose menace they now could sense.

"Take the horse!" called Banion. "I'll get the man!"

He was coiling the thin, braided hide *reata*, soft as a glove and strong as steel, which always hung at the Spanish saddle.

He cast, and cast again—yet again, the loop at forty feet gone to nothing. The very silence of the victim nerved him to haste, and he stepped in knee deep, finding only mud, the trickle of black sands being farther out. The rope sped once more, and fell within reach—was caught. A sob or groan came, the first sound. Even then from the imprisoned animal beyond him came that terrifying sound, the scream of a horse in mortal terror. Jackson's rope fell short.

"Get the rope under your arms!" called Banion to the blackened, sodden figure before him. Slowly, feebly, his order was obeyed. With much effort the victim got the loop below one arm, across a shoulder, and then paused.

"Your rope, quick, Bill!"

Jackson hurried and they joined the ends of the two ropes.

"Not my horse—he's wild. Dally on to your own saddle, Bill, and go slow or you'll tear his head off."

The scout's pony, held by the head and backed slowly, squatted to its haunches, snorting, but heaving strongly. The head of the victim was drawn oddly toward his shoulder by the loop, but slowly, silently, his hands clutching at the rope, his body began to rise, to slip forward.

Banion, deep as he dared, at last caught him by the collar, turned up his face. He was safe. Jackson heard the rescuer's deep exclamation, but was busy.

"Cast free, Will, cast free quick, and I'll try for the horse!"

He did try, with the lengthened rope, cast after cast, paying little attention to the work of Banion, who dragged out his man and bent over him as he lay motionless on the safe edge of the treacherous sunken sands which still half buried him.

"No use!" exclaimed the older man. He ran to his saddle and got his deadly double barrel, then stepped as close as possible to the sinking animal as he could. There came a roar. The head of the horse dropped flat, began to sink. "Pore

critter!" muttered the old man, capping his reloaded gun. He
now hastened to aid Banion.

The latter turned a set face toward him and pointed. The
rescued man had opened his eyes. He reached now convulsively for a tuft of grass, paused, stared.

"Hit's Sam Woodhull!" ejaculated the scout. Then, suddenly, "Git away, Will—move back!"

Banion looked over his shoulder as he stood, his own
hands and arms, his clothing, black with mire. The old
man's gray eye was like a strange gem, gleaming at the far
end of the deadly double tube, which was leveled direct at
the prostrate man's forehead.

"No!" Banion's call was quick and imperative. He flung
up a hand, stepped between. "No! You'd kill him—now?"

With a curse Jackson flung his gun from him, began to
recoil the muddied ropes. At length, without a word, he
came to Banion's side. He reached down, caught an arm and
helped Banion drag the man out on the grass. He caught off
a handful of herbage and thrust it out to Woodhull, who
remained silent before what seemed his certain fate.

"Wipe off yore face, you skunk!" said the scout. Then he
seated himself, morosely, hands before knees.

"Will Banion," said he, "ye're a fool—a nacherl-borned,
congenual, ingrain damned fool! Ye're flyin' in the face o'
Proverdence, which planted this critter right here fer us ter
leave where no one'd ever be the wiser, an' where he
couldn't never do no more devilment. Ye idjit, leave me kill
him, ef ye're too chicken-hearted yoreself! Or leave us
throw him back in again!"

Banion would not speak at first, though his eyes never
left Woodhull's streaked, ghastly face.

"By God!" said he slowly, at length, "if we hadn't joined
Scott and climbed Chapultepec together, I'd kill you like a
dog, right here! Shall I give you one more chance to square
things for me? You know what I mean! Will you promise?"

"Promise?" broke in Jackson. "Ye damned fool, would ye
believe ary promise he made, even now? I tellee, boy, he'll
murder ye the fust chanct he gits! He's tried hit one night
afore. Leave me cut his throat, Will! Ye'll never be safe

ontel I do. Leave me cut his throat er kill him with a rock. Hit's only right."

Banion shook his head.

"No," he said slowly, "I couldn't, and you must not."

"Do you promise?" he repeated to the helpless man. "Get up—stand up! Do you promise—will you swear?"

"Swear? Hell!" Jackson also rose as Woodhull staggered to his feet. "Ye knew this man orto kill ye, an' ye sneaked hit, didn't ye? Whar's yer gun?"

"There!" Woodhull nodded to the bog, over which no object now showed. "I'm helpless! I'll promise! I'll swear!"

"Then we'll not sound the No-quarter charge that you and I have heard the Spanish trumpets blow. You will remember the shoulder of a man who fought with you? You'll do what you can now—at any cost?"

"What cost?" demanded Woodhull thickly.

Banion's own white teeth showed as he smiled.

"What difference?" said he. "What odds?"

"That's hit!" Again Jackson cut in, inexorable. "Hit's no difference to him what he sw'ars, yit he'd bargain even now. Hit's about the gal!"

"Hush!" said Banion sternly. "Not another word!"

"Figure on what it means to you." He turned to Woodhull. "I know what it means to me. I've got to have my own last chance, Woodhull, and I'm saving you for that only. Is your last chance now as good as mine? This isn't mercy—I'm trading now. You know what I mean."

Woodhull had freed his face of the mud as well as he could. He walked away, stooped at a trickle of water to wash himself. Jackson quietly rose and kicked the shotgun back farther from the edge. Woodhull now was near to Banion's horse, which, after his fashion, always came and stood close to his master. The butts of the two dragoon revolvers showed in their holsters at the saddle. When he rose from the muddy margin, shaking his hands as to dry them, he walked toward the horse. With a sudden leap, without a word, he sprang beyond the horse, with a swift clutch at both revolvers, all done with a catlike quickness not to have been predicted. He stood clear of the plunging horse, both weapons leveled, covering his two rescuers.

"Evener now!" His teeth bared. "Promise *me!*"

Jackson's deep curse was his answer. Banion rose, his arms folded.

"You're a liar and a coward, Sam!" said he. "Shoot, if you've got the nerve!"

Incredible, yet the man was a natural murderer. His eye narrowed. There came a swift motion, a double empty click!

"Try again, Sam!" said Banion, taunting him. "Bad luck— you landed on an empty!"

He did try again. Swift as an adder, his hands flung first one and then the other weapon into action.

Click after click, no more; Jackson sat dumb, expecting death.

"They're all empty, Sam," said Banion at last as the murderer cast down the revolvers and stood with spread hands. "For the first time, I didn't reload. I didn't think I'd need them."

"You can't blame me!" broke out Woodhull. "You said it was no quarter! Isn't a prisoner justified in trying to escape?"

"You've not escaped," said Banion, coldly now. "Rope him, Jackson."

The thin, soft hide cord fell around the man's neck, tightened.

"Now," shrilled Jackson, "I'll give ye a dog's death!"

He sprang to the side of the black Spaniard, who by training had settled back, tightening the rope.

Chapter XXII

A SECRET OF TWO

Catching the intention of the maddened man, now bent only on swift revenge, Banion sprang to the head of his horse, flinging out an arm to keep Jackson out of the saddle. The horse, frightened at the stubborn struggle between the two, sprang away. Woodhull was pulled flat by the rope about his neck, nor could he loosen it now with his hands, for the horse kept steadily away. Any instant and he might be off in a mad flight, dragging the man to his death.

"Ho! Pronto—*¡Vien aqui!*"

Banion's command again quieted the animal. His ears forward, he came up, whickering his own query as to what really was asked of him.

Banion caught the bridle rein once more and eased the rope. Jackson by now had his shotgun and was shouting, crazed with anger. Woodhull's life chance was not worth a bawbee.

It was his enemy who saved it once again, for inscrutable but unaltered reasons of his own.

"Drop that, Jackson!" called Banion. "Do as I tell you! This man's mine!"

Cursing himself, his friend, their captive, the horse, his gun and all animate and inanimate Nature in his blood rage, the old man, livid in wrath, stalked away at length. "I'll kill him sometime, ef ye don't yerself!" he screamed, his beard trembling. "Ye damned fool!"

"Get up, Woodhull!" commanded Banion. "You've tried once more to kill me. Of course, I'll not take any oath or promise from you now. You don't understand such things. The blood of a gentleman isn't anywhere in your strain. But I'll give you one more chance—give myself that chance too. There's only one thing you understand. That's fear. Yet I've seen you on a firing line, and you started with Doniphan's men. We didn't know we had a coward with us. But you are a coward.

"Now I leave you to your fear! You know what I want— more than life it is to me; but your life is all I have to offer for it. I'm going to wait till then.

"Come on, now! You'll have to walk. Jackson won't let you have his horse. My own never carried a woman but once, and he's never carried a coward at all. Jackson shall not have the rope. I'll not let him kill you."

"What do you mean?" demanded the prisoner, not without his effrontery.

The blood came back to Banion's face, his control breaking.

"I mean for you to walk, trot, gallop, damn you! If you don't you'll strangle here instead of somewhere else in time."

He swung up, and Jackson sullenly followed.

"Give me that gun," ordered Banion, and took the shotgun and slung it in the pommel loop of his own saddle.

The gentle amble of the black stallion kept the prisoner at a trot. At times Banion checked, never looking at the man following, his hands at the rope, panting.

"Ye'll try him in the camp council, Will?" began Jackson once more. "Anyways that? He's a murderer. He tried to kill us both, an' he will yit. Boy, ye rid with Doniphan, an' don't know the *ley refugio?* Hasn't the prisoner tried to escape?

Ain't that old as Mayheeco Veeayho? Take this skunk in on a good rope like that? Boy, ye're crazy!"

"Almost," nodded Banion. "Almost. Come on. It's late."

It was late when they rode down into the valley of the Platte. Below them twinkled hundreds of little fires of the white nation, feasting. Above, myriad stars shone in a sky unbelievably clear. On every hand rose the roaring howls of the great gray wolves, also feasting now; the lesser chorus of yapping coyotes. The savage night of the Plains was on. Through it passed three savage figures, one a staggering, stumbling man with a rope around his neck.

They came into the guard circle, into the dog circle of the encampment; but when challenged, answered and were not stopped.

"Here, Jackson," said Banion at length, "take the rope. I'm going to our camp. I'll not go into this train. Take this pistol—it's loaded now. Let off the *reata*, walk close to this man. If he runs, kill him. Find Molly Wingate. Tell her Will Banion has sent her husband to her—once more. It's the last time."

He was gone in the dark. Bill Jackson, having first meticulously exhausted the entire vituperative resources of the English, the Spanish and all the Indian languages he knew, finally poked the muzzle of the pistol into Woodhull's back.

"Git, damn ye!" he commanded. "Center, guide! Forrerd, march! Ye—"

He improvised now, all known terms of contempt having been heretofore employed.

Threading the way past many feast fires, he did find the Wingate wagons at length, did find Molly Wingate. But there his memory failed him. With a skinny hand at Sam Woodhull's collar, he flung him forward.

"Here, Miss Molly," said he, "this thing is somethin' Major Banion sont in ter ye by me. We find hit stuck in the mud. He said ye're welcome."

But neither he nor Molly really knew why that other man had spared Sam Woodhull's life, or what it was he awaited in return for Sam Woodhull's life.

All that Jackson could do he did. As he turned in the dark

he implanted a heartfelt kick which sent Sam Woodhull on his knees before Molly Wingate as she stood in wondering silence.

Then arose sudden clamorings of those who had seen part of this—seen an armed man assault another, unarmed and defenseless, at their very firesides. Men came running up. Jesse Wingate came out from the side of his wagon.

"What's all this?" he demanded. "Woodhull, what's up? What's wrong here?"

Chapter XXIII

AN ARMISTICE

To the challenge of Wingate and his men Jackson made answer with a high-pitched fighting yell. Sweeping his pistol muzzle across and back again over the front of the closing line, he sprang into saddle and wheeled away.

"Hit means we've brung ye back a murderer. Git yer own rope—ye kain't have mine! If ye-all want trouble with Old Missoury over this, er anything else, come runnin' in the mornin'. Ye'll find us sp'ilin' fer a fight!"

He was off in the darkness.

Men clustered around the draggled man, one of their own men, recently one in authority. Their indignation rose, well grounded on the growing feeling between the two segments of the train. When Woodhull had told his own story, in his own way, some were for raiding the Missouri detachment forthwith. Soberer counsel prevailed. In the morning Price, Hall and Kelsey rode over to the Missouri encampment and asked for their leader. Banion met them while the work of breaking camp went on, the cattle herd being already driven in and held at the rear by lank, youthful riders, themselves sp'lin' fer a fight.

"Major Banion," began Caleb Price, "we've come over to get some sort of understanding between your men and ours. It looks like trouble. I don't want trouble."

"Nor do I," rejoined Banion. "We started out for Oregon as friends. It seems to me that should remain our purpose. No little things should alter that."

"Precisely. But little things have altered it. I don't propose to pass on any quarrel between you and one of our people— a man from your own town, your own regiment. But that has now reached a point where it might mean open war between two parts of our train. That would mean ruin. That's wrong."

"Yes," replied Banion, "surely it is. You see, to avoid that, I was just ordering my people to pull out. I doubt if we could go on together now. I don't want war with any friends. I reckon we can take care of any enemies. Will this please you?"

Caleb Price held out his hand.

"Major, I don't know the truth of any of the things I've heard, and I think those are matters that may be settled later on. But I am obliged to say that many of our people trust you and your leadership more than they do our own. I don't like to see you leave."

"Well, then we won't leave. We'll hold back and follow you. Isn't that fair?"

"It is more than fair, for you can go faster now than we can, like enough. But will you promise me one thing, sir?"

"What is it?"

"If we get in trouble and send back for you, will you come?"

"Yes, we'll come. But pull on out now, at once. My men want to travel. We've got our meat slung on lines along the wagons to cure as we move. We'll wait till noon for you."

"It is fair." Price turned to his associates. "Ride back, Kelsey, and tell Wingate we all think we should break camp at once.

"You see," he added to Banion, "he wouldn't even ride over with us. I regret this break between you and him. Can't it be mended?"

A sudden spasm passed across Will Banion's browned face.

"It cannot," said he, "at least not here and now. But the women and children shall have no risk on that account. If we can ever help, we'll come."

The two again shook hands, and the Wingate lieutenants rode away, so ratifying a formal division of the train.

"What do you make of all this, Hall?" asked sober-going Caleb Price at last. "What's the real trouble? Is it about the girl?"

"Oh, yes; but maybe more. You heard what Woodhull said. Even if Banion denied it, it would be one man's word against the other's. Well, it's wide out here, and no law."

"They'll fight?"

"Will two roosters that has been breasted?"

Chapter XXIV

THE ROAD WEST

Came now once more the notes of the bugle in signal for the assembly. Word passed down the scattered Wingate lines, "Catch up! Catch up!"

Riders went out to the day guards with orders to round up the cattle. Dark lines of the driven stock began to dribble in from the edge of the valley. One by one the corralled vehicles broke park, swung front or rear, until the columns again held on the beaten road up the valley in answer to the command, "Roll out! Roll out!" The Missourians, long aligned and ready, fell in far behind and pitched camp early. There were two trains, not one.

Now, hour after hour and day by day, the toil of the trail through sand flats and dog towns, deadly in its monotony, held them all in apathy. The light-heartedness of the start in early spring was gone. By this time the spare spaces in the wagons were kept filled with meat, for always there were buffalo now. Lines along the sides of the wagons held loads of rudely made jerky—pieces of meat slightly salted and exposed to the clear dry air to finish curing.

But as the people fed full there began a curious sloughing off of the social compact, a change in personal attitude. A dozen wagons, short of supplies or guided by faint hearts, had their fill of the Far West and sullenly started back east. Three dozen broke train and pulled out independently for the West, ahead of Wingate, mule and horse transport again rebelling against being held back by the ox teams. More and more community cleavages began to define. The curse of flies by day, of mosquitoes by night added increasing miseries for the travelers. The hot midday sun wore sore on them. Restless high spirits, grief over personal losses, fear of the future, alike combined to lessen the solidarity of the great train; but still it inched along on its way to Oregon, putting behind mile after mile of the great valley of the Platte.

The grass now lay yellow in the blaze of the sun, the sandy dust was inches deep in the great road, cut by thousands of wheels. Flotsam and jetsam, wreckage, showed more and more. Skeletons of cattle, bodies not yet skeletons, aroused no more than a casual look. Furniture lay cast aside, even broken wagons, their wheels fallen apart, showing intimate disaster. The actual hardships of the great trek thrust themselves into evidence on every hand, at every hour. Often was passed a little cross, half buried in the sand, or the tail gate of a wagon served as head board for some ragged epitaph of some ragged man.

It was decided to cross the South Fork at the upper ford, so called. Here was pause again for the Wingate train. The shallow and fickle stream, fed by the June rise in the mountains, now offered a score of channels, all treacherous. A long line of oxen, now wading and now swimming, dragging a long rope to which a chain was rigged—the latter to pull the wagon forward when the animals got footing on ahead— made a constant sight for hours at a time. One wagon after another was snaked through rapidly as possible. Once bogged down in a fast channel, the fluent sand so rapidly filled in the spokes that the settling wagon was held as though in a giant vise. It was new country, new work for them all; but they were Americans of the frontier.

The men were in the water all day long, for four days, swimming, wading, digging. Perhaps the first plow furrow west of the Kaw was cast when some plows eased down the precipitous bank which fronted one of the fording places. Beyond that lay no mark of any plow for more than a thousand miles.

They now had passed the Plains, as first they crossed the Prairie. The thin tongue of land between the two forks, known as the Highlands of the Platte, made vestibule to the mountains. The scenery began to change, to become rugged, semi-mountainous. They noted and held in sight for a day the Courthouse Rock, the Chimney Rock, long known to the fur traders, and opened up wide vistas of desert architecture new to their experiences.

They were now amid great and varied abundance of game. A thousand buffalo, five, ten, might be in sight at one time, and the ambition of every man to kill his buffalo long since had been gratified. Black-tailed deer and antelope were common, and even the mysterious bighorn sheep of which some of them had read. Each tributary stream now had its delicious mountain trout. The fires at night had abundance of the best of food, cooked for the most part over the native fuel of the *bois des vackes*.

The grass showed yet shorter, proving the late presence of the toiling Mormon caravan on ahead. The weather of late June was hot, the glare of the road blinding. The wagons began to fall apart in the dry, absorbent air of the high country. And always skeletons lay along the trail. An ox abandoned by its owners as too footsore for further travel might better have been shot than abandoned. The gray wolves would surely pull it down before another day. Continuously such tragedies of the wilderness went on before their wearying eyes.

Breaking down from the highlands through the Ash Hollow gap, the train felt its way to the level of the North Fork of the great river which had led them for so long. Here some trapper once had built a cabin—the first work of the sort in six hundred miles—and by some strange concert this deserted cabin had years earlier been constituted a post office of the desert. Hundreds of letters, bundles of papers were addressed to people all over the world, east and west. No government recognized this office, no postage was employed in it. Only, in the hope that someone passing east or west would carry on the inclosures without price, folk here sent out their souls into the invisible.

"How far'll we be out, at Laramie?" demanded Molly Wingate of the train scout, Bridger, whom. Banion had sent on to Wingate in spite of his protest.

"Nigh onto six hundred an' sixty-seven mile they call hit, ma'am, from Independence to Laramie, an' we'll be two months a-makin' hit, which everges around ten mile a day."

"But it's most to Oregon, hain't it?"

"Most to Oregon? Ma'am, it's nigh three hundred mile beyond Laramie to the South Pass, an' the South Pass hain't half-way to Oregon. Why, ma'am, we ain't well begun!"

Chapter XXV

OLD LARAMIE

An old gray man in buckskins sat on the ground in the shade of the adobe stockade at old Fort Laramie, his knees high in front of him, his eyes fixed on the ground. His hair fell over his shoulders in long curls which had once been brown. His pointed beard fell on his breast. He sat silent and motionless, save that constantly he twisted a curl around a forefinger, over and over again. It was his way. He was a long-hair, a man of another day. He had seen the world change in six short years, since the first wagon crossed yonder ridges, where now showed yet one more wagon train approaching.

He paid no attention to the debris and discard of this new day which lay all about him as he sat and dreamed of the days of trap and packet. Near at hand were pieces of furniture leaning against the walls, not bought or sold, but abandoned as useless here at Laramie. Wagon wheels, tireless, their fellies falling apart, lay on the ground, and other ruins of great wagons, dried and disjointed now.

Dust lay on the ground. The grass near by was all cropped

short. Far off, a village of the Cheyennes, come to trade, and sullen over the fact that little now could be had for robes or peltries, grazed their ponies aside from the white man's road. Six hundred lodges of the Sioux were on the tributary river a few miles distant. The old West was making a last gallant stand at Laramie.

Inside the gate a mob of white men, some silent and businesslike, many drunken and boisterous, pushed here and there for access to the trading shelves, long since almost bare of goods. Six thousand emigrants passed that year.

It was the Fourth of July in Old Laramie, and men in jeans and wool and buckskin were celebrating. Old Laramie had seen life—all of life, since the fur days of La Ramée in 1821. Having now superciliously sold out to these pilgrims, reserving only alcohol enough for its own consumption, Old Laramie was willing to let the world wag, and content to twiddle a man curl around a finger.

But yet another detachment of the great army following the hegira of the Mormons was now approaching Laramie. In the warm sun of mid-morning, its worn wheels rattling, its cattle limping and with lolling tongues, this caravan forded and swung wide into corral below the crowded tepees of the sullen tribesmen.

Ahead of it now dashed a horseman, swinging his rifle over his head and uttering Indian yells. He pulled up at the very door of the old adobe guard tower with its mounted swivel guns; swung off, pushed on into the honeycomb of the inner structure.

The famous border fortress was built around a square, the living quarters on one side, the trading rooms on another. Few Indians were admitted at one time, other than the Indian wives of the *engagés*, the officials of the fur company or of the attached white or halfbreed hunters. Above some of the inner buildings were sleeping lofts. The inner open space served as a general meeting ground. Indolent but on guard, Old Laramie held her watch, a rear guard of the passing West in its wild days before the plow.

All residents here knew Jim Bridger. He sought out the man in charge.

"How, Bordeaux?" he began. "Whar's the bourgeois, Papin?"

"Down river—h'east h'after goods."

The trader, hands on his little counter, nodded to his shelves.

"Nada!" he said in his polyglot speech. "Hi'll not got a damned thing lef'. How many loads you'll got for your h'own post, Jeem?"

"Eight wagons. Iron, flour and bacon."

"Hi'll pay ye double here what you'll kin git retail there, Jeem, and take it h'all h'off your hand. This h'emigrant, she'll beat the fur."

"I'll give ye half," said Bridger. "Thar's people here needs supplies that ain't halfway acrost. But what's the news, Bordeaux? Air the Crows down?"

"H'on the Sweetwater, h'awaitin' for the peelgrim. Hi'll heard of your beeg fight on the Platte. Plenty beeg fight on ahead, too, maybe-so. You'll bust h'up the trade, Jeem. My Sioux, she's scare to come h'on the post h'an' trade. He'll stay h'on the veelage, her."

"Every dog to his own yard. Is that all the news?"

"Five thousand Mormons, he'll gone by h'aready. H'wornans pullin' the han'cart, *sacre Enfant!* News—you'll h'ought to know the news. You'll been h'on the settlement six mont'!"

"Hit seemed six year. The hull white nation's movin'. So. That all?"

"Well, go h'ask Keet. He's come h'up South Fork yesterdays. Maybe-so *quelq' cho' des nouvelles* h'out West. I dunno, me."

"Kit—Kit Carson, you mean? What's Kit doing here?"

"*Oui.* I dunno, me."

He nodded to a door. Bridger pushed past hint. In an inner room a party of border men were playing cards at a table. Among these was a slight, sandy-haired man of middle age and mild, blue eye. It was indeed Carson, the redoubtable scout and guide, a better man even than Bridger in the work of the wilderness.

"How are you, Jim?" he said quietly, reaching up a hand

as he sat. "Haven't seen you for five years. What are you doing here?"

He rose now and put down his cards. The game broke up. Others gathered around Bridger and greeted him. It was some time before the two mountain men got apart from the others.

"What brung ye north, Kit?" demanded Bridger at length. "You was in Californy in '47, with the General."

"Yes, I was in California this spring. The treaty's been signed with Mexico. We get the country from the Rio Grande west, including California. I'm carrying dispatches to General Kearny at Leavenworth. There's talk about taking over Laramie for an Army post. The tribes are up in arms. The trade's over, Jim."

"What I know, an' have been sayin'! Let's have a drink, Kit, fer old times."

Laughing, Carson turned his pockets inside out. As he did so something heavy fell from his pocket to the floor. In courtesy as much as curiosity Bridger stooped first to pick it up. As he rose he saw Carson's face change as he held out his hand.

"What's this stone, Kit—yer medicine?"

But Bridger's own face altered suddenly as he now guessed the truth. He looked about him suddenly, his mouth tight. Kit Carson rose and they passed from the room.

"Only one thing heavy as that, Mister Kit!" said Bridger fiercely. "Where'd you git hit? My gran'pap had some o' that. Hit come from North Carliny years ago. I know what hit is—hit's gold! Kit Carson, damn ye, hit's the gold!"

"Shut your mouth, you fool!" said Carson. "Yes, it's gold. But do you want me to be a liar to my General? That's part of my dispatches."

"Hit come from Californy?"

"Curse me, yes, California! I was ordered to get the news to the Army first. You're loose-tongued, Jim. Can you keep this?"

"Like a grave, Kit."

"Then here!"

Carson felt inside his shirt and pulled out a meager and

ill-printed sheet which told the most epochal news that this
or any country has known—the midwinter discovery of gold
at Sutter's Mills.

A flag was flying over Laramie stockade, and this flag the
mountain men saw fit to salute with many libations, hearing
now that it was to fly forever over California as over
Oregon. Crowding the stockade inclosure full was a motley
throng—border men in buckskins, *engagés* swart as Indians,
French breeds, full-blood Cheyennes and Sioux of the northern hills, all mingling with the curious emigrants who had
come in from the wagon camps. Plump Indian girls, many
of them very comely, some of them wives of the trappers
who still hung about Laramie, ogled the newcomers, laughing, giggling together as young women of any color do, their
black hair sleek with oil, their cheeks red with vermilion,
their wrists heavy with brass or copper or pinchbeck circlets,
their small moccasined feet peeping beneath gaudy calico
given them by their white lords. Older squaws, envious but
perforce resigned, muttered as their own stern-faced stolid
red masters ordered them to keep close. Of the full-bloods,
whether Sioux or Cheyennes, only those drunk were other
than sullenly silent and resentful as they watched the white
man's orgy at Old Laramie on the Fourth of July of 1848.

Far flung along the pleasant valley lay a vast picture possible in no other land or day. The scattered covered wagons,
the bands of cattle and horses, the white tents rising now in
scores, the blue of many fires, all proved that now the white
man had come to fly his flag over a new frontier.

Bridger stood, chanting an Indian song. A group of men
came out, all excited with patriotic drink. A tall man in
moccasins led, his fringed shirt open over a naked breast,
his young squaw following him.

"Let me see one o' them damned things!" he was exclaiming. "That's why I left home fifty year ago. Pap wanted to
make me plow! I ain't seed one since, but I'll bet a pony I
kin run her right now! Go git yer plow things, boys, an'
fotch on ary sort of cow critter suits ye. I'll bet I kin hook
'em up an' plow with 'em, too, right yere!"

The old gray man at the gate sat and twisted his long curls.

The sweet wind of the foothills blew aslant the smokes of a thousand fires. Over the vast landscape passed many moving figures. Young Indian men, mostly Sioux, some Cheyennes, a few Gros Ventres of the Prairie, all peaceable under the tacit truce of the trading post, rode out from their villages to their pony herds. From the post came the occasional note of an inharmonic drum, struck without rhythm by a hand gone lax. The singers no longer knew they sang. The border feast had lasted long. Keg after keg had been broached. The Indian drums were going. Came the sound of monotonous chants, broken with staccato yells as the border dance, two races still mingling, went on with aboriginal excesses on either side. On the slopes as dusk came twinkled countless tepee fires. Dogs barked mournfully a-distant. The heavy half roar of the buffalo wolves, superciliously confident, echoed from the broken country.

Now and again a tall Indian, naked save where he clutched his robe to him unconsciously, came staggering to his tepee, his face distorted, yelling obscene words and not knowing what he said. Patient, his youngest squaw stood by his tepee, his spear held aloft to mark his door plate, waiting for her lord to come. Wolfish dogs lay along the tepee edges, noses in tails, eyeing the master cautiously. A grumbling old woman mended the fire at her own side of the room, nearest the door, spreading smooth robes where the man's medicine hung at the willow tripod, his slatted lazyback near by. In due time all would know whether at the game of "hands," while the feast went on, the little elusive bone had won or lost for him. Perhaps he had lost his horses, his robes, his weapons—his squaws. The white man's medicine was strong, and there was much of it on his feasting day.

From the stockade a band of mounted Indians, brave in new finery, decked with eagle bonnets and gaudy in beaded shirts and leggings, rode out into the slopes, chanting maudlin songs. They were led by the most beautiful young woman of the tribe, carrying a wand topped by a gilded ball, and ornamented with bells, feathers, natural flowers. As the wild pageant passed the proud savages paid no attention to the white men.

The old gray man at the gate sat and twisted his long curls.

And none of them knew the news from California.

Chapter XXVI

THE FIRST GOLD

The purple mantle of the mountain twilight was dropping on the hills when Bridger and Carson rode out together from the Laramie stockade to the Wingate encampment in the valley. The extraordinary capacity of Bridger in matters alcoholic left him still in fair possession of his faculties; but some new purpose, born of the exaltation of alcohol, now, held his mind.

"Let me see that little dingus ye had, Kit," said he—"that piece o' gold."

Carson handed it to him.

"Ye got any more o' hit, Kit?"

"Plenty! You can have it if you'll promise not to tell where it came from, Jim."

"If I do, Jim Bridger's a liar, Kit!"

He slipped the nugget into his pocket. They rode to the head of the train, where Bridger found Wingate and his aids, and presented his friend. They all, of course, knew of Frémont's famous scout, then at the height of his reputation, and greeted him with enthusiasm. As they gathered around

him Bridger slipped away. Searching among the wagons, he
at last found Molly Wingate and beckoned her aside with
portentous injunctions of secrecy.

In point of fact, a sudden maudlin inspiration had seized Jim
Bridger, so that a promise to Kit Carson seemed infinitely less
important than a promise to this girl, whom, indeed, with an
old man's inept infatuation, he had worshiped afar after the
fashion of white men long gone from society of their kind. Liquor now made him bold. Suddenly he reached out a hand and
placed in Molly's palm the first nugget of California gold that
ever had come thus far eastward. Physically heavy it was; of
what tremendous import none then could have known.

"I'll give ye this!" he said. "An' I know whar's plenty
more."

She dropped the nugget because of the sudden weight in
her hand; picked it up

"Gold!" she whispered, for there is no mistaking gold.

"Yes, gold!"

"Where did you get it?"

She was looking over her shoulder instinctively.

"Listen! Ye'll never tell? Ye mustn't! I swore to Kit
Carson, that give hit to me, I'd never tell no one. But I'll
set you ahead o' any livin' bein', so maybe some day ye'll
remember old Jim Bridger.

"Yes, hit's gold! Kit Carson brung it from Sutter's Fort,
on the Sacramenty, in Californy. They've got it that in wag-
onloads. Kit's on his way east now to tell the Army!"

"Everyone will know!"

"Yes, but not now! Ef ye breathe this to a soul thar won't
be two wagons left together in the train. Thar'll be bones o'
womern from here to Californy!"

Wide-eyed, the girl stood, weighing the nugget in her
hands.

"Keep hit, Miss Molly," said Bridger simply. "I don't
want hit no more. I only got hit fer a bracelet fer ye, or
something. Good-by. I've got to leave the train with my own
wagons afore long an' head fer my fort. Ye'll maybe see
me—old Jim Bridger—when ye come through.

"Yes, Miss Molly, I ain't as old as I look, and I got a fort o' my own beyant the Green River. This year, what I'll take in for my cargo, what I'll make cash money fer work fer the immygrints, I'll salt down anyways ten thousand; next year maybe twicet that, or even more. I sartainly will do a good trade with them Mormons."

"I suppose," said the girl, patient with what she knew was alcoholic garrulity.

"An' out there's the purtiest spot west o' the Rockies. My valley is ever'thing a man er a womern can ask or want. And me, I'm a permanent man in these yere parts. It's me, Jim Bridger, that fust diskivered the Great Salt Lake. It's me, Jim Bridger, fust went through Colter's Hell up in the Yellowstone. Ain't a foot o' the Rockies I don't know. I eena-most built the Rocky Mountains, me." He spread out his hands. "And I've got to be eena' most all Injun myself."

"I suppose." The girl's light laugh cut him.

"But never so much as not to rever'nce the white woman, Miss Molly. Ye're all like angels to us wild men out yere. We—we never have forgot. And so I give ye this, the fust gold from Californy. There may be more. I don't know."

"But you're going to leave us? What are you going to do?" A sudden kindness was in the girl's voice.

"I'm a-goin' out to Fort Bridger, that's what I'm a-goin' to do; an' when I git thar I'm a-goin' to lick hell out o' both my squaws, that's what I'm a-goin' to do! One's named Blast Yore Hide, an' t'other Dang Yore Eyes. Which, ef ye ask me, is two names right an' fitten, way I feel now."

All at once Jim Bridger was all Indian again. He turned and stalked away. She heard his voice rising in his Indian chant as she turned back to her own wagon fire.

But now shouts were arising, cries coming up the line. A general movement was taking place toward the lower end of the camp, where a high quavering call rose again and again.

"There's news!" said Carson to Jesse Wingate quietly. "That's old Bill Jackson's war cry, unless I am mistaken. Is he with you?"

"He was," said Wingate bitterly. "He and his friends

broke away from the train and have been flocking by themselves since then."

Three men rode up to the Wingate wagon, and two flung off. Jackson was there, yes, and Jed Wingate, his son. The third man still sat his horse. Wingate straightened.

"Mr. Banion! So you see fit to come into my camp?" For the time he had no answer.

"How are you, Bill?" said Kit Carson quietly, as he now stepped forward from the shadows. The older man gave him a swift glance.

"Kit! You here—why?" he demanded. "I've not seed ye, Kit, sence the last Rendyvous on the Green. Ye've been with the Army on the coast?"

"Yes. Going east now."

"Allus ridin' back and forerd acrost the hull country. I'd hate to keep ye in buckskin breeches, Kit. But ye're carryin' news?"

"Yes," said Carson. "Dispatches about new Army posts— to General Kearny. Some other word for him, and some papers to the Adjutant General of the Army. Besides, some letters from Lieutenant Beale in Mexico, about war matters and the treaty, like enough. You know, we'll get all the southern country to the Coast?"

"An' welcome ef we didn't! Not a beaver to the thousand miles, Kit. I'm goin' to Oregon—goin' to settle in the Nez Percé country, whar there's horses an' beaver."

"But wait a bit afore you an' me gits too busy talkin'. Ye see, I'm with Major Banion, yan, an' the Missoury train. We're in camp ten mile below. We wouldn't mix with these people no more—only one way—but I reckon the Major's got some business o' his own that brung him up. I rid with him. We met the boy an' ast him to bring us in. We wasn't sure how friendly our friends is feelin' towards him an' me."

He grinned grimly. As he spoke they both heard a woman's shrilling, half greeting, half terror. Wingate turned in time to see his daughter fall to the ground in a sheer faint.

Will Banion slipped from his saddle and hurried forward.

Chapter XXVII

TWO WHO LOVED

Jesse Wingate made a swift instinctive motion toward the revolver which swung at his hip. But Jed sprang between him and Banion.

"No! Hold on, Pap—stop!" cried Jed. "It's all right. I brought him in."

"As a prisoner?"

"I am no man's prisoner, Captain Wingate," said Banion's deep voice.

His eyes were fixed beyond the man to whom he spoke. He saw Molly, to whom her mother now ran, to take the white face in her own hands. Wingate looked from one to the other.

"Why do you come here? What do I owe you that you should bring more trouble, as you always have? And what do you owe me?"

"I owe you nothing!" said Banion. "You owe me nothing at all. I have not traveled in your train, and I shall not travel in it. I tell you once more, you're wrong in your beliefs; but till I can prove that I'll not risk any argument about it."

"Then why do you come to my camp now?"

"You should know."

"I do know. It's Molly!"

"It's Molly, yes. Here's a letter from her. I found it in the cabin at Ash Hollow. Your friend Woodhull could have killed me—we passed him just now. Jed could have killed me—you can now; it's easy. But that wouldn't change me. Perhaps it wouldn't change her."

"You come here to face me down?"

"No, sir. I know you for a brave man, at least. I don't believe I'm a coward—I never asked. But I came to see Molly, because here she's asked it. I don't know why. Do you want to shoot me like a coyote?"

"No. But I ask you, what do I owe you?"

"Nothing. But can we trade? If I promise to leave you with my train?"

"You want to steal my girl!"

"No! I want to earn her—some day."

The old Roman before him was a man of quick and strong decisions. The very courage of the young man had its appeal.

"At least you'll eat," said he. "I'd not turn even a black Secesh away hungry—not even a man with your record in the Army."

"No, I'll not eat with you."

"Wait then! I'll send the girl pretty soon, if you are here by her invitation. I'll see she never invites you again."

Wingate walked toward his wagon. Banion kept out of the light circle and found his horse. He stood, leaning his head on his arms in the saddle, waiting, until after what seemed an age she slipped out of the darkness, almost into his arms, standing pale, her fingers lacing and unlacing—the girl who had kissed him once—to say good-by.

"Will Banion!" she whispered. "Yes, I sent for you. I felt you'd find the letter."

"Yes, Molly." It was long before he would look at her. "You're the same," said he. "Only you've grown more beautiful every day. It's hard to leave you—awfully hard. I couldn't, if I saw you often."

He reached out again and took her in his arms, softly,

kissed her tenderly on each cheek, whispered things that lovers do say. But for his arms she would have dropped again, she was so weak. She fought him off feebly.

"No! No! It is not right! No! No!"

"You're not going to be with us any more?" she said at last.

He shook his head. They both looked at his horse, his rifle, swung in its sling strap at the saddle horn. She shook her head also.

"Is this the real good-by, Will?"·Her lips trembled.

"It must be. I have given my word to your father. But why did you send for me? Only to torture me? I must keep my word to hold my train apart. I've promised my men to stick with them."

"Yes, you mustn't break your word. And it was fine just to see you a minute, Will; just to tell you—oh, to say I love you, Will! But I didn't think that was why I sent. I sent to warn you—against him. It seems always to come to the same thing."

She was trying not to sob. The man was in but little better case. The stars did not want them to part. All the somber wilderness world whispered for them to love and not to part at all. But after a time they knew that they again had parted, or now were able to do so.

"Listen, Will," said the girl at last, putting back a lock of her fallen hair. "I'll have to tell you. We'll meet in Oregon? I'll be married then. I've promised. Oh, God help me! I think I'm the wickedest woman in all the·world, and the most unhappy. Oh, Will Banion, I—I love a thief! Even as you are, I love you! I guess that's why I sent for you, after all.

"Go find the scout—Jim Bridger!" she broke out suddenly. "He's going on ahead. Go on to his fort with him— he'll have wagons and horses. He knows the way. Go with Bridger, Will! Don't go to Oregon! I'm afraid for you. Go to California—and forget me! Tell Bridger—"

"Why, where is it?" she exclaimed.

She was feeling˚in the pocket of her apron, and it was empty.

"I've lost it!" she repeated. "I lose everything!"

"What was it, Molly?"

She leaned her lips to his ear.

"It was gold!"

He stood, the magic name of that metal which shows the color in the shade electrifying even his ignorance of the truth.

"Gold?"

She told him then, breaking her own promise magnificently, as a woman will.

"Go, ride with Bridger," she went on. "Don't tell him you ever knew me. He'll not be apt to speak of me. But they found it, in California, the middle of last winter—gold! Gold! Carson's here in our camp—Kit Carson. He's the first man to bring it to the valley of the Platte. He was sworn to keep it secret; so was Bridger, and so am I. Not to Oregon, Will—California! You can live down your past. If we die, God bless the man I do love. That's you, Will! And I'm going to marry—him. Ten days! On the trail! And he'll kill you, Will! Oh, keep away!"

She paused, breathless from her torrent of incoherent words, jealous of the passing moments. It was vague, it was desperate, it was crude. But they were in a world vague, desperate and crude.

"I've promised my men I'd not leave them," he said at last. "A promise is a promise."

"Then God help us both! But one thing—when I'm married, that's the end between us. So good-by."

He leaned his head back on his saddle for a time, his tired horse turning back its head. He put out his hand blindly; but it was the muzzle of his horse that had touched his shoulder. The girl was gone.

The Indian drums at Laramie thudded through the dark. The great wolf in the breaks lifted his hoarse, raucous roar once more. The wilderness was afoot or bedding down, according to its like.

Chapter XXVIII

WHEN A MAID MARRIES

Carson, Bridger and Jackson, now reunited after years, must pour additional libations to Auld Lang Syne at Laramie, so soon were off together. The movers sat around their thrifty cooking fires outside the wagon corral. Wingate and his wife were talking heatedly, she in her nervousness not knowing that she fumbled over and over in her fingers the heavy bit of rock which Molly had picked up and which was in her handkerchief when it was requisitioned by her mother to bathe her face just now. After a time she tossed the nugget aside into the grass. It was trodden by a hundred feet ere long.

But gold will not die. In three weeks a prowling Gros Ventre squaw found it and carried it to the trader, Bordeaux, asking, "Shoog?"

"Non, non!" replied the Laramie trader. "Pas de shoog!" But he looked curiously at the thing, so heavy.

"How, cola!" wheedled the squaw. "Shoog!" She made the sign for sugar, her finger from her palm to her lips. Bordeaux tossed the thing into the tin can on the shelf and gave her what sugar would cover a spoon.

"Where?" He asked her, his fingers loosely shaken, meaning, "Where did you get it?"

The Gros Ventre lied to him like a lady, and told him, on the South Fork, on the Creek of Bitter Cherries—near where Denver now is; and where placers once were. That was hundreds of miles away. The Gros Ventre woman had been there once in her wanderings and had seen some heavy metal.

Years later, after Fort Laramie was taken over by the Government, Bordeaux as sutler sold much flour and bacon to men hurrying down the South Fork to the early Colorado diggings. Meantime in his cups he often had told the mythical tale of the Gros Ventre woman—long after California, Idaho, Nevada, Montana were all afire. But one of his half-breed children very presently had commandeered the tin cup and its contents, so that to this day no man knows whether the child swallowed the nugget or threw it into the Laramie River or the Platte River or the sagebrush. Some depose that an emigrant bought it of the baby; but no one knows.

What all men do know is that gold does not die; nay, nor the news of it. And this news now, like a multiplying germ, was in the wagon train that had started out for Oregon.

As for Molly, she asked no questions at all about the lost nugget, but hurried to her own bed, supperless, pale and weeping. She told her father nothing of the nature of her meeting with Will Banion, then nor at any time for many weeks.

"Molly, come here, I want to talk to you."

Wingate beckoned to his daughter the second morning after Banion's visit.

The order for the advance was given. The men had brought in the cattle and the yoking up was well forward. The rattle of pots and pans was dying down. Dogs had taken their places on flank or at the wagon rear, women were climbing up to the seats, children clinging to pieces of dried meat. The train was waiting for the word.

The girl followed him calmly, high-headed.

"Molly, see here," he began. "We're all ready to move on. I don't know where Will Banion went, but I want you to know, as I told him, that he can't travel in our train."

"He'll not ask to, father. He's promised to stick to his own men."

"He's left you at last! That's good. Now I want you to drop him from your thoughts. Hear that, and heed it. I tell you once more, you're not treating Sam Woodhull right."

She made him no answer.

"You're still young, Molly," he went on. "Once you're settled you'll find Oregon all right. Time you were marrying. You'll be twenty and an old maid first thing you know. Sam will make you a good husband. Heed what I say."

But she did not heed, though she made no reply to him. Her eye, scornful, threatening and young, looked yonder where she knew her lover was; nor was it in her soul ever to return from following after him. The name of her intended husband left her cold as ice.

"Roll out! Roll out! Ro-o-o-ll ou-t!"

The call went down the line once more. The pistolry of the wagon whips made answer, the drone of the drivers rose as the sore-necked oxen bowed their heads again, with less strength even for the lightened loads.

The old man who sat by the gate at Fort Laramie, twisting a curl around his finger, saw the plain clearing now, as the great train swung out and up the river trail. He perhaps knew that Jim Bridger, with his own freight wagons, going light and fast with mules, was on west, ahead of the main caravan. But he did not know the news Jim Bridger carried, the same news that Carson was carrying east. The three old mountain men, for a few hours meeting after years, now were passing far apart, never to meet again. Their chance encountering meant much to hundreds of men and women then on the road to Oregon; to untold thousands yet to come.

As for one Samuel Woodhull, late column captain, it was to be admitted that for some time he had been conscious of certain buffetings of fate. But as all thoroughbred animals are thin-skinned, so are all the short-bred pachydermatous, whereby they endure and mayhap arrive at the manger well as the next. True, even Woodhull's vanity and self-content had everything asked of them in view of his late series of mishaps; but by now he had somewhat chirked up under rest and good food, and was once more the dandy and hail fellow. He felt assured that very presently bygones would be bygones. Moreover—so he reasoned—if he, Sam Woodhull, won the spoils, what matter who had won any sort of victory? He knew, as all these others knew and as all the world knows, that a beautiful woman is above all things *spolia opima* of war. Well, in ten days he was to marry Molly Wingate, the most beautiful woman of the train and the belle of more than one community. Could he not afford to laugh best, in spite of all events, even if some of them had not been to his own liking?

But the girl's open indifference was least of all to his liking. It enraged his vain, choleric nature to its inner core. Already he planned dominance; but willing to wait and to endure for ten days, meantime he employed innocence, reticence, dignity, attentiveness, so that he seemed a suitor misunderstood, misrepresented, unjustly used—to whose patient soul none the less presently must arrive justice and exoneration, after which all would be happier even than a marriage bell. After the wedding bells he, Samuel Woodhull, would show who was master.

Possessed once more of horse, arms and personal equipment, and having told his own story of persecution to good effect throughout the train, Woodhull had been allowed to resume a nominal command over a part of the Wingate wagons. The real control lay in the triumvirate who once had usurped power, and who might do so again.

Wingate himself really had not much more than nominal control of the general company, although he continued to give what Caleb Price called the easy orders. His wagons, now largely changed to ox transport, still traveled at the head of the train, Molly continuing to drive her own light wagon and Jed remaining on the cow column.

The advance hardly had left Fort Laramie hidden by the rolling ridges before Woodhull rode up to Molly's wagon and made excuse to pass his horse to a boy while he himself climbed up on the seat with his fiancée.

She made room for him in silence, her eyes straight ahead.

The wagon cover made good screen behind, the herdsmen were far in the rear, and from the wagons ahead none could see them. Yet when, after a moment, her affianced husband dropped an arm about her waist the girl flung it off impatiently.

"Don't!" she exclaimed. "I detest love-making in public. We see enough of it that can't be hid. It's getting worse, more open, the farther we get out."

"The train knows we are to be married at the halfway stop, Molly. Then you'll change wagons and will not need to drive."

"Wait till then."

"I count the hours. Don't you, dearest?"

She turned a pallid face to him at last, resentful of his endearments.

"Yes, I do," she said. But he did not know what she meant, or why she was so pale.

"I think we'll settle in Portland," he went on. "The travelers' stories say that place, at the head of navigation on the Willamette, has as good a chance as Oregon City, at the Falls. I'll practice law. The goods I am taking out will net us a good sum, I'm hoping. Oh, you'll see the day when you'll not regret that I held you to your promise! I'm not playing this Oregon game to lose it."

"Do you play any game to lose it?"

"No! Better to have than to explain have not—that's one of my mottoes."

"No matter how?"

"Why do you ask?"

"I was only wondering."

"About what?"

"About men—and the differences."

"My dear, as a school-teacher you have learned to use a map, a blackboard. Do you look on us men as ponderable, measurable, computable?"

"A girl ought to if she's going to marry."

"Well, haven't you?"

"Have I?"

She still was staring straight ahead, cold, making no silent

call for a lover's arms or arts. Her silence was so long that
at length even his thick hide was pierced.

"Molly!" he broke out. "Listen to me! Do you want the
engagement broken? Do you want to be released?"

"What would they all think?"

"Not the question. Answer me!"

"No, I don't want it broken. I want it over with. Isn't that
fair?"

"Is it?"

"Didn't you say you wanted me on any terms?"

"Surely!"

"Don't you now?"

"Yes, I do, and I'm going to have you, too!"

His eye, covetous, turned to the ripe young beauty of the
maid beside him. He was willing to pay any price.

"Then it all seems settled."

"All but one part. You've never really and actually told
me you loved me."

A wry smile.

"I'm planning to do that after I marry you. I suppose
that's the tendency of a woman? Of course, it can't be true
that only one man will do for a woman to marry, or one
woman for a man? If anything went wrong on that basis—
why, marrying would stop?That would be foolish, wouldn't
it? I suppose women do adjust? Don't you think so?"

His face grew hard under this cool reasoning.

"Am I to understand that you are marrying me as a second
choice, and so that you can forget some other man?"

"Couldn't you leave a girl a secret if she had one?
Couldn't you be happier if you did? Couldn't you take your
chance and see if there's anything under the notion about
more than one man and more than one woman in the world?
Love? Why, what is love? Something to marry on? They
say it passes. They tell me that marriage is more adjustable,
means more interests than love; that the woman who marries
with her eyes open is apt to be the happiest in the long run.
Well, then you said you wanted me on any terms. Does not
that include open eyes?"

"You're making a hard bargain—the hardest a man can be obliged to take."

"It was not of my seeking."

"You said you loved me—at first."

"No. Only a girl's in love with love—at first. I've not really lied to you. I'm trying to be honest before marriage. Don't fear I'll not be afterward. There's much in that, don't you think? Maybe there's something, too, in a woman's ability to adjust and compromise? I don't know. We ought to be as happy as the average married couple, don't you think? None of them are happy for so very long, they say. They say love doesn't last long. I hope not. One thing, I believe marriage is easier to beat than love is."

"How old are you, really, Molly?"

"I am just over nineteen, sir."

"You are wise for that; you are old."

"Yes—since we started for Oregon."

He sat in sullen silence for a long time, all the venom of his nature gathering, all his savage jealousy.

"You mean since you met that renegade, traitor and thief, Will Banion! Tell me, isn't that it?"

"Yes, that's true. I'm older now. I know more."

"And you'll marry me without love. You love him without marriage? Is that it?"

"I'll never marry a thief."

"But you love one?"

"I thought I loved you."

"But you do love him, that man!"

Now at last she turned to him, gazing straight through the mist of her tears.

"Sam, if you really loved me, would you ask that? Wouldn't you just try to be so gentle and good that there'd no longer be any place in my heart for any other sort of love, so I'd learn to think that our love was the only sort in the world? Wouldn't you take your chance and make good on it, believing that it must be in nature that a woman can love more than one man, or love men in more than one way? Isn't marriage broader and with more chance for both? If you love me and not just yourself alone, can't you take your chance as I am taking mine? And after all, doesn't a woman give the odds? If you do love me—"

"If I do, then my business is to try to make you forget Will Banion."

"There is no other way you could. He may die. I promise you I'll never see him after I'm married.

"And I'll promise you another thing"—her strained nerves now were speaking truth for her—"if by any means I ever learn—if I ever believe—that Major Banion is not what I now think him, I'll go on my knees to him. I'll know marriage was wrong and love was right all the time."

"Fine, my dear! Much happiness! But unfortunately for Major Banion's passing romance, the official records of a military court-martial and a dishonorable discharge from the Army are facts which none of us can doubt or deny."

"Yes, that's how it is. So that's why."

"What do you really mean then, Molly—you say, that's why?"

"That's why I'm going to marry you, Sam. Nine days from today, at the Independence Rock, if we are alive. And from now till then, and always, I'm going to be honest, and I'm going to pray God to give you power to make me forget every other man in all the world except my—my—" But she could not say the word "husband."

"Your husband!"

He said it for her, and perhaps then reached his zenith in approximately unselfish devotion, and in good resolves at least.

The sun shone blinding hot. The white dust rose in clouds. The plague of flies increased. The rattle and creak of wheel, the monotone of the drivers, the cough of dust-afflicted kine made the only sounds for a long time.

"You can't kiss me, Molly?"

He spoke not in dominance but in diffidence. The girl awed him.

"No, not till after, Sam; and I think I'd rather be left alone from now till then. After—Oh, be good to me, Sam! I'm trying to be honest as a woman can. If I were not that I'd not be worth marrying at all."

Without suggestion or agreement on his part she drew tighter the reins on her mules. He sprang down over the wheel. The sun and the dust had their way again; the monotony of life, its drab discontent, its yearnings and its sense of failure once more resumed sway in part or all of the morose caravan. They all sought new fortunes, each of these. One day each must learn that, travel far as he likes, a man takes himself with him for better or for worse.

Chapter XXIX

THE BROKEN WEDDING

Banion allowed the main caravan two days' start before he moved beyond Fort Laramie. Every reason bade him to cut entirely apart from that portion of the company. He talked with every man he knew who had any knowledge of the country on ahead, read all he could find, studied such maps as then existed, and kept an open ear for advice of old-time men who in hard experience had learned how to get across a country.

Two things troubled him: The possibility of grass exhaustion near the trail and the menace of the Indians. Squaw men in from the north and west said that the Arapahoes were hunting on the Sweetwater, and sure to make trouble; that the Blackfeet were planning war; that the Bannacks were east of the Pass; that even the Crows were far down below their normal range and certain to harass the trains. These stories, not counting the hostility of the Sioux and Cheyennes of the Platte country, made it appear that there was a tacit suspense of intertribal hostility, and a general and joint uprising against the migrating whites.

These facts Banion did not hesitate to make plain to all his men; but, descendants of pioneers, with blood of the wilderness in their veins, and each tempted by adventure as much as by gain, they laughed long and loud at the thought of danger from all the Indians of the Rockies. Had they not beaten the Sioux? Could they not in turn humble the pride of any other tribe? Had not their fathers worked with rifle lashed to the plow beam? Indians? Let them come!

Founding his own future on this resolute spirit of his men, Banion next looked to the order of his own personal affairs. He found prices so high at Fort Laramie, and the stock of all manner of goods so low, that he felt it needless to carry his own trading wagons all the way to Oregon, when a profit of 400 per cent lay ready not a third of the way across and less the further risk and cost. He accordingly cut down his own stocks to one wagon, and sold off wagons and oxen as well, until he found himself possessed of considerably more funds than when he had started out.

He really cared little for these matters. What need had he for a fortune or a future now? He was poorer than any jeans-clad ox driver with a sunbonnet on the seat beside him and tow-headed children on the flour and bacon sacks, with small belongings beyond the plow lashed at the tail gate, the ax leaning in the front corner of the box and the rifle swinging in its loops at the wagon bows. They were all beginning life again. He was done with it.

The entire caravan now had passed in turn the Prairies and the Plains. In the vestibule of the mountains they had arrived in the most splendid out-of-doors country the world has ever offered. The climate was superb, the scenery was a constant succession of changing beauties new to the eyes of all. Game was at hand in such lavish abundance as none of them had dreamed possible. The buffalo ranged always within touch, great bands of elk now appeared, antelope always were in sight. The streams abounded in noble game fish, and the lesser life of the open was threaded across continually by the presence of the great predatory animals— the grizzly, the gray wolf, even an occasional mountain lion. The guarding of the cattle herds now required continual exertion, and if any weak or crippled draft animal fell out, its bones were clean within the hour. The feeling of the wilderness now was distinct enough for the most adventurous. They fed fat, and daily grew more like savages in look and practice.

Wingate's wagons kept well apace with the average schedule of a dozen miles a day, at times spurting to fifteen or twenty miles, and made the leap over the heights of land between the North Platte and the Sweetwater, which latter stream, often winding among defiles as well as pleasant meadows, was to lead them to the summit of the Rockies at the South Pass, beyond which they set foot on the soil of Oregon, reaching thence to the Pacific. Before them now lay the entry mark of the Sweetwater Valley, that strange oblong upthrust of rock, rising high above the surrounding plain, known for two thousand miles as Independence Rock.

At this point, more than eight hundred miles out from the Missouri, a custom of unknown age seemed to have decreed a pause. The great rock was an unmistakable landmark, and time out of mind had been a register of the wilderness. It carried hundreds of names, including every prominent one ever known in the days of fur trade or the new day of the wagon trains. It became known as a resting place; indeed, many rested there forever, and never saw the soil of Oregon. Many an emigrant woman, sick well-nigh to death, held out so that she might be buried among the many other graves that clustered there. So, she felt, she had the final company of her kind. And to those weak or faint of heart the news that this was not halfway across often smote with despair and death, and they, too, laid themselves down here by the road to Oregon.

But here also were many scenes of cheer. By this time the new life of the trail had been taken on, rude and simple. Frolics were promised when the wagons should reach the Rock. Neighbors made reunions there. Weddings, as well as burials, were postponed till the train got to Independence Rock.

Here then, a sad-faced girl, true to her promise and true to some strange philosophy of her own devising, was to become the wife of a suitor whose persistency had brought him little comfort beyond the wedding date. All the train knew that Molly Wingate was to be married there to Sam Woodhull, now restored to trust and authority. Some said it was a good match, others shook their heads, liking well to see a maid either blush or smile in such case as Molly's, whereas she did neither.

At all events, Mrs. Wingate was two days baking cakes at the train stops. Friends got together little presents for the bride. Jed, Molly's brother, himself a fiddler of parts, organized an orchestra of a dozen pieces. The Rev. Henry Doak, a Baptist divine of much nuptial diligence en route, made ready his best coat. They came into camp. In the open spaces of the valley hundreds of wagons were scattered, each to send representatives to Molly Wingate's wedding. Some insisted that the ceremony should be performed on the top of the Rock itself, so that no touch of romance should lack.

Then approached the very hour—ten of the night, after duties of the day were done. A canopy was spread for the ceremony. A central camp fire set the place for the wedding feast. Within a half hour the bride would emerge from the secrecy of her wagon to meet at the canopy under the Rock the impatient groom, already clad in his best, already giving largess to the riotous musicians, who now attuned instruments, now broke out into rude jests or pertinent song.

But Molly Wingate did not appear, nor her father, nor her mother. A hush fell on the rude assemblage. The minister of the gospel departed to the Wingate encampment to learn the cause of the delay. He found Jesse Wingate irate to open wrath, the girl's mother stony calm, the girl herself white but resolute.

"She insists on seeing the marriage license, Mr. Doak," began Jesse Wingate. "As though we could have one! As though she should care more for that than her parents!"

"Quite so," rejoined the reverend man. "That is something I have taken up with the happy groom. I have with all the couples I have joined in wedlock on the trail. Of course, being a lawyer, Mr. Woodhull knows that even if they stood before the meeting and acknowledged themselves man and wife it would be a lawful marriage before God and man. Of course, also we all know that since we left the Missouri River we have been in unorganized territory, with no courts and no form of government, no society as we understand it at home. Very well. Shall loving hearts be kept asunder for those reasons? Shall the natural course of life be thwarted until we get to Oregon? Why, sir, that is absurd! We do not even know much of the government of Oregon itself, except that it is provisional."

The face of Molly Wingate appeared at the drawn curtains of her transient home. She stepped from her wagon and came forward. Beautiful, but not radiant, she was; cold and calm, but not blushing and uncertain. Her wedding gown was all in white, true enough to tradition, though but of delaine, pressed new from its packing trunk by her mother's hands. Her bodice, long and deep in front and at back, was plain entirely, save for a treasure of lace from her mother's trunk and her mother's wedding long ago. Her hands had no gloves, but white short-fingered mitts, also cherished remnants of days of schoolgirl belledom, did service. Over white stockings, below the long and full-bodied skirt, showed the crossed bands of long elastic tapes tied in an ankle bow to hold in place her little slippers of black high-finished leather. Had they seen her, all had said that Molly Wingate was the sweetest and the most richly clad bride of any on all the long, long trail across the land that had no law. And all she lacked for her wedding costume was the bride's bouquet, which her mother now held out to her, gathered with care that day of the mountain flowers—blue hare-bells, forget-me-nots of varied blue and the blossom of the gentian, bold and blue in the sunlight, though at night infolded and abashed, its petals turning in and waiting for the sun again to warm them.

Molly Wingate, stout and stern, full bosomed, wet eyed, held out her one little present to her girl, her ewe lamb, whom she was now surrendering. But no hand of the bride was extended for the bride's bouquet. The voice of the bride was not low and diffident, but high pitched, insistent.

"Provisional? Provisional? What is it you are saying, sir? Are you asking me to be married in a provisional wedding? Am I to give all I have provisionally? Is my oath provisional, or his?"

"Now, now, my dear!" began the minister.

Her father broke out into a half-stifled oath.

"What do you mean?"

Her mother's face went pale under its red bronze.

"I mean this," broke out the girl, still in the strained high tones that betokened her mental state: "I'll marry no man in any halfway fashion! Why didn't you tell me? Why didn't I think? How could I have forgotten? Law, organization, society, convention, form, custom—haven't I got even those things to back me? No? Then I've nothing! It was—it was those things—form, custom—that I was going to have to support me. I've got nothing else. Gone—they're gone, too! And you ask me to marry him—provisionally—provisionally! Oh, my God! what awful thing was this? I wasn't even to have that solid thing to rest on, back of me, after it all was over!"

They stood looking at her for a time, trying to catch and weigh her real intent, to estimate what it might mean as to her actions.

"Like images, you are!" she went on hysterically, her physical craving for one man, her physical loathing of another, driving her well-nigh mad. "You wouldn't protect your own daughter!"—to her stupefied parents. "Must I think for you at this hour of my life? How near—oh, how near! But not now—not this way! No! No!"

"What do you mean, Molly?" demanded her father sternly. "Come now, we'll have no woman tantrums at this stage! This goes on! They're waiting! He's waiting!"

"Let him wait!" cried the girl in sudden resolution.

All her soul was in the cry, all her outraged, self-punished heart. Her philosophy fell from her swiftly at the crucial moment when she was to face the kiss, the embrace of another man. The great inarticulate voice of her woman nature suddenly sounded, imperative, terrifying, in her own ears—"Oh, Will Banion, Will Banion, why did you take away my heart?" And now she had been on the point of doing this thing! An act of God had intervened.

Jesse Wingate nodded to the minister. They drew apart. The holy man nodded assent, hurried away—the girl sensed on what errand.

"No use!" she said. "I'll not!"

Stronger and stronger in her soul surged the yearning for the dominance of one man, not this man yonder—a yearning too strong now for her to resist.

"But Molly, daughter," her mother's voice said to her, "girls has—girls does. And like he said, it's the promise, it's the agreement they both make, with witnesses."

"Yes, of course," her father chimed in. "It's the consent in the contract when you stand before them all."

"I'll not stand before them. I don't consent! There is no agreement!"

Suddenly the girl reached out and caught from her mother the pitiful little bride's bouquet.

"Look!" she laughed. "Look at these!"

One by one, rapidly, she tore out and flung down the folded gentian flowers.

"Closed, closed! When the night came, they closed! They couldn't! They couldn't! I'll not—I can't!"

She had the hand's clasp of mountain blossoms stripped down to a few small flowers of varied blooms. They heard the coming of the groom, half running. A silence fell over all the great encampment. The girl's father made a half step forward, even as her mother sank down, cowering, her hands at her face.

Then, without a word, with no plan or purpose, Molly Wingate turned, sprang away from them and fled out into a night that was black indeed.

Truly she had but one thought, and that in negation only. Yonder came to claim her a man suddenly odious to her senses. It could not be. His kiss, his arms—if these were of this present time and place, then no place in all the world, even the world of savage blackness that lay about, could be so bad as this. At the test her philosophy had forsaken her, reason now almost as well, and sheer terrified flight remained her one reaction.

She was gone, a white ghost in her wedding gown, her little slippers stumbling over the stones, her breath coming sobbingly as she ran. They followed her. Back of them, at the great fire whose illumination deepened the shadows here, rose a murmur, a rising of curious people, a pressing forward to the Wingate station. But of these none knew the truth, and it was curiosity that now sought answer for the delay in the anticipated divertisement.

Molly Wingate ran for some moments, to some distance— she knew of neither. Then suddenly all her ghastly nightmare of terror found climax in a world of demons. Voices of the damned rose around her. There came a sudden shock, a blow. Before she could understand, before she could determine the shadowy form that rose before her in the dark, she fell forward like the stricken creature.

Chapter XXX

THE DANCE IN THE DESERT

There was no wedding that night at the Independence Rock. The Arapahoes saw to that. But there were burials the day following, six of them—two women, a child, three men. The night attack had caught the company wholly off guard, and the bright fire gave good illumination for shaft and ball.

"Put out the fires! Corral! Corral!"

Voices of command arose. The wedding guests rushed for the shelter of their own wagons. Men caught up their weapons and a steady fire at the unseen foe held the latter at bay after the first attack.

Indeed, a sort of panic seized the savages. A warrior ran back exclaiming that he had seen a spirit, all in white, not running away from the attack, but toward them as they lay in cover. He had shot an arrow at the spirit, which then had vanished. It would be better to fall back and take no more like chances.

For this reason the family of Molly Wingate, pursuing her closely as they could, found her at last, lying face down in

the grass, her arms outspread, her white wedding gown red
with blood. An arrow, its shaft cracked by her fall, was
imbedded in her shoulder, driven deep by the savage bowman who had fired in fear at an object he did not recognize.
So they found her, still alive, still unmutilated, still no prisoner. They carried the girl back to her mother, who reached
out her arms and laid her child down behind the barricaded
wagon wheels.

"Bring me a candle, you!" she called to the nearest man.
It chanced to be Sam Woodhull.

Soon a woman came with a light.

"Go away now!" the mother commanded the disappointed
man.

He passed into the dark. The old woman opened the bodice over the girl's heart, stripped away the stained lace that
had served in three weddings on two sides of the Appalachians, and so got to the wound.

"It's in to the bone," she said. "It won't come out. Get
me my scissors out of my bag. It's hanging right 'side the
seat, our wagon.

"Ain't there no doctor?" she demanded, her own heart
weakening now. But none could tell. A few women grouped
around her.

"It won't come out of that little hole it went in," said
stout Molly Wingate, not quite sobbing. "I got to cut it
wider."

Silence held them as she finished the shreds of the ashen
shaft and pressed to one side the stub of it. So with what
tools she knew best she cut into the fabric of her own weaving, out of her own blood and bone; cut mayhap in steady
snippings at her own heart, pulling and wrenching until the
flesh, now growing purple, was raised above the girl's white
breast. Both arms, in their white sleeves, lay on the trodden
grass motionless, and had not shock and strain left the victim
unconscious the pain must now have done so.

The sinew wrappings held the strap-iron head, wetted as
they now were with blood. The sighing surgeon caught the
base of the arrowhead in thumb and finger. There was no
stanching of the blood. She wrenched it free at last, and the

blood gushed from a jagged hole which would have meant death in any other air or in any patient but the vital young.

Now they disrobed the bride that was no bride, even as the rifle fire died away in the darkness. Women brought frontier drafts of herbs held sovereign, and laid her upon the couch that was not to have been hers alone.

She opened her eyes, moaning, held out her arms to her mother, not to any husband; and her mother, bloody, unnerved, weeping, caught her to her bosom.

"My lamb! My little lamb! Oh, dear me! Oh, dear me!"

The wailing of others for their dead arose. The camp dogs kept up a continual barking, but there was no other sound. The guards now lay out in the dark. A figure came creeping toward the bridal tent.

"Is she alive? May I come in? Speak to me, Molly!"

"Go on away, Sam!" answered the voice of the older woman. "You can't come in."

"But is she alive? Tell me !" His voice was at the door which he could not pass.

"Yes, more's the pity!" he heard the same voice say.

But from the girl who should then have been his, to have and to hold, he heard no sound at all, nor could he know her frightened gaze into her mother's face, her tight clutch on her mother's hand.

This was no place for delay. They made graves for the dead, pallets for the wounded. At sunrise the train moved on, grim, grave, dignified and silent in its very suffering. There was no time for reprisal or revenge. The one idea as to safety was to move forward in hope of shaking off pursuit.

But all that morning and all that day the mounted Arapahoes harassed them. At many bends of the Sweetwater they paused and made sorties; but the savages fell back, later to close in, sometimes under cover so near that their tauntings could be heard.

Wingate, Woodhull, Price, Hall, Kelsey stationed themselves along the line of flankers, and as the country became flatter and more open they had better control of the pursuers, so that by nightfall the latter began to fall back.

The end of the second day of forced marching found them at the Three Crossings of the Sweetwater, deep in a cheerless alkaline desert, and on one of the most depressing reaches of the entire journey. That night such gloom fell on their council as had not yet been known.

"The Watkins boy died today," said Hall, joining his colleagues at the guarded fire. "His leg was black where it was broke. They're going to bury him just ahead, in the trail. It's not best to leave headboards here."

Wingate had fallen into a sort of apathy. For a time Woodhull did not speak to him after he also came in.

"How is she, Mr. Wingate?" he asked at last. "She'll live?"

"I don't know," replied the other. "Fever. No one can tell. We found a doctor in one of the Iowa wagons. He don't know."

Woodhull sat silent for a time, exclaimed at last, "But she will—she must! This shames me! We'll be married yet."

"Better wait to see if she lives or dies," said Jesse Wingate succinctly.

"I know what I wish," said Caleb Price at last as he stared moodily at the coals, "and I know it mighty well—I wish the other wagons were up. Yes, and—"

He did not finish. A nod or so was all the answer he got. A general apprehension held them all.

"If Bridger hadn't gone on ahead, damn him!" exclaimed Kelsey at last.

"Or if Carson hadn't refused to come along, instead of going on east," assented Hall. "What made him so keen?"

Kelsey spoke morosely.

"Said he had papers to get through. Maybe Kit Carson'll sometime carry news of our being wiped out somewhere."

"Or if we had Bill Jackson to trail for us," ventured the first speaker again. "If we could send back word—"

"We can't, so what's the use?" interrupted Price. "We were all together, and had our chance—once."

But buried as they were in their gloomy doubts, regrets, fears, they got through that night and the next in safety. They dared not hunt, though the buffalo and antelope were in swarms, and though they knew they now were near the western limit of the buffalo range. They urged on, mile after mile. The sick and the wounded must endure as they might.

Finally they topped the gentle incline which marked the heights of land between the Sweetwater and the tributaries of the Green, and knew they had reached the South Pass, called halfway to Oregon. There was no timber here. The pass itself was no winding cañon, but only a flat, broad valley. Bolder views they had seen, but none of greater interest.

Now they would set foot on Oregon, passing from one great series of waterways to another and even vaster, leading down to the western sea—the unknown South Sea marked as the limits of their possessions by the gallants of King Charles when, generations earlier, and careless of all these intervening generations of toil and danger, they had paused at the summit of Rockfish Gap in the Appalachians and waved a gay hand each toward the unknown continent that lay they knew not how far to the westward.

But these, now arrived halfway of half that continent, made no merriment in their turn. Their wounded and their sick were with them. The blazing sun tried them sore. Before them also lay they knew not what.

And now, coming in from the northeast in a vast braided tracing of travois poles and trampling hoofs, lay a trail which fear told them was that of yet another war party waiting for the white-topped wagons. It led on across the Pass. It could not be more than two days old.

"It's the Crows!" exclaimed Sam Woodhull, studying the broad trail. "They've got their women and children with them."

"We have ours with us," said Caleb Price simply.

Every man who heard him looked back at the lines of gaunt cattle, at the dust-stained canvas coverings that housed their families. They were far afield from home or safety.

"Call Wingate. Let's decide what to do," exclaimed Price again. "We'll have to vote."

They voted to go on, fault of any better plan. Some said Bridger's post was not far ahead. A general impatience, fretful, querulous, manifested itself. Ignorant, many of these wanted to hurry on to Oregon, which for most meant the Williamette Valley, in touch with the sea, marked as the usual end of the great trek. Few knew that they now stood on the soil of the Oregon country. The maps and journals of Molly Wingate were no more forthcoming, for Molly Wingate no more taught the evening school, but lay delirious under the hothouse canvas cover that intensified the rays of the blazing sun. It was life or death, but by now life-and-death issue had become no unusual experience.

It was August, midsummer, and only half the journey done. The heat was blinding, blistering. For days now, in the dry sage country, from the ford of the North Fork of the Platte, along the Sweetwater and down the Sandy, the white alkali dust had sifted in and over everything. Lips cracked open, hands and arms either were raw or black with tan. The wagons were ready to drop apart. A dull silence had fallen on the people; but fatuously following the great Indian trail they made camp at last at the ford of the Green River, the third day's march down the Pacific Slope. No three days of all the slow trail had been harder to endure than these.

"Play for them, Jed," counseled Caleb Price, when that hardy youth, leaving his shrunken herd, came in for his lunch that day at the ford.

"Yes, but keep that fiddle in the shade, Jed, or the sun certainly will pop it open."

Jed's mother, her apron full of broken bits of sagebrush, turned to see that her admonishment was heeded before she began her midday coffee fire. As for Jed himself, with a wide grin he crouched down at the side of the wagon and leaned against a wheel as he struck up a lively air, roaring joyously to his accompaniment:

> Git out o' the way, old Dan Tucker,
> You're too late to git yore supper!

Unmindful of the sullen apathy of men and women, the wailing of children stifling under the wagon tops, the moans of the sick and wounded in their ghastly discomfort, Jed sang with his cracked lips as he swung from one jig to the next, the voice of the violin reaching all the wagons of the shortened train.

"Choose yore pardners!" rang his voice in the joyous jesting of youth. And—marvel and miracle—then and there, those lean brown folk did take up the jest, and laughingly gathered on the sun-seared sands. They formed sets and danced—danced a dance of the indomitable, at high noon, the heat blinding, the sand hot under feet not all of which were shod. Molly Wingate, herself fifty and full-bodied, cast down her firewood, caught up her skirt with either hand and made good an old-time jig to the tune of the violin and the roaring accompaniment of many voices and of patted hands. She paused at length, dropping her calico from between her fingers, and hastened to a certain wagon side as she wiped her face with her apron.

"Didn't you hear it, Molly?" she demanded, parting the curtain and looking in.

"Yes, I did. I wanted—I almost wanted to join. Mother, I almost wanted to hope again. Am I to live? Where are we now?"

"By a right pretty river, child, and eena'most to Oregon. Come, kiss your mother, Molly. Let's try."

Whereupon, having issued her orders and set everyone to work at something after her practical fashion, the first lady of the train went frizzling her shaved buffalo meat with milk in the frying pan; grumbling that milk now was almost at the vanishing point, and that now they wouldn't see another buffalo; but always getting forward with her meal. This she at last amiably announced.

"Well, come an' git it, people, or I'll throw it to the dogs."

Flat on the sand, on blankets or odds and ends of hide, the emigrants sat and ate, with the thermometer—had they had one—perhaps a hundred and ten in the sun. The men were silent for the most part, with now and then a word about the ford, which they thought it would be wise to make at once, before the river perchance might rise, and while it still would not swim the cattle.

"We can't wait for anyone, not even the Crows," said

Wingate, rising and ending the mealtime talk. "Let's get across."

Methodically they began the blocking up of the wagon bodies to the measurement established by a wet pole.

"Thank the Lord," said Wingate, "they'll just clear now if the bottom is hard all the way."

One by one the teams were urged into the ticklish crossing. The line of wagons was almost all at the farther side when all at once the rear guard came back, spurring.

"Corral! Corral!" he called.

He plunged into the stream as the last driver urged his wagon up the bank. A rapid dust cloud was approaching down the valley.

"Indians!" called out a dozen voices. "Corral, men! For God's sake, quick—corral!"

They had not much time or means to make defense, but with training now become second nature they circled and threw the dusty caravan into the wonted barricade, tongue to tail gate. The oxen could not all be driven within, the loose stock was scattered, the horses were not on picket lines at that time of day; but driving what stock they could, the boy herders came in at a run when they saw the wagons parking.

There was no time to spare. The dust cloud swept on rapidly. It could not spell peace, for no men would urge their horses at such pace under such a sun save for one purpose—to overtake this party at the ford.

"It's Bill Jackson!" exclaimed Caleb Price, rifle in hand, at the river's edge. "Look out, men! Don't shoot! Wait! There's fifty Indians back of him, but that's Jackson ahead. Now what's wrong?"

The riddle was not solved even when the scout of the Missouri train, crowded ahead by the steady rush of the shouting and laughing savages, raised his voice as though in warning and shouted some word, unintelligible, which made them hold their fire.

The wild cavalcade dashed into the stream, crowding their prisoner—he was no less—before them, bent bows back of him, guns ready.

They were stalwart, naked men, wide of jaw, great of chest, not a woman or child among them, all painted and full armed.

"My God, men!" called Wingate, hastening under cover. "Don't let them in! Don't let them in! It's the Crows!"

Chapter XXXI

HOW, COLA!

How, cola!" exclaimed the leader of the band of Indians, crowding up to the gap in the corral where a part of the stock had just been driven in. He grinned maliciously and made the sign for "Sioux"—the edge of the hand across the throat.

But men, rifles crosswise, barred him back, while others were hurrying, strengthening the barricade. A half dozen rifles, thrust out through wheels or leveled across wagon togues, now covered the front rank of the Crows; but the savages, some forty or fifty in number, only sat their horses laughing. This was sport to them. They had no doubt at all that they would have their will of this party of the whites as soon as they got ready, and they planned further strategy. To drive a prisoner into camp before killing him was humorous from their point of view, and practical withal, like driving a buffalo close to the village before shooting it.

But the white men were not deceived by the trading-post salutation.

"He's a liar!" called out the voice of Jackson. "They're

not Sioux—they're Crows, an' out for war! Don't let 'em in, boys! For God's sake, keep 'em out!"

It was a brave man's deed. The wonder was his words were not his last, for though the Crows did not understand all his speech, they knew well enough what he meant. One brave near him struck him across the mouth with the heavy wooden stock of his Indian whip, so that his lips gushed blood. A half dozen arrows turned toward him, trembling on the strings. But the voice of their partisan rose in command. He preferred a parley, hoping a chance might offer to get inside the wagon ring. The loose stock he counted safe booty any time they liked. He did not relish the look of the rifle muzzles at a range of twenty feet. The riders were now piled in almost against the wheels.

"Swap!" exclaimed the Crow leader ingratiatingly, and held out his hand. "How, cola!"

"Don't believe him! Don't trust him, men!"

Again Jackson's voice rose. As the savages drew apart from him, to hold him in even better bow range, one young brave, hideously barred in vermilion and yellow, all the time with an arrow at the prisoner's back, the men in the wagon corral now saw that Jackson's hands were tied behind his back, so that he was helpless. But still he sat his own horse, and still he had a chance left to take.

"Look out!" he called high and clear. "Get away from the hole! I'm comin' in!"

Before anyone fully caught his meaning he swung his horse with his legs, lifted him with his heels and made one straight, desperate plunge for the gap, jostling aside the nearest two or three of his oppressors.

It was a desperate man's one hope—no hope at all, indeed, for the odds were fifty to one against him. Swift as was his movement, and unprepared as his tormentors were for it, just as the horse rose to his leap over the wagon tongue, and as the rider flung himself low on his neck to escape what he knew would come, a bow twanged back of him. They all heard the zhut! of the arrow as it struck. Then, in a stumbling heap, horse and rider fell, rolled over, as a sleet of arrows followed through.

Jackson rolled to one side, rose to his knees. Molly Wingate chanced to be near. Her scissors, carefully guarded always, because priceless, hung at her neck. Swiftly she began to saw at the thong which held Jackson's wrists, bedded almost to the bone and twisted with a stick. She severed the cord somehow and the man staggered up. Then they saw the arrow standing out at both sides of his shoulder, driven through the muscles with the hasty snap of the painted bowman's shot.

"Cut it—break it!" he demanded of her; for all the men now were at the edge, and there was no one else to aid. And staunch Molly Wingate, her eyes staring again in horror, took the bloody stem and tried to break it off, in her second case of like surgery that week. But the shaft was flexible, tough and would not break.

"A knife—quick! Cut it off above the feather!"

He himself caught the front of the shaft and pushed it back, close to the head. By chance she saw Jed's knife at his belt as he kneeled, and drew it. Clumsily but steadily she slashed into the shaft, weakened it, broke it, pushed the point forward. Jackson himself unhesitatingly pulled it through, a gush of blood following on either side the shoulder. There was no time to notice that. Crippled as he was, the man only looked for weapons. A pistol lay on the ground and he caught it up.

But for the packs and bales that had been thrown against the wheels, the inmates of the corral would all have fallen under the rain of arrows that now slatted and thudded in. But they kept low, and the Indians were so close against the wagons that they could not see under the bodies or through the wheels. The chocks had not yet been taken out from under the boxes, so that they stood high. Against such a barricade cavalry was helpless. There was no warrior who wanted to follow Jackson's example of getting inside.

For an instant there came no order to fire. The men were reaching into the wagons to unsling their rifles from the riding loops fastened to the bows. It all was a trample and a tumult and a whirl of dust under thudding hoofs outside and in, a phase which could last no more than an instant.

Came the thin crack of a squirrel rifle from the far corner of the wagon park. The Crow partisan sat his horse just a moment, the expression on his face frozen there, his mouth slowly closing. Then he slid off his horse close to the gap, now piled high with goods and gear.

A boy's high quaver rose.

"You can't say nothing this time! You didn't shoot at all now!"

An emigrant boy was jeering at his father.

But by that time no one knew or cared who shot. The fight was on. Every rifle was emptied in the next instant, and at that range almost every shot was fatal or disabling. In sudden panic at the powder flare in their faces, the Crows broke and scattered, with no time to drag away their wounded.

The fight, or this phase of it, was over almost before it was begun. It all was one more repetition of border history. Almost never did the Indians make a successful attack on a trading post, rarely on an emigrant train in full corral. The cunning of the Crow partisan in driving in a prisoner as a fence had brought him close, yes—too close. But the line was not yet broken.

Firing with a steady aim, the emigrants added to the toll they took. The Crows bent low and flogged their horses. Only in the distant willow thickets did they pause. They even left their dead.

There were no wounded, or not for long. Jackson, the pistol in his hand, his face gray with rage and pain, stepped outside the corral. The Crow chief, shot through the chest, turned over, looked up dully.

"How, cola!" said his late prisoner, baring his teeth.

And what he did with this brave he did with all the others of the wounded able to move a hand. The debt to savage treachery was paid, savagely enough, when he turned back to the wagons, and such was the rage of all at this last assault that no voice was raised to stay his hand.

"There's nothing like tobacker," asserted Jackson coolly when he had reentered the corral and it came to the question of caring for his arrow wound. "Jest tie on a good chaw o' tobacker on each side o' that hole an' 'twont't be long afore she's all right. I'm glad it went plumb through. I've knowed a arrerhead to pull off an' stay in when the sinew wroppin's got loose from soakin'.

"Look at them wrists," he added, holding up his hands. "They twisted that rawhide clean to the bone, damn their skins! Pertendin' to be friends! They put me in front sos't you'd let 'em ride up clost—that's the Crow way, to come right inter camp if they can, git in close an' play friends. But, believe me, this ain't but the beginnin'. They'll be back, an' plenty with 'em. Them Crows ain't west of the Pass fer only one thing, an' that's this wagon train."

They gathered around him now, plying him with questions. Sam Woodhull was among those who came, and him Jackson watched narrowly every moment, his own weapon handy, as he now described the events that had brought him hither.

"Our train come inter the Sweetwater two days back o' you all," he said. "We seed you'd had a fight but had went on. We knowed some was hurt, fer we picked up some womern fixin's—tattin', hit were—with blood on hit. And we found buryin's, the dirt different color."

They told him now of the first fight, of their losses, of the wounded; told him of the near escape of Molly Wingate, though out of courtesy to Woodhull, who stood near, they said nothing of the interrupted wedding. The old mountain man's face grew yet more stern.

"That gal!" he said. "Her shot by a sneakin' 'Rapahoe? Ain't that a shame! But she's not bad—she's comin' through?"

Molly Wingate, who stood ready now with bandages, told him how alike the two arrow wounds had been.

"Take an' chaw tobacker, ma'am," said he. "Put a hunk on each side, do-ee mind, an' she'll be well."

"Go on and tell us the rest," someone demanded.

"Not much to tell that ye couldn't of knew, gentlemen," resumed the scout. "Ef ye'd sont back fer us we'd of jined ye, shore, but ye didn't send."

"How could we send, man?" demanded Woodhull savagely. "How could we know where you were, or whether you'd come—or whether you'd have been of any use if you had?"

"Well, we knew whar you-all was, 't any rate," rejoined Jackson. "We was two days back o' ye, then one day. Our captain wouldn't let us crowd in, fer he said we wasn't welcome an' we wasn't needed.

"That was ontel we struck the big Crow trail, with you all a follerin' o' hit blind, a-chasin' trouble as hard as ye could. Then he sont me on ahead to warn ye an' to ask ef we should jine on. We knowed the Crows was down atter the train.

"I laid down to sleep, I did, under a sagebrush, in the sun, like a fool. I was beat out an' needed sleep, an' I thought I was safe fer a leetle while. When I woke up it was a whoop that done hit. They was around me, laughin', twenty arrers p'inted, an' some shot inter the ground by my face. I taken my chance, an' shook hands. They grabbed me an' tied me. Then they made me guide them in, like ye seen. They maybe didn't know I come from the east an' not from the west.

"Their village is on some creek above here. I think they're on a visit to the Shoshones. Eight hundred men they are, or more. Hit's more'n what it was with the Sioux on the Platte, fer ye're not so many now. An' any time now the main band may come. Git ready, men. Fer me, I must git back to my own train. They may be back twenty mile, or thirty. Would ary man want to ride with me? Would ye, Sam Woodhull?"

The eyes of his associates rested on Woodhull.

"I think one man would be safer than two," said he. "My own place is here if there's sure to be a fight."

"Mebbe so," assented Jackson. "In fack, I don't know as more'n one'd git through if you an' me both started." His cold gray eye was fixed on Woodhull carelessly. "An' ef hit was the wrong man got through he'd never lead them Missouri men for'rerd to where this fight'll be.

"An' hit'll be right here. Look yan!" he added.

He nodded to the westward, where a great dust cloud arose.

"More is comin'," said he. "Yan's Bannack's like as not,

er even the Shoshones, all I know, though they're usual quiet. The runners is out atween all the tribes. I must be on my way."

He hurried to find his own horse, looked to its welfare, for it, too, had an arrow wound. As he passed a certain wagon he heard a voice call to him, saw a hand at the curtained front.

"Miss Molly! Hit's you! Ye're not dead no ways, then?"

"Come," said the girl.

He drew near, fell back at sight of her thin face, her pallor; but again she commanded him.

"I know," said she. "He's—he's safe?"

"Yes, Miss Molly, a lot safer'n any of us here."

"You're going back to him?"

"Yes. When he knows ye're hurt he'll come. Nothin'll stop him, oncet I tell him."

"Wait!" she whispered. "I heard you talk. Take him this." She pushed into his hand a folded paper, unsealed, without address. "To him!" she said, and fell back on the blankets of her rude pallet.

At that moment her mother was approaching, and at her side walked Woodhull, actuated by his own suspicions about Jackson. He saw the transaction of the passed note and guessed what he could not know. He tapped Jackson on the shoulder, drew him aside, his own face pale with anger.

"I'm one of the officers of this train," said he. "I want to know what's in that note. We have no truck with Banion, and you know that. Give it to me."

Jackson calmly tucked the paper into the fire bag that hung at his belt.

"Come an' take it, Sam, damn ye!" said he. "I don't know what's in hit, an' won't know. Who it's to ain't none o' yore damn business!"

"You're a cursed meddler!" broke out Woodhull. "You're a spy in our camp, that's all you are!"

"So! Well, cussed meddler er not, I'm a cussed shore shot. An' I advise ye to give over on all this an' mind yore business. Ye'll have plenty to do by midnight, an' by that time all yore womern an' children, all yore old men an' all yore cowards'll be prayin' fer Banion an' his men to come. That there includes you somewhere's, Sam. Don't temp' me too much ner too long. I'll kill ye yit ef ye do! Git on away!"

They parted, each with eye over shoulder. Their talk had been aside and none had heard it in full. But when Woodhull again joined Mrs. Wingate that lady conveyed to him Molly's refusal to see him or to set a time for seeing him. Bitterly angered, humiliated to the core, he turned back to the men who were completing the defenses of the wagon park.

"I kain't start now afore dark," said Jackson to the train command. "They're a-goin' to jump the train. When they do come they'll surround ye an' try to keep ye back from the water till the stock goes crazy. Lay low an' don't let a Injun inside. Hit may be a hull day, er more, but when Banion's men come they'll come a-runnin'—allowin' I git through to tell 'em.

"Dig in a trench all the way aroun'," he added finally. "Put the womern an' children in hit an' pile up an' pile up all yer flour on top. Don't waste no powder—let 'em come up clost as they will. Hold on ontel we come."

At dusk he slipped away, the splash of his horse's feet in the ford coming fainter and fainter, even as the hearts of some felt fainter as his wise and sturdy counsel left them. Naught to do now but to wait.

They did wait—the women and children, the old, the ill and the wounded huddled shivering and crying in the scooped-out sand, hardest and coldest of beds; the men in line against the barricade, a circle of guards outside the wagon park. But midnight passed, and the cold hours of dawn, and still no sign came of an attack. Men began to believe the dust cloud of yesterday no more than a false alarm, and the leaders were of two minds, whether to take Jackson's counsel and wait for the Missourians, or to hook up and push on as fast as possible to Bridger's fort, scarce more than two hard days' journey on ahead. But before this breakfast hour discussion had gone far events took the decision out of their hands.

"Look!" cried a voice. "Open the gate!"

The cattle guards and outposts who had just driven the
herd to water were now spurring for shelter and hurrying on
the loose stock ahead of them. And now, from the willow
growth above them, from the trail that led to the ford and
from the more open country to the westward there came, in
three great detachments, not a band or a body, but an army
of the savage tribesmen, converging steadily upon the
wagon train.

They came slowly, not in a wild charge, not yelling, but
chanting. The upper and right-hand bodies were Crows.
Their faces were painted black, for war and for revenge. The
band on the left were wild men, on active half-broke horses,
their weapons for the most part bows and arrows. They later
found these to be Bannacks, belonging anywhere but here,
and in any alliance rather than with the Crows from east of
the Pass.

Nor did the latter belong here to the south and west, far
off their own great hunting range. Obviously what Carson,
Bridger, Jackson had said was true. All the tribes were in
league to stop the great invasion of the white nation, who
now were bringing their women and children and this thing
with which they buried the buffalo. They meant extermi-
nation now. They were taking their time and would take
their revenge for the dead who lay piled before the white
man's barricade.

The emigrants rolled back a pair of wagons, and the cattle
were crowded through, almost over the human occupants of
the oblong. The gap was closed. All the remaining cargo
packages were piled against the wheels, and the noncom-
batants sheltered in that way. Shovels deepened the trench
here or there as men sought better to protect their families.

And now in a sudden *melée* of shouts and yells, of trampling hoofs and whirling colors, the first bands of the Crows
came charging up in the attempt to carry away their dead of
yesterday. Men stooped to grasp a stiffened wrist, a leg, a
belt; the ponies squatted under ghastly dragging burdens.

But this brought them within pistol range. The reports of
the white men's weapons began, carefully, methodically,
with deadly accuracy. There was no panic. The motionless

or the struggling blotches ahead of the wagon park grew and grew. Only a few of the Crows got off with bodies of their friends or relatives. One warrior after another dropped. They were used to killing buffalo at ten yards. The white rifles killed their men now regularly at a hundred. They drew off, out of range.

Meantime the band from the westward was rounding up and driving off every animal that had not been corralled. The emigrants saw themselves in fair way to be set on foot.

Now the savage strategy became plain. The fight was to be a siege.

"Look!" Again a leader pointed.

Crouched now, advancing under cover of the shallow cut-bank, the headdresses of a score of the Western tribesmen could be seen. They sank down. The ford was held, the water was cut off! The last covering fringe of willows also was held. On every side the black-painted savages sat their ponies, out of range. There could be no more water or grass for the horses and cattle, no wood for the camp.

There was no other concerted charge for a long time. Now and then some painted brave, chanting a death song, would ride slowly toward the wagon park, some dervish vow actuating him or some bravado impelling him. But usually he fell.

It all became a quiet, steady, matter-of-fact performance on both sides. This very freedom from action and excitement, so different from the gallant riding of the Sioux, was more terrifying than direct attack *en masse*, so that when it came to a matter of shaken morale the whites were in as bad case as their foes, although thus far they had had no casualty at all.

There lacked the one leader, cool, calm, skilled, experienced, although courage did not lack. Yet even the best courage suffers when a man hears the wailing of his children back of him, the groans of his wife. As the hours passed, with no more than an occasional rifle shot or the zhut! of an arrow ending its high arc, the tension on the nerves of the beleaguered began to manifest itself.

At midday the children began to cry for water. They were

appeased with milk from the few cows offering milk; but how long might that last, with the cattle themselves beginning to moan and low?

"How far are they back?"

It was Hall, leader of the Ohio wagons. But none could tell him where the Missouri train had paused. Wingate alone knew why Banion had not advanced. He doubted if he would come now.

"And this all was over the quarrel between two men," said Caleb Price to his friend Wingate.

"The other man is a thief, Cale," reiterated Wingate. "He was court-martialed and broke, dishonorably discharged from the Army. He was under Colonel Doniphan, and had control of subsistence in upper Mexico for some time. He had the regimental funds. Doniphan was irregular. He ran his regiment like a mess, and might order first this officer, then that, of the line or staff, to take on his free-for-all quartermaster trains. But he was honest. Banion was not. He had him broke. The charges were filed by Captain Woodhull. Well, is it any wonder there is no love lost? And is it any wonder I wouldn't train up with a thief, or allow him to visit in my family? By God! right now I wouldn't; and I didn't send for him to help us!"

"So!" said Caleb Price. "So! And that was why the wedding—"

"Yes! A foolish fancy of a girl. I don't know what passed between her and Banion. I felt it safer for my daughter to be married, as soon as could be, to another man, an honest man. You know how that came out. And now, when she's as apt to die as live, and we're all as apt to, you others send for that renegade to save us! I have no confidence that he will come. I hope he will not. I'd like his rifles, but I don't want him."

"Well," said Caleb Price, "it is odd how his rifles depend on him and not on the other man. Yet they both lived in the same town."

"Yes, one man may be more plausible than another."

"Yes? I don't know that I ever saw a man more plausible with his fists than Major Banion was. Yes, I'll call him plausible. I wish some of us—say, Sam Woodhull, now—could be half as plausible with these Crows. Difference in men, Jess!" he concluded. "Woodhull was there—and now he's here. He's here—and now we're sending there for the other man."

"You want that other man, thief and dishonest as he is?"

"By God! yes! I want his rifles and him too. Women, children and all, the whole of us, will die if that thief doesn't come inside of another twenty-four hours."

Wingate flung out his arms, walked away, hands clasped behind his back. He met Woodhull.

"Sam, what shall we do?" he demanded. "You're sort of in charge now. You've been a soldier, and we haven't had much of that."

"There are fifteen hundred or two thousand of them," said Woodhull slowly—"a hundred and fifty of us that can fight. Ten to one, and they mean no quarter."

"But what shall we do?"

"What can we but lie close and hold the wagons?"

"And wait?"

"Yes."

"Which means only the Missouri men!"

"There's no one else. We don't know that they're alive. We don't know that they will come."

"But one thing I do know"—his dark face gathered in a scowl—"if he doesn't come it will not be because he was not asked! That fellow carried a letter from Molly to him. I know that. Well, what do you-all think of me? What's my standing in all this? If I've not been shamed and humiliated, how can a man be? And what am I to expect?"

"If we get through, if Molly lives, you mean?"

"Yes. I don't quit what I want. I'll never give her up. You give me leave to try again? Things may change. She may consider the wrong she's done me, an honest man. It's his hanging around all the time, keeping in her mind. And now we've sent for him—and so has she!"

They walked apart, Wingate to his wagon.

"How is she?" he asked of his wife, nodding to Molly's wagon.

"Better some ways, but low," replied his stout helpmate, herself haggard, dark circles of fatigue about her eyes. "She won't eat, even with the fever down. If we was back home where we could get things! Jess, what made us start for Oregon?"

"What made us leave Kentucky for Indiana, and Indiana for Illinois? I don't know. God help us now!"

"It's bad, Jesse."

"Yes, it's bad." Suddenly he took his wife's face in his hands and kissed her quietly. "Kiss Little Molly for me," he said. "I wish—I wish—"

"I wish them other wagons'd come," said Molly Wingate. "Then we'd see!"

Chapter XXXII

THE FIGHT AT THE FORD

Jackson, wounded and weary as he was, drove his crippled horse so hard all the night through that by dawn he had covered almost fifty miles, and was in sight of the long line of wagons, crawling like a serpent down the slopes west of the South Pass, a cloud of bitter alkali dust hanging like a blanket over them. No part of the way had been more cheerless than this gray, bare expanse of more than a hundred miles, and none offered less invitation for a bivouac. But now both man and horse were well-nigh spent.

Knowing that he would be reached within an hour or so at best, Jackson used the last energies of his horse in riding back and forth at right angles across the trail, the Plains sign of "Come to me!" He hoped it would be seen. He flung himself down across the road, in the dust, his bridle tied to his wrist. His horse, now nearly gone, lay down beside him, nor ever rose again. And here, in the time a gallop could bring them up, Banion and three of his men found them, one dead, the other little better.

"Bill! Bill!"

The voice of Banion was anxious as he lightly shook the shoulder of the prone man, half afraid that he, too, had died. Stupid in sleep, the scout sprang up, rifle in hand.

"Who's thar?"

"Hold, Bill! Friends! Easy now!"

The old man pulled together, rubbed his eyes.

"I must of went to sleep again," said he. "My horse—pshaw now, pore critter, do-ee look now!"

In rapid words he now told his errand. They could see the train accelerating its speed. Jackson felt in the bag at his belt and handed Banion the folded paper. He opened the folds steadily, read the words again and again.

" 'Come to us,' " is what it says. He spoke to Jackson.

"Ye're a damned liar, Will," remarked Jackson.

"I'll read it all!" said Banion suddenly.

" 'Will Banion, come to me, or it may be too late. There never was any wedding. I am the most wicked and most unhappy woman in the world. You owe me nothing! But come! M. W.'

"That's what it says. Now you know. Tell me—you heard of no wedding back at Independence Rock? They said nothing? He and she—"

"Ef they was ever any weddin' hit was a damned pore sort, an' she says thar wasn't none. She'd orto know."

"Can you ride, Jackson?"

"Span in six fast mules for a supply wagon, such as kin gallop. I'll sleep in that a hour or so. Git yore men started, Will. We may be too late. It's nigh fifty mile to the ford o' the Green."

It came near to mutiny when Banion ordered a third of his men to stay back with the ox teams and the families. Fifty were mounted and ready in five minutes. They were followed by two fast wagons. In one of these rolled Bill Jackson, unconscious of the roughness of the way.

On the Sandy, twenty miles from the ford, they wakened him.

"Now tell me how it lies," said Banion. "How's the country?"

Jackson drew a sketch on the sand.

"They'll surround, an' they'll cut off the water."

"Can we ford above and come in behind them?"

"We mout. Send half straight to the ford an' half come in behind, through the willers, huh? That'd put 'em atween three fires. Ef we driv' 'em on the wagons they'd get hell thar, an' ef they broke, the wagons could chase 'em inter us again. I allow we'd give 'em hell. Hit's the Crows I'm most a-skeered of. The Bannacks—ef that's who they was—'ll run easy."

At sunset of that day the emigrants, now half mad of thirst, and half ready to despair of succor or success, heard the Indian drums sound and the shrilling of the eagle-bone whistles. The Crows were chanting again. Whoops arose along the river bank.

"My God! they're coming!" called out a voice.

There was a stir of uneasiness along the line, an ominous thing. And then the savage hosts broke from their cover, more than a thousand men, ready to take some loss in their hope that the whites were now more helpless. In other circumstances it must have been a stirring spectacle for any who had seen it. To these, cowering in the sand, it brought terror.

But before the three ranks of the Crows had cleared the cover the last line began to yell, to whip, to break away. Scattering but continuous rifle fire followed them, war cries arose, not from savages, but white men. A line of riders emerged, coming straight through to the second rank of the Crow advance. Then the beleaguered knew that the Missourians were up.

"Banion, by God!" said a voice which few stopped to recognize as Woodhull's.

He held his fire, his rifle resting so long through the wagon wheel that Caleb Price in one swift motion caught it away from him.

"No harm, friend," said he, "but you'll not need this just now!"

His cold eye looked straight into that of the intending murderer.

The men in the wagon park rose to their work again. The

hidden Bannacks began to break away from their lodgment under the river bank. The sound of hoofs and of shouts came down the trail. The other wing of the Missourians flung off and cleared the ford before they undertook to cross, their slow, irregular, deadly rifle fire doing its work among the hidden Bannacks until they broke and ran for their horses in the cottonwoods below. This brought them partly into view, and the rifles of the emigrants on that side bore on them till they broke in sheer terror and fled in a scattered *sauve qui peut*.

The Crows swerved under the enfilading fire of the men who now crossed the ford. Caught between three fires, and meeting for their first time the use of the revolver, then new to them, they lost heart and once more left their dead, breaking away into a mad flight west and north which did not end till they had forded the upper tributaries of the Green and Snake, and found their way back west of the Tetons to their own country far east and north of the two-go-tee crossing of the Wind River Mountains; whence for many a year they did not emerge again to battle with the white nation on the Medicine Road. At one time there were forty Crow squaws, young and old, with gashed breasts and self-amputated fingers, given in mourning over the unreturning brave.

What many men had not been able to do of their own resources, less than a fourth their number now had done. Side by side Banion, Jackson, a half dozen others, rode up to the wagon gap, now opened. They were met by a surge of the rescued. Women, girls threw themselves upon them, kissing them, embracing them hysterically. Where had been gloom, now was rejoicing, laughter, tears.

The leaders of the emigrants came up to Banion and his men, Wingate in advance. Banion still sat his great black horse, coldly regarding them.

"I have kept my promise, Captain Wingate," said he. "I have not come until you sent for me. Let me ask once more, do I owe you anything now?"

"No, sir, you do not," replied the older man.

"And do you owe me anything?"

Wingate did not answer.

"Name what you like, Major Banion," said a voice at his shoulder—Caleb Price.

Banion turned to him slowly.

"Some things have no price, sir," said he. "For other things I shall ask a high price in time. Captain Wingate, your daughter asked me to come. If I may see her a moment, and carry back to my men the hope of her recovery, we shall all feel well repaid."

Wingate made way with the others. Banion rode straight through the gap, with no more than one unseeing glance at Woodhull, near whom sat Jackson, a pistol resting on his thigh. He came to the place under a wagon where they had made a hospital cot for Molly Wingate. It was her own father and mother who lifted her out as Will Banion sprang down, hat in hand, pale in his own terror at seeing her so pale.

"No, don't go!" said the girl to her parents. "Be here with us—and God."

She held out her arms and he bent above her, kissing her forehead gently and shyly as a boy.

"Please get well, Molly Wingate," said he. "You are Molly Wingate?"

"Yes. At the end—I couldn't! I ran away, all in my wedding clothes, Will. In the dark. Someone shot me. I've been sick, awfully sick, Will."

"Please get well, Molly Wingate! I'm going away again. This time, I don't know where. Can't you forget me, Molly Wingate?"

"I'm going to try, Will. I did try. Go on ahead, Will," she added. "You know what I mean. Do what I told you. I—why, Will!"

"My poor lamb!" said the strong voice of her mother, who gathered her in her arms, looking over her shoulder at this man to whom her child had made no vows. But Banion, wet eyed, was gone once more.

Jackson saw his leader out of the wagon gap, headed for a camping spot far apart. He stumbled up to the cot where Molly lay, her silent parents still close by.

"Here, Miss Molly, gal," said he, holding out some object in his hand. "We both got a arrer through the shoulder, an' mine's a'most well a'ready. Ain't nothin' in the world like a good chaw o' tobackerr to put on a arrer cut. Do-ee, now!"

Chapter XXXIII

THE FAMILIES ARE COMING!

The Missourians camped proudly and coldly apart, the breach between the two factions by no means healed, but rather deepened, even if honorably so, and now well understood of all.

Most men of both parties now knew of the feud between Banion and Woodhull, and the cause underlying it. Woman gossip did what it might. A half dozen determined men quietly watched Woodhull. As many continually were near Banion, although for quite a different reason. All knew that time alone must work out the answer to this implacable quarrel, and that the friends of the two men could not possibly train up together.

After all, when in sheer courtesy the leaders of the Wingate train came over to the Missouri camp on the following day there came nearer to being a good understanding than there ever had been since the first break. It was agreed that all the wagons should go on together as far as Fort Bridger, and that beyond that point the train should split into two or perhaps three bodies—a third if enough Woodhull adherents could be found to make him up a train. First place, second and third were to be cast by lot. They all talked soberly, fairly, with the dignity of men used to good standing among men. These matters concluded, and it having been agreed that all should lie by for another day, they resolved the meeting into one of better fellowship.

Old Bill Jackson, lying against his blanket roll, fell into reminiscence.

"Times past," said he, "the Green River Rendyvous was helt right in here. I've seed this place spotted with tepees—hull valley full o' Company men an' free trappers an' pack-train people—time o' Ashley an' Sublette an' my Uncle Jackson an' all them traders. That was right here on the Green. Ever'body drunk an' happy, like I ain't now. Mounting men togged out, new leggin's an' moccasins their womern had made, warriors painted up a inch o' their lives, an' women with brass wire an' calico all they wanted—maybe two-three thousand people in the Rendyvous.

"But I never seed the grass so short, an' I never seed so much fightin' afore in all my life as I have this trip. This is the third time we're jumped, an' this time we're lucky, shore as hell. Pull on through to Bridger an' fix yer wagons afore they tumble apart. Leave the grass fer them that follows, an' git on fur's you kin, every wagon. We ain't likely to have no more trouble now. Pile up them braves in one heap fer a warnin' to any other bunch o' reds that may come along to hide around the wagon ford. New times has come on the Green."

"Can you travel, Jackson?" asked Hall of Ohio. "You've had a hard time."

"Who? Me? Why shouldn't I? Give me time to pick up some o' them bows an' arrers an' I'm ready to start. I noticed a right fine horn bow one o' them devils had—the Crows allus had good bows. That's the yaller-an'-red brave that was itchin' so long to slap a arrer through my ribs from behind. I'd like to keep his bow fer him, him not needin' it now."

Before the brazen sun had fully risen on the second day these late peaceful farmers of Ohio, Iowa, Illinois, Indiana,

Missouri were plodding along once more beside their sore-footed oxen; passing out unaided into a land which many leading men in the Government, North and South, and quite aside from political affiliations, did not value at five dollars for it all, though still a thousand miles of it lay ahead.

"Oh, then, Susannah!" roared Jed Wingate, trudging along beside Molly's wagon in the sand. "Don't you cry fer me—I'm going through to Oregon, with my banjo on my knee!"

Fair as a garden to the sun-seared eyes of the emigrants seemed the mountain post, Fort Bridger, when its rude stockade separated itself from the distortions of the desert mirage, whose citadels of silence, painted temples fronted with colossal columns, giant sphinxes, vast caryatids, lofty arches, fretwork façades, fantastically splendid castles and palaces now resolved themselves into groups of squat pole structures and a rude stock corral.

The site of the post itself could not better have been chosen. Here the flattened and dividing waters of the Black's Fork, icy cold and fresh from the Uintah Mountains to the southward, supported a substantial growth of trees, green now and wonderfully refreshing to desert-weary eyes.

"The families are coming!"

Bridger's clerk, Chardon, raised the new cry of the trading post.

"Broke an' hungry, I'll bet!" swore old Jim Bridger in his beard.

But he retired into his tepee and issued orders to his Shoshone squaw, who was young and pretty. Her name, as he once had said, was Dang Yore Eyes—and she was very proud of it. Philosophical withal, though smarting under recent blows of her white lord, she now none the less went out and erected once more in front of the tepee the token Bridger had kicked down—the tufted lance, the hair-fringed bull-neck shield, the sacred medicine bundle which had stood in front of Jeem's tepee in the Rendezvous on Horse Creek, what time he had won her in a game of hands. Whereupon the older squaw, not young, pretty or jealous, abused him in Ute and went out after wood. Her name was Blast Your Hide, and she also was very proud of her white name. Whereafter both Dang Yore Eyes and Blast Yore Hide, female, and hence knowing the moods of man, wisely hid out for a while. They knew when Jeem had the long talk with the sick white squaw, who was young, but probably needed bitter bark of the cottonwood to cure her fever.

Painted Utes and Shoshones stood about, no more silent than the few local mountaineers, bearded, beaded and fringed, who still after some mysterious fashion clung to the old life at the post. Against the newcomers, profitable as they were, still existed the ancient antipathy of the resident for the nonresident.

"My land sakes alive!" commented stoical Molly Wingate after they had made some inquiries into the costs of staples here. "This store ain't no place to trade. They want fifty dollars a sack for flour—what do you think of that? We got it for two dollars back home. And sugar a dollar a tin cup, and just plain salt two bits a pound, and them to guess at the pound. Do they think we're Indians, or what?"

"It's the tenth day of August, and a thousand miles ahead," commented Caleb Price. "And we're beyond the buffalo now."

"And Sis is in trouble," added Jed Wingate. "The light wagon's got one hind spindle half in two, and I've spliced the hind ex for the last time."

Jackson advanced an idea.

"At Fort Hall," he said, "I've seed 'em cut a wagon in two an' make a two-wheel cart out'n hit. They're easier to git through mountains that way."

"Now listen to that, Jesse!" Mrs. Wingate commented. "It's getting down to less and less every day. But I'm going to take my bureau through, and my wheat, and my rose plants, if I have to put wheels on my bureau."

The men determined to saw down three wagons of the train which now seemed doubtful of survival as quadrupeds, and a general rearrangement of cargoes was agreed. Now they must jettison burden of every dispensable sort. Some of the sore-necked oxen were to be thrown into the loose herd and their places taken for a time by cows no longer offering milk.

A new soberness began to sit on all. The wide reaches of desert with which they here were in touch appalled their hearts more than anything they yet had met. The grassy valley of the Platte, where the great fourfold tracks of the trail cut through a waving sea of green belly deep to the oxen, had seemed easy and inviting, and since then hardship had at least been spiced with novelty and change. But here was a new and forbidding land. This was the Far West itself; silent, inscrutable, unchanged, irreducible. The mightiness of its calm was a smiting thing. The awesomeness of its chill, indifferent nights, the unsparing ardors of its merciless noons, the measureless expanses of its levels, the cold barrenness of its hills—these things did not invite as to the bosom of a welcoming mother; they repelled, as with the chill gesture of a stranger turning away outcasts from the door.

"Here resolution almost faints!" wrote one.

A general requisition was made on the scant stores Bridger had hurried through. To their surprise, Bridger himself made no attempt at frontier profits.

"Chardon," commanded the moody master of the post to his head clerk, "take down your tradin' bar an' let my people in. Sell them their flour an' meal at what it has cost us here—all they want, down to what the post will need till my partner Vasquez brings in more next fall, if he ever does. Sell 'em their flour at four dollars a sack, an' not at fifty, boy. Git out that flag I saved from Sublette's outfit, Chardon. Put it on a pole for these folks, an' give it to them so's they kin carry it on acrost to Oregon. God's got some use for them folks out yan or hit wouldn't be happenin' this way. I'm goin' to help 'em acrost. Ef I don't, old Jim Bridger is a liar!"

That night Bridger sat in his lodge alone, moodily smoking. He heard a shaking at the pegs of the door flap.

"Get out!" he exclaimed, thinking that it was his older associate, or else some intruding dog.

His order was not obeyed. Will Banion pulled back the flap, stooped and entered.

"How!" exclaimed Bridger, and with fist smitten on the

blankets made the sign to "Sit!" Banion for a time also smoked in silence, knowing the moody ways of the old-time men.

"Ye came to see me about her, Miss Molly, didn't ye?" began Bridger after a long time, kicking the embers of the tepee fire together with the toe of his moccasin.

"How do you know that?"

"I kin read signs."

"Yes, she sent me."

"When?"

"That was at Laramie. She told me to come on with you then. I could not."

"Pore child, they mout 'a' killed her! She told me she'd git well, though—told me so today. I had a talk with her." His wrinkled face broke into additional creases. "She told me more!"

"I've no wonder."

"Ner me. Ef I was more young and less Injun I'd love that gal! I do, anyhow, fer sake o' what I might of been ef I hadn't had to play my game the way the cards said fer me.

"She told me she was shot on her weddin' night, in her weddin' clothes—right plum to the time an' minute o' marryin', then an' thar. She told me she thanked God the Injun shot her, an' she wished to God he'd killed her then an' thar. I'd like such fer a bride, huh? That's one hell of a weddin', huh? Why?"

Banion sat silent, staring at the embers.

"I know why, or part ways why. Kit an' me was drunk at Laramie. I kain't remember much. But I do ree-colleck Kit said something to me about you in the Army, with Donerphan in Mayheeco. Right then I gits patriotic. 'Hooray!' says I. Then we taken another drink. After that we fell to arguin' how much land we'd git out o' Mayheeco when the treaty was signed. He said hit war done signed now, or else hit warn't. I don't ree-colleck which, but hit was one or t'other. He had papers. Ef I see Kit agin ary time now I'll ast him what his papers was. I don't ree-colleck exact.

"All that, ye see, boy," he resumed, "was atter I was over

to the wagons at Laramie, when I seed Miss Molly to say good-by to her. I reckon maybe I was outside o' sever'l horns even then."

"And that was when you gave her the California nugget that Kit Carson had given you!" Banion spoke at last.

"Oh, ye spring no surprise, boy! She told me today she'd told you then; said she'd begged you to go on with me an' beat all the others to Californy; said she wanted you to git rich; said you an' her had parted, an' she wanted you to live things down. I was to tell ye that.

"Boy, she loves ye—not me ner that other man. The Injun womern kin love a dozen men. The white womern kain't. I'm still fool white enough fer to believe that. Of course she'd break her promise not to tell about the gold. I might 'a' knowed she'd tell the man she loved. Well, she didn't wait long. How long was hit afore she done so—about ten minutes? Boy, she loves ye. Hit ain't no one else."

"I think so. I'm afraid so."

"Why don't ye marry her then, damn ye, right here? Ef a gal loves a man he orto marry her, ef only to cure her o' bein' a damn fool to love any man. Why don't you marry her right now?"

"Because I love her!"

Bridger sat in disgusted silence for some time.

"Well," said he at last, "there's some kinds o' damned fools that kain't be cured noways. I expect you're one o' them. Me, I hain't so highfalutin'. Ef I love a womern, an' her me, somethin's goin' to happen. What's this here like? Nothin' happens. Son, it's when nothin' happens that somethin' else does happen. She marries another man—barrin' 'Rapahoes. A fool fer luck—that's you. But there mightn't always be a Injun hidin' to shoot her when she gits dressed up agin an' the minister is a-waitin' to pernounce 'em man an' wife. Then whar air ye?"

He went on more kindly after a time, as he reached out a hard, sinewy hand.

"Such as her is fer the young man that has a white man's full life to give her. She's purty as a doe fawn an' kind as a thoroughbred filly. In course ye loved her, boy. How could

ye a-help hit? An' ye was willin' to go to Oregon—ye'd
plow rather'n leave sight o' her? I don't blame ye, boy. Such
as her is not supported by rifle an' trap. Hit's the home
smoke, not the tepee fire, for her. I ask ye nothin' more,
boy. I'll not ask ye what ye mean. Man an' boy, I've follered
the tepee smokes—blue an' a-movin' an' a-beckonin' they
was—an' I never set this hand to no plow in all my life.
But in my heart two things never was wiped out—the sight
o' the white womern's face an' the sight o' the flag with
stars. I'll help ye all I can, an' good luck go with ye. Work
hit out yore own way. She's worth more'n all the gold Californy's got buried!"

This time it was Will Banion's hand that was suddenly
extended.

"Take her secret an' take her advice then," said Bridger
after a time. "Ye must git in ahead to Californy. Fust come
fust served, on any beaver water. Fer me 'tis easy. I kin hold
my hat an' the immigrints'll throw money into hit. I've got
my fortune here, boy. I can easy spare ye what ye need, ef
ye do need a helpin' out'n my plate. Fer sake o' the finest
gal that ever crossed the Plains, that's what we'll do! Ef I
don't, Jim Bridger's a putrefied liar, so help me God!"

Banion made no reply at once, but could not fail of understanding.

"I'll not need much," said he. "My place is to go on ahead
with my men. I don't think there'll be much danger now
from Indians, from what I hear. At Fort Hall I intend to split
off for California. Now I make you this proposition, not in
payment for your secret, or for anything else: If I find gold
I'll give you half of all I get, as soon as I get out or as soon
as I can send it."

"What do ye want o' me, son?"

"Six mules and packs. All the shovels and picks you have
or can get for me at Fort Hall. There's another thing."

"An' what is that?"

"I want you to find out what Kit Carson said and what
Kit Carson had. If at any time you want to reach me—six
months, a year—get word through by the wagon trains next

year, in care of the District Court at Oregon City, on the Willamette."

"Why, all right, all right, son! We're all maybe talkin' in the air, but I more'n half understand ye. One thing, ye ain't never really intendin' to give up Molly Wingate! Ye're a fool not to marry her now, but ye're reckonin' to marry her sometime—when the moon turns green, huh? When she's old an' shriveled up, then ye'll marry her, huh?"

Banion only looked at him, silent.

"Well, I'd like to go on to Californy with ye, son, ef I didn't know I'd make more here, an' easier, out'n the crazy fools that'll be pilin' in here next year. So good luck to ye."

"Kit had more o' that stuff," he suddenly added. "He give me some more when I told him I'd lost that fust piece he give me. I'll give ye a piece fer sample, son. I've kep' hit close."

He begun fumbling in the tobacco pouch which he found under the head of his blanket bed. He looked up blankly, slightly altering the name of his youngest squaw.

"Well, damn her hide!" said he fervently. "Ye kain't keep nothin' from 'em! An' they kain't keep nothin' when they git hit."

Chapter XXXIV

A MATTER OF FRIENDSHIP

Once more the train, now permanently divided into two, faced the desert, all the men and many women now afoot, the kine low-headed, stepping gingerly in their new rawhide shoes. Gray, grim work, toiling over the dust and sand. But at the head wagon, taking over an empire foot by foot, flew the great flag. Half fanatics? That may be. Fanatics, so called, also had prayed and sung and taught their children, all the way across to the Great Salt Lake. They, too, carried books. And within one hour after their halt near the Salt Lake they began to plow, began to build, began to work, began to grow and make a country.

The men at the trading post saw the Missouri wagons pull out ahead. Two hours later the Wingate train followed, as the lot had determined. Woodhull remained with his friends in the Wingate group, regarded now with an increasing indifference, but biding his time.

Bridger held back his old friend Jackson even after the last train pulled out. It was mid afternoon when the start was made.

"Don't go just yet, Bill," said he. "Ride on an' overtake 'em. Nothin' but rattlers an' jack rabbits now fer a while. The Shoshones won't hurt 'em none. I'm powerful lone-some, somehow. Let's you an' me have one more drink."

"That sounds reas'nble," said Jackson. "Shore that sounds reas'nble to me."

They drank of a keg which the master of the post had hidden in his lodge, back of his blankets; drank again of high wines diluted but uncolored—the "likker" of the fur trade.

They drank from tin cups, until Bridger began to chant, a deepening sense of his old melancholy on him.

"Good-by!" he said again and again, waving his hand in general vagueness to the mountains.

"We was friends, wasn't we, Bill?" he demanded again and again; and Jackson, drunk as he, nodded in like maudlin gravity. He himself began to chant. The two were savages again.

"Well, we got to part, Bill. This is Jim Bridger's last Rendyvous. I've rid around an' said good-by to the mount-ings. Why don't we do it the way the big partisans allus done when the Rendyvous was over? 'Twas old Mike Fink an' his friend Carpenter begun hit, fifty year ago. Keel-boat men on the river, they was. There's as good shots left to-day as then, an' as good friends. You an' me has seed hit; we seed hit at the very last meetin' o' the Rocky Mountain Company men, before the families come. An 'nary a man spilled the whiskey on his partner's head."

"That's the truth," assented Jackson. "Though some I wouldn't trust now."

"Would ye trust me, Bill, like I do you, fer sake o' the old times, when friends was friends?"

"Shore I would, no matter how come, Jim. My hand's stiddy as a rock, even though my shootin' shoulder's a leetle stiff from that Crow arrer."

Each man held out his firing arm, steady as a bar.

"I kin still see the nail heads on the door, yan. Kin ye, Bill?"

"Plain! It's a waste o' likker, Jim, fer we'd both drill the cups."

"Are ye a-skeered?"

"I told ye not."

"Chardon!" roared Bridger to his clerk. "You, Chardon, come here!"

The clerk obeyed, though he and others had been discreet about remaining visible as this bout of old-timers at their cups went on. Liquor and gunpowder, usually went together.

"Chardon, git ye two fresh tin cups an' bring 'em here. Bring a piece o' charcoal to spot the cups. We're goin' to shoot 'em off each other's heads in the old way. You know what I mean."

Chardon, trembling, brought the two tin cups, and Bridger with a burnt ember sought to mark plainly on each a black bull's-eye. Silence fell on the few observers, for all the emigrants had now gone and the open space before the rude trading building was vacant, although a few faces peered around corners. At the door of the tallest tepee two native women sat, a young and an old, their blankets drawn across their eyes, accepting fate, and not daring to make a protest.

"How!" exclaimed Bridger as he filled both cups and put them on the ground. "Have ye wiped yer bar'l?"

"Shore I have. Let's wipe agin."

Each drew his ramrod from the pipes and attached the cleaning worm with its twist of tow, kept handy in belt pouch in muzzle-loading days.

"Clean as a whistle!" said Jackson, holding out the end of the rod.

"So's mine, pardner. Old Jim Bridger never disgraced his-self with a rifle."

"Ner me," commented Jackson. "Hold a hair full, Jim, an' cut nigh the top o' the tin. That'll be safer, fer my skelp, an' hit'll let less whisky out'n the hole. We got to drink what's left. S'pose'n we have a snort now?"

"Atter we both shoot we kin drink," rejoined his friend, with a remaining trace of judgment. "Go take stand whar we marked the scratch. Chardon, damn ye, carry the cup down an' set hit on his head, an' ef ye spill a drop I'll drill ye, d'ye hear?"

The *engagé's* face went pale.

"But Monsieur Jim—" he began.

"Don't 'Monsieur Jim' me or I'll drill a hole in ye anyways! Do-ee-do what I tell ye, boy! Then if ye crave fer to see some ol'-time shootin' come on out, the hull o' ye, an' take a lesson, damn ye!"

"Do-ee ye shoot first, Bill," demanded Bridger. "The light's soft, an' we'll swap atter the fust fire, to git hit squar' for the hindsight, an' no shine on the side o' the front sight."

"No, we'll toss fer fust," said Jackson, and drew out a Spanish dollar. "Tails fer me last!" he called as it fell. "An' I win! You go fust, Jim."

"Shore I will ef the toss-up says so," rejoined his friend. "Step off the fifty yard. What sort o' iron ye carryin', Bill?"

"Why do ye ask? Ye know ol' Mike Sheets in Virginia never bored a better. I've never changed."

"Ner I from my old Hawken. Two good guns, an' two good men, Bill, o' the ol' times—the ol' times! We kain't say fairer'n this, can we, at our time o' life, fer favor o' the old times, Bill? We got to do somethin', so's to kind o' git rested up."

"No man kin say fairer," said his friend.

They shook hands solemnly and went onward with their devil-may-care test, devised in a historic keel-boat man's brain, as inflamed then by alcohol as their own were now.

Followed by the terrified clerk, Bill Jackson, tall, thin and grizzled, stoical as an Indian, and too drunk to care much for consequences, so only he proved his skill and his courage, walked steadily down to the chosen spot and stood, his arms folded, after leaning his own rifle against the door of the trading room. He faced Bridger without a tremor, his head bare, and cursed Chardon for a coward when his hand trembled as he balanced the cup on Jackson's head.

"Damn ye," he exclaimed, "there'll be plenty lost without any o' your spillin'!"

"Air ye all ready, Bill?" called Bridger from his station, his rifle cocked and the delicate triggers set, so perfect in their mechanism that the lightest touch against the trigger edge would loose the hammer.

"All ready!" answered Jackson.

The two, jealous still of the ancient art of the rifle, which nowhere in the world obtained nicer development than among men such as these, faced each other in what always was considered the supreme test of nerve and skill; for naturally a man's hand might tremble, sighting three inches above his friend's eyes when it would not move a hair sighting center between the eyes of an enemy.

Bridger spat out his tobacco chew and steadily raised his rifle. The man opposite him stood steady as a pillar, and did not close his eyes. The silence that fell on those who saw became so intense that it seemed veritably to radiate, reaching out over the valley to the mountains as in a hush of leagues.

For an instant, which to the few observers seemed an hour, these two figures, from which motion seemed to have passed forever, stood frozen. Then there came a spurt of whitish-blue smoke and the thin dry crack of the border rifle.

The hand and eye of Jim Bridger, in spite of advancing years, remained true to their long training. At the rifle crack the tin cup on the head of the statue-like figure opposite him was flung behind as though by the blow of an invisible hand. The spin of the bullet acting on the liquid contents, ripped apart the seams of the cup and flung the fluid wide. Then and not till then did Jackson move.

He picked up the empty cup, bored center directly through the black spot, and turning walked with it in his hand toward Bridger, who was wiping out his rifle once more.

"I call hit mighty careless shootin'," said he, irritated. "Now lookee what ye done to the likker! Ef ye'd held a leetle higher, above the level o' the likker, like I told ye, she wouldn't o' busted open thataway now. It's nacherl, thar warn't room in the cup fer both the likker an' the ball. That's wastin' likker, Jim, an' my mother told me when I was a boy, 'Willful waste makes woeful want!' "

"I call hit a plum-center shot," grumbled Bridger. "Do-ee

look now! Maybe ye think ye kin do better shoot'in yerself than old Jim Bridger!"

"Shore I kin, an' I'll show ye! I'll bet my rifle aginst yourn—ef I wanted so sorry a piece as yourn—I kin shoot that clost to the mark an' not spill no likker a-tall! An' ye can fill her two-thirds full an' put yer thumb in fer the balance ef ye like."

"I'll just bet ye a new mule agin yer pony ye kain't do nothin' o' the sort!" retorted Bridger.

"All right, I'll show ye. O' course, ye got to hold still."

"Who said I wouldn't hold still?"

"Nobody. Now you watch me."

He stooped at the little water ditch which had been led in among the buildings from the stream and kneaded up a little ball of mud. This he forced into the handle of the tin cup, entirely filling it, then washed off the body of the cup.

"I'll shoot the fillin' out'n the handle an' not out'n the cup!" said he. "Mud's cheap, an' all the diff'runce in holdin' is, ef I nicked the side o' yer haid it'd hurt ye 'bout the same as ef what I nicked the center o' hit. Ain't that so? We'd orto practice inderstry an' 'conomy, Jim. Like my mother said, 'Penny saved is er penny yearned.' 'Little drops o' water, little gains o' sand,' says she, 'a-makes the mighty o-o-ocean, an the plea-ea-sant land.' "

"I never seed it tried," said Bridger, with interest, "but I don't see why hit hain't practical. Whang away, an ef' ye spill the whisky shootin' to one side, or cut har shootin' too low, your *caballo* is mine—an' he hain't much!"

With no more argument, he in turn took up his place, the two changing positions so that the light would favor the rifleman. Again the fear-smitten Chardon adjusted the filled cup, this time on his master's bared head.

"Do-ee turn her sideways now, boy," cautioned Bridger. "Set the han'le sideways squar', so she looks wide. Give him a fa'r shot now, fer I'm interested in this yere thing, either way she goes. Either I lose ha'r er a mule."

But folding his arms he faced the rifle without batting an eye, as steady as had been the other in his turn.

Jackson extended his long left arm, slowly and steadily

raising the silver bead up from the chest, the throat, the chin, the forehead of his friend, then lowered it, rubbing his sore shoulder.

"Tell him to turn that han'le squar' to me, Jim!" he called. "The damn fool has got her all squegeed eroun' to one side."

Bridger reached up a hand and straightened the cup himself.

"How's that?" he asked.

"All right! Now hold stiddy a minute."

Again the Indian women covered their faces, sitting motionless. And at last came again the puff of smoke, the faint crack of the rifle, never loud in the high, rarefied air.

The straight figure of the scout never wavered. The cup still rested on his head. The rifleman calmly blew the smoke from his barrel, his eye on Bridger as the latter now raised a careful hand to his head. Chardon hastened to aid, with many ejaculations.

The cup still was full, but the mud was gone from inside the handle as though poked out with a finger!

"That's what I call shootin', Jim," said Jackson, "an' reas'nable shootin' too. Now spill half o' her where she'll do some good, an' give me the rest. I got to be goin' now. I don't want yer mule. I fust come away from Missouri to git shet o' mules."

Chardon, cupbearer, stood regarding the two wild souls whom he never in his own more timid nature was to understand. The two mountain men shook hands. The alcohol had no more than steadied them in their rifle work, but the old exultation of their wild life came to them now once more. Bridger clapped hand to mouth and uttered his old war cry before he drained his share of the fiery fluid.

"To the ol' days, friend!" said he once more; "the days that's gone, when men was men, an' a friend could trust a friend!"

"To the ol' days!" said Jackson in turn. "An' I'll bet two better shots don't stand today on the soil o' Oregon! But I got to be goin', Jim. I'm goin' on to the Columby. I may not see ye soon. It's far."

He swung into his saddle, the rifle in its loop at the horn.

But Bridger came to him, a hand on his knee.

"I hate to see ye go, Bill."

"Shore!" said Jackson. "I hate to go. Take keer yerself, Jim."

The two Indian women had uncovered their faces and gone inside the lodge. But old Jim Bridger sat down, back against a cottonwood, and watched the lopping figure of his friend jog slowly out into the desert. He himself was singing now, chanting monotonously an old Indian refrain that lingered in his soul from the days of the last Rendezvous.

At length he arose, and animated by a sudden thought sought out his tepee once more. Dang Yore Eyes greeted him with shy smiles of pride.

"Heap shoot, Jeem!" said she. "No kill-um. Why?"

She was decked now in her finest, ready to use all her blandishments on her lord and master. Her cheeks were painted red, her wrists were heavy with copper. On a thong at her neck hung a piece of yellow stone which she had bored through with an awl, or rather with three or four awls, after much labor, that very day.

Bridger picked up the ornament betwen thumb and finger. He said no word, but his fingers spoke.

"Other pieces. Where?"

"White man. Gone—out there." She answered in the same fashion.

"How, cola!" she spoke aloud. "Him say, 'How, cola,' me." She smiled with much pride over her conquest, and showed two silver dollars. "Swap!"

In silence Bridger went into the tepee and pulled the door flaps.

Chapter XXXV

GEE—WHOA—HAW!

Midsummer in the desert. The road now, but for the shifting of the sands, would have been marked by the bodies of dead cattle, in death scarcely more bone and parchment than for days they had been while alive. The horned toad, the cactus, the rattlesnake long since had replaced the prairie dogs of the grassy floor of the eastern Plains. A scourge of great black crickets appeared, crackling loathsomely under the wheels. Sagebrush and sand took the place of trees and grass as they left the river valley and crossed a succession of ridges or plateaus. At last they reached vast black basaltic masses and lava fields, proof of former subterranean fires which seemingly had forever dried out the life of the earth's surface. The very vastness of the views might have had charm but for the tempering feeling of awe, of doubt, of fear.

They had followed the trail over the immemorial tribal crossings over heights of land lying between the heads of streams. From the Green River, which finds the great cañons of the Colorado, they came into the vast horseshoe valley of the Bear, almost circumventing the Great Salt Lake, but unable to forsake it at last. West and south now rose bold mountains around whose northern extremity the river had felt its way, and back of these lay fold on fold of lofty ridges, now softened by the distances. Of all the splendid landscapes of the Oregon Trail, this one had few rivals. But they must leave this and cross to yet another though less inviting vast river valley of the series which led them across the continent.

Out of the many wagons which Jesse Wingate originally had captained, now not one hundred remained in his detachment when it took the sagebrush plateaus below the great Snake River. They still were back of the Missouri train, no doubt several days, but no message left on a cleft stick at camp cheered them or enlightened them. And now still another defection had cut down the train.

Woodhull, moody and irascible, feverish and excited by turns, ever since leaving Bridger had held secret conclaves with a few of his adherents, the nature of which he did not disclose. There was no great surprise and no extreme regret when, within safe reach of Fort Hall, he had announced his intention of going on ahead with a dozen wagons. He went without obtaining any private interview with Molly Wingate.

These matters none the less had their depressing effect. Few illusions remained to any of them now, and no romance. Yet they went on—ten miles, fifteen sometimes, though rarely twenty miles a day. Women fell asleep, babes in arms, jostling on the wagon seats; men almost slept as they walked, ox whip in hand; the cattle slept as they stumbled on, tongues dry and lolling. All the earth seemed strange, unreal. They advanced as though in a dream through some inferno of a crazed imagination.

About them now often rose the wavering images of the mirage, offering water, trees, wide landscapes; beckoning in such desert deceits as they often now had seen. One day as the brazen sun mocked them from its zenith they saw that they were not alone on the trail.

"Look, mother!" exclaimed Molly Wingate—she now

rode with her mother on the seat of the family wagon, Jed driving her cart when not on the cow column. "See! There's a caravan!"

Her cry was echoed or anticipated by scores of voices of others who had seen the same thing. They pointed west and south.

Surely there was a caravan—a phantom caravan! Far off, gigantic, looming and lowering again, it paralleled the advance of their own train, which in numbers it seemed to equal. Slowly, steadily, irresistibly, awesomely, it kept pace with them, sending no sign to them, mockingly indifferent to them—mockingly so, indeed; for when the leaders of the Wingate wagons paused the riders of the ghostly train paused also, biding their time with no action to indicate their intent. When the advance was resumed the uncanny *pari passu* again went on, the rival caravan going forward as fast, no faster than those who regarded it in a fascinated interest that began to become fear. Yonder caravan could bode no good. Without doubt it planned an ambush farther on, and this sinister indifference meant only its certainty of success.

Or were there, then, other races of men out here in this unknown world of heat and sand? Was this a treasure train of old Spanish *cargadores?* Did ghosts live and move as men? If not, what caravan was this, moving alone, far from the beaten trail? What purpose had it here?

"Look, mother!"

The girl's voice rose eagerly again, but this time with a laugh in it. And her assurance passed down the line, others laughing in relief at the solution.

"It's ourselves!" said Molly. "It's the Fata Morgana—but how marvelous! Who could believe it?"

Indeed, the mirage had taken that rare and extraordinary form. The mirage of their own caravan, rising, was reflected, mirrored, by some freak of the desert sun and air, upon the fine sand blown in the air at a distance from the train. It was, indeed, themselves they saw, not knowing it, in a vast primordial mirror of the desert gods. Nor did the discovery of the truth lessen the feeling of discomfort, of apprehension. The laughter was at best uneasy until at last a turn in the trail, a shift in the wizardry of the heat waves, broke up the ghostly caravan and sent it, figure by figure, vehicle by vehicle, into the unknown whence it had come.

"This country!" exclaimed Molly Wingate's mother. "It scares me! If Oregon's like this—"

"It isn't, mother. It is rich and green, with rains. There are great trees, many mountains, beautiful rivers where we are going, and there are fields of grain. There are—why, there are homes!"

The sudden pathos of her voice drew her mother's frowning gaze.

"There, there, child!" said she. "Don't you mind. We'll always have a home for you, your paw and me."

The girl shook her head.

"I sometimes think I'd better teach school and live alone."

"And leave your parents?"

"How can I look my father in the face every day, knowing what he feels about me? Just now he accuses me of ruining Sam Woodhull's life—driving him away, out of the train. But what could I do? Marry him, after all? I can't—I can't! I'm glad he's gone, but I don't know why he went."

"In my belief you haven't heard or seen the last of Sam Woodhull yet," mused her mother. "Sometimes a man gets sort of peeved—wants to marry a girl that jilts him more'n if she hadn't. And you certainly jilted him at the church door, if there'd been any church there. It was an awful thing, Molly. I don't know as I see how Sam stood it long as he did."

"Haven't I paid for it, mother?"

"Why, yes, one way of speaking. But that ain't the way men are going to call theirselves paid. Until he's married, a man's powerful set on having a woman. If he don't, he thinks he ain't paid, it don't scarcely make no difference what the woman does. No, I don't reckon he'll forget. About Will Banion—"

"Don't let's mention him, mother. I'm trying to forget him."

"Yes? Where do you reckon he is now—how far ahead?"

"I don't know. I can't guess."

The color on her cheek caught her mother's gaze.

"Gee-whoa-haw! Git along Buck and Star!" commanded the buxom dame to the swaying ox team that now followed the road with no real need of guidance. They took up the heat and burden of the desert.

Chapter XXXVI

Two Love Letters

The families are coming—again the families!" It was again the cry of the passing fur post, looking eastward at the caravan of the west-bound plows; much the same here at old Fort Hall, on the Snake River, as it was at Laramie on the North Platte, or Bridger on the waters tributary to the Green.

The company clerks who looked out over the sandy plain saw miles away a dust cloud which meant but one thing. In time they saw the Wingate train come on, slowly, steadily, and deploy for encampment a mile away. The dusty wagons, their double covers stained, mildewed, torn, were scattered where each found the grass good. Then they saw scores of the emigrants, women as well as men, hastening into the post.

It was now past midsummer, around the middle of the month of August, and the Wingate wagons had covered some twelve hundred and eighty miles since the start at mid-May of the last spring—more than three months of continuous travel; a trek before which the passage over the

Appalachians, two generations earlier, wholly pales.

What did they need, here at Fort Hall, on the Snake, third and last settlement of the two thousand miles of toil and danger and exhaustion? They needed everything. But one question first was asked by these travel-sick home-loving people: What was the news?

News? How could there be news when almost a year would elapse before Fort Hall would know that on that very day—in that very month of August, 1848—Oregon was declared a territory of the Union?

News? How could there be news, when these men could not know for much more than a year that, as they outspanned here in the sage, Abraham Lincoln had just declined the governorship of the new territory of Oregon? Why? He did not know. Why had these men come here? They did not know.

But news—the news! The families must have the news. And here—always there was news! Just beyond branched off the trail to California. Here the supply trains from the Columbia brought news from the Oregon settlements. News? How slow it was, when it took a letter more than two years to go one way from edge to edge of the American continent!

They told what news they knew—the news of the Mormons of 1847 and 1848; the latest mutterings over fugitive negro slaves; the growing feeling that the South would one day follow the teachings of secession. They heard in payment the full news of the Whitman massacre in Oregon that winter; they gave back in turn their own news of the battles with the Sioux and the Crows; the news of the new Army posts then moving west into the Plains to clear them for the whites. News? Why, yes, large news enough, and on either hand, so the trade was fair.

But these matters of the outside world were not the only ones of interest, whether to the post traders or the newly arrived emigrants. Had others preceded them? How many? When? Why, yes, a week earlier fifty wagons of one train, Missouri men, led by a man on a great black horse and an old man, a hunter. Banion? Yes, that was the name, and the scout was Jackson—Bill Jackson, an old-time free trapper. Well, these two had split off for California, with six good pack mules, loaded light. The rest of the wagons had gone on to the Snake. But why these two had bought the last shovels and the only pick in all the supplies at old Fort Hall no man could tell. Crazy, of course; for who could pause to work on the trail with pick or shovel, with winter coming on at the Sierra crossing?

But not crazier than the other band who had come in three days ago, also ahead of the main train. Woodhull? Yes, that was the name—Woodhull. He had twelve or fifteen wagons with him, and had bought supplies for California, though they all had started for Oregon. Well, they soon would know more about the Mary's River and the Humboldt Desert. Plenty of bones, there, sure!

But even so, a third of the trains, these past five years, had split off at the Raft River and given up hope of Oregon. California was much better—easier to reach and better when you got there. The road to Oregon was horrible. The crossings of the Snake, especially the first crossing, to the north bank, was a gamble with death for the whole train. And beyond that, to the Blue Mountains, the trail was no trail at all. Few ever would get through, no one knew how many had perished. Three years ago Joe Meek had tried to find a better trail west of the Blues. All lost, so the story said. Why go to Oregon? Nothing there when you got there. California, now, had been settled and proved a hundred years and more. Every year men came this far east to wait at Fort Hall for the emigrant trains and to persuade them to go to California, not to Oregon.

But what seemed strange to the men at the trading post was the fact that Banion had not stopped or asked a question. He appeared to have made up his mind long earlier, and beyond asking for shovels he had wanted nothing. The same way with Woodhull. He had come in fast and gone out fast, headed for the Raft River trail to California, the very next morning. Why? Usually men stopped here at Fort Hall, rested, traded, got new stock, wanted to know about the trail ahead. Both Banion and Woodhull struck Fort Hall with their minds already made up. They did not talk. Was there any new word about the California trail, down at Bridger? Had a new route over the Humboldt Basin been found, or something of that sort? How could that be? If so, it must be rough and needing work in places, else why the need for so many shovels? But maybe the emigrants themselves knew about these singular matters, or would when they had read their letters. Yes, of course, the Missouri movers had left a lot of letters, some for their folks back East next year maybe, but some for people in the train. Banion, Woodhull—had they left any word? Why, yes, both of them. The trader smiled. One each. To the same person, yes. Well, lucky girl! But that black horse now—the Nez Percés would give a hundred ponies for him. But he wouldn't trade. A sour young man. But Woodhull, now, the one with the wagons, talked more. And they each had left a letter for the same girl! And this was Miss Molly Wingate? Well, the trader did not blame them! These American girls! They were like roses to the old traders, cast away this lifetime out here in the desert.

News? Why, yes, no train ever came through that did not bring news and get news at old Fort Hall—and so on.

The inclosure of the old adobe fur-trading post was thronged by the men and women of the Wingate train. Molly Wingate at first was not among them. She sat, chin on her hand, on a wagon tongue in the encampment, looking out over the blue-gray desert to the red-and-gold glory of the sinking sun. Her mother came to her and placed in her lap the two letters, stood watching her.

"One from each," said she sententiously, and turned away.

The girl's face paled as she opened the one she had felt sure would find her again, somewhere, somehow. It said:

Dearest: I write to Molly Wingate, because and only because I know she still is Molly Wingate. It might be kinder to us both if I did not write at all but went my way and left it all to time and silence. I found I could not. There will be no other woman, in all my life, for me. I cannot lay any vow on you. If I could, if I dared, I would say: "Wait for a year, while I pray for a year—and God help us both."

As you know, I now have taken your advice. Bridger and I are joined for the California adventure. If the gold is there, as Carson thinks, I may find more fortune than I have earned. More than I could earn you gave me—when I was young. That was two months ago. Now I am old.

Keep the news of the gold, if it can be kept, as long as you can. No doubt it will spread from other sources, but so far as I know—and thanks only to you—I am well ahead of any other adventurer from the East this season, and, as you know, winter soon will seal the trails against followers. Next year, 1849, will be the big rush, if it all does not flatten.

I can think of no one who can have shared our secret. Carson will be East by now, but he is a government man, and close of mouth with strangers. Bridger, I am sure—for the odd reason that he worships you—will tell no one else, especially since he shares profits with me, if I survive and succeed. One doubt only rests in my mind. At his post I talked with Bridger, and he told me he had a few other bits of gold that Carson had given him at Laramie. He looked for them but had lost them. He suspected his Indian women, but he knew nothing. Of course, it would be one chance in a thousand that any one would know the women had these things, and even so no one could tell where the gold came from, because not even the women would know that; not even Bridger does, exactly; not even I myself.

In general I am headed for the valley of the Sacramento. I shall work north. Why? Because that will be toward Oregon!

I write as though I expected to see you again, as though I had a right to expect or hope for that. It is only the dead young man, Will Banion, who unjustly and wrongly craves and calls out for the greatest of all fortune for a man—who unfairly and wrongly writes you now, when he ought to remember your word, to go to a land far from you, to forget you and to live down his past. Ah, if I could! Ah, if I did not love you!

But being perhaps about to die, away from you, the truth only must be between you and me. And the truth is I never shall forget you. The truth is I love you more than anything else and everything else in all the world.

If I were in other ways what the man of your choice should be, would this truth have any weight with you? I do not know and I dare not ask. Reason does tell me how selfish it would be to ask you to hold in your heart a memory and not a man. That is for me to do—to have a memory, and not you. But my memory never can content me.

It seems as though time had been invented so that, through all its aeons, our feet might run in search, one for the other—to meet, where? Well, we did meet—for one instant in the uncounted ages, there on the prairie. Well, if ever you do see me again you shall say whether I have been, indeed, tried by fire, and whether it has left me clean— whether I am a man and not a memory.

That I perhaps have been a thief, stealing what never could be mine, is my great agony now. But I love you. Good-by.   WILLIAMS HAYS BANION.
TO MARGARET WINGATE,
  Fort Hall, in Oregon.

For an hour Molly sat, and the sun sank. The light of the whole world died.

The other letter rested unopened until later, when she broke the seal and read by the light of a sagebrush fire. she frowned. Could it be that in the providence of God she once had been within one deliberate step of marrying Samuel Payson Woodhull?

My Darling Molly: This I hope finds you well after the hard journey from Bridger to Hall.

They call it Cruel to keep a Secret from a Woman. If so, I have been Cruel, though only in Poor pay for your Cruelty to me. I have had a Secret—and this is it: I have left for California from this Point and shall not go to Oregon. I have learned of Gold in the State of California, and have departed to that State in the hope of early Success in Achieving a Fortune. So far as I know, I am the First to have this news of Gold, unless a certain man whose name and thought I execrate has by his Usual dishonesty fallen on the same information. If so, we two may meet where none can Interfear.

I do not know how long I may be in California, but be Sure I go for but the one purpose of amassing a Fortune for the Woman I love. I never have given you Up and never shall. Your promise is mine and our Engagement never has been Broken, and the Mere fact that accident for the time Prevented our Nuptials by no means shall ever mean that we shall not find Happy Consumation of our most Cherished Desire at some later Time.

I confidently Hope to arrive in Oregon a rich man not later than one or two years from Now. Wait for me. I am mad without you and shall count the Minutes until then when I can take you in my Arms and Kiss you a thousand Times. Forgive me; I have not Heretofore told you of these Plans, but it was best not and it was for You. Indeed you are so much in my Thought, my Darling, that each and Everything I do is for You and You only.

No more at present then, but should Opportunity offer I shall get word to you addressed to Oregon City which your father said was his general Desstination, it being my own present purpose Ultimately to engage in the Practise of law either at that Point or the settlement of Portland which I understand is not far Below. With my Means, we should soon be Handsomely Settled.

May God guard you on the Way Thither and believe me, Darling, with more Love than I shall be ever able to Tell and a Thousand Kisses.

Your Affianced and Impatient Lover
SAM'L. PAYSON WOODHULL

The little sagebrush fire flared up brightly for an instant as Molly Wingate dropped one of her letters on the embers.

Chapter XXXVII

JIM BRIDGER FORGETS

What's wrong with the people, Cale?" demanded Jesse Wingate of his stouthearted associate, Caleb Price. The sun was two hours high, but not all the breakfast fires were going. Men were moody, truculent, taciturn, as they went about their duties.

Caleb Price bit into his yellow beard as he gazed down the irregular lines of the encampment.

"Do you want me to tell you the truth, Jesse?"

"Why, yes!"

"Well, then, it seems to me the truth is that this train has lost focus."

"I don't know what you mean."

"I don't know that I'm right—don't know I can make my guess plain. Of course, every day we lay up, the whole train goes to pieces. The thing to do is to go a little way each day—get into the habit. You can't wear out a road as long as this one by spurts—it's steady does it.

"But I don't think that's all. The main trouble is one that I don't like to hint to you, especially since none of us can help it."

"Out with it, Cale!"

"The trouble is, the people don't think they've got a leader."

Jesse Wingate colored above his beard.

"That's pretty hard," said he.

"I know it's hard, but I guess it's the truth. You and I and Hall and Kelsey—we're accepted as the chief council. But there are four of us, and all this country is new to all of us. The men now are like a bunch of cattle ready to stampede. They're nervous, ready to jump at anything. Wrong way, Jesse. They ought to be as steady as any of the trains that have gone across; 1843, when the Applegates crossed; 1846, when the Donners went—every year since. Our folks—well, if you ask me, I really think they're scared."

"That's hard, Cale!"

"Yes, hard for me to say to you, with your wife sad and your girl just now able to sit up—yes, it's hard. Harder still since we both know it's your own personal matter—this quarrel of those two young men, which I don't need explain. That's at the bottom of the train's uneasiness."

"Well, they've both gone now."

"Yes, both. If half of the both were here now you'd see the people quiet. Oh, you can't explain leadership, Jesse! Some have it, most don't. He had. We know he had. I don't suppose many of those folks ever figured it out, or do now. But they'd fall in, not knowing why."

"As it is, I'll admit, there seems to be something in the air. They say birds know when an earthquake is coming. I feel uneasy myself, and don't know why. I started for Oregon. I don't know why. Do you suppose—"

The speculations of either man ceased as both caught sight of a little dust cloud far off across the sage, steadily advancing down the slope.

"Hum! And who's that, Jesse?" commented the Ohio leader. "Get your big glass, Jesse."

Wingate went to his wagon and returned with the great telescope he sometimes used, emblem of his authority.

"One man, two packs," said he presently. "All alone so

far as I can see. He's Western enough—some post-trapper, I suppose. Rides like an Indian and dressed like one, but he's white, because he has a beard."

"Let me see." Price took the glass. "He looks familiar! See if you don't think it's Jim Bridger. What's he coming for—two hundred miles away from his own post?"

It was Jim Bridger, as the next hour proved, and why he came he himself was willing to explain after he had eaten and smoked.

"I camped twelve mile back," said he, "an' pushed in this mornin'. I jest had a idee I'd sornter over in here, see how ye was gittin' along. Is your hull train made here?"

"No," Wingate answered. "The Missouri wagons are ahead."

"Is Woodhull with ye?"

"No."

"Whar's he at?"

"We don't know. Major Banion and Jackson, with a half dozen packs, no wagons, have given up the trip. They've split off for California—left their wagons."

"An' so has Sam Woodhull, huh?"

"We suppose so. That's the word. He took about fifteen wagons with him. That's why we look cut down."

"Rest of ye goin' on through, huh?"

"I am. I hope the others will."

"Hit's three days on to whar the road leaves for California—on the Raft River. Mebbe more'll leave ye thar, huh?"

"We don't know. We hope not. I hear the fords are bad, especially the crossing of the Snake. This is a big river. My people are uneasy about it."

"Yes, hit's bad enough, right often. Thar's falls in them cañons hundreds o' feet high, makin' a roarin' ye kin hear forty mile, mebbe. The big ford's erroun' two hunderd mile ahead. That'd make me four hunderd mile away from home, an' four hunderd to ride back agin' huh? Is that fur enough fer a ol' man, with snow comin' on soon?"

"You don't mean you'd guide us on that far? What charge?"

"I come fer that, mainly. Charge ye? I won't charge ye nothin'. What do ye s'pose Jim Bridger'd care ef ye all was drownded in the Snake? Ain't thar plenty more pilgrims whar ye all come from? Won't they be out here next year, with money ter spend with my pardner Vasquez an' me?"

"Then how could we pay you?"

"Ye kain't. Whar's Miss Molly?"

"You want to see her?"

"Yes, else why'd I ask?"

"Come," said Wingate, and led the way to Molly's little cart. The girl was startled when she saw the old scout, her wide eyes asking her question. "Mornin', Miss Molly!" he began, his leathery face wrinkling in a smile. "Ye didn't expect me, an' I didn't neither. I'm glad ye're about well o' that arrer wound. I kerried a arrerhead under my shoulder blade sever'l years oncet, ontel Preacher Whitman cut hit out. Hit felt right crawly all the time till then.

"Yes, I jest sorntered up couple hundred mile this mornin', Miss Molly, ter see how ye all was gettin' along—one thing er another."

Without much regard to others, he now led Molly a little apart and seated her on the sage beside him.

"Will Banion and Bill Jackson has went on to Californy, Miss Molly," said he. "You know why."

Mollie nodded.

"Ye'd orto! Ye told him."

"Yes, I did."

"I know. Him an' me had a talk. Owin' you an' me all he'll ever make, he allowed to pay nothin'! Which is, admittin' he loves you, he don't take no advice, ter finish that weddin' with another man substertuted. No, says he, 'I kain't marry her, because I love her!' says he. Now, that's crazy. Somethin' deep under that, Miss Molly."

"Let's not talk about it, please."

"All right. Let's talk erbout Sam Woodhull, huh?"

"No!"

"Then mebbe I'd better be goin'. I know you don't want ter talk erbout me!" His wrinkling smile said he had more to tell.

"Miss Molly," said he at last, "I mout as well tell ye. Sam Woodhull is on the way atter Will Banion. He's like enough picked out a fine bunch o' horse thiefs ter go erlong with him. He knows somethin' erbout the gold—I jest found out how.

"Ye see, some men ain't above shinin' up to a Injun womern even, such bein' mebbe lonesome. Sam Woodhull wasn't. He seed one o' my fam'ly wearin' a shiny thing on her neck. Hit were a piece o' gold Kit give me atter I give you mine. He trades the womern out o' her necklace—fer all o' two pesos, Mexican. But she not talkin' Missoury, an' him not talkin' Shoshone, they don't git fur on whar the gold come from.

"She done told him she got hit from me, but he don't say a word ter me erbout that; he's too wise. But she did tell him how Will Banion gits some mules an' packs o' me. From then, plain guessin', he allows ter watch Banion.

"My womern keeps sayin'—not meanin' no harm—thet thar's plenty more necklaces in Cal'for; because she's heard me an' Banion say that word, 'Californy.'

"Slim guessin' hit were, Miss Molly, but enough fer a man keen as Sam, that's not pertickler, neither. His plan was ter watch whar the packs went. He knowed ef Banion went ter Oregon he'd not use packs.

"Huh! Fine time he'll have, follerin' that boy an' them mules with wagons! I'm easier when I think o' that. Because, Miss Molly, ef them two does meet away from friends o' both, thar's goin' to be trouble, an' trouble only o' one kind."

Again Molly Wingate nodded, pale and silent.

"Well, a man has ter take keer o' his own self," went on Bridger. "But that ain't all ner most what brung me here."

"What was it then?" demanded Molly. "A long ride!"

"Yeh. Eight hunderd mile out an' back, ef I see ye across the Snake, like I allow I'd better do. I'm doin' hit fer you, Miss Molly. I'm ol' an' ye're young; I'm a wild man an' ye're one o' God's wimern. But I had sisters oncet—white they was, like you. So the eight hunderd mile is light. But thet ain't why I come, neither, or all why, yit."

"What is it then you want to tell me? Is it about—him?"

Bridger nodded. "Yes. The only trouble is, I don't know what it is."

"Now you're foolish!"

"Shore I am! Ef I had a few drinks o' good likker mebbe I'd be foolisher—er wiser. Leastways, I'd be more like I was when I plumb forgot what 'twas Kit Carson said to me when we was spreein' at Laramie. He had somethin' ter do, somethin' he was goin' ter do, somethin' I was ter do fer him, er mebee-so, next season, atter he got East an' got things done he was goin' ter do. Ye see, Kit's in the Army."

"Was it about—him?"

"That's what I kain't tell. I jest sorntered over here a few hunderd mile ter ask ye what ye s'pose it is that I've plumb fergot, me not havin' the same kind o' likker right now.

"When me an' Bill was havin' a few afore he left I was right on the p'int o' rememberin' what it was I was fergittin'. I don't make no doubt, ef Kit an' me er Bill an' me could only meet an' drink along day er so hit'd all come plain to me. But all by myself, an' sober, an' not sociable with Dang Yore Eyes jest now, I sw'ar, I kain't think o' nothin'. What's a girl's mind fer ef hit hain't to think o' things?"

"It was about—him? It was about Kit Carson, something he had—was it about the gold news?"

"Mebbe. I don't know."

"Did he—Mr. Banion—say anything?"

"Mostly erbout you, an' not much. He only said ef I ever got any mail to send it ter the Judge in the Willamette settlements."

"He does expect to come back to Oregon!"

"How can I tell? My belief, he'd better jump in the Percific Ocean. He's a damn fool, Miss Molly. Ef a man loves a womern, that's somethin' that never orto wait. Yit he goes teeterin' erroun' like he had from now ter doomsday ter marry the girl which he loves too much fer ter marry her. That makes me sick. Yit he has resemblances ter a man, too, some ways—faint resemblances, yes. Fer instance, I'll bet a gun flint these here people that's been hearin' erbout the

ford o' the Snake'd be a hull lot gladder ef they knew Will
Banion was erlong. Huh?"

Molly Wingate was looking far away, pondering many
things.

"Well, anyways, hit's even-Stephen fer them both two
now," went on Bridger, "an' may God perteck the right an'
the devil take the hin'mostest. They'll like enough both
marry Injun wimern an' settle down in Californy. Out o'
sight, out o' mind. Love me little, love me long. Lord Lov-
ell, he's mounted his milkwhite steed. Farewell, sweet sir,
partin' is such sweet sorrer; like ol' Cap'n Bonneville uster
say. But o' all the messes any fool bunch o' pilgrims ever
got inter, this is the worstest, an' hit couldn't be no worser.

"Now, Miss Molly, ye're a plumb diserpintment ter me.
I jest drapped in ter see ef ye couldn't tell me what hit was
Kit done told me. But ye kain't. What is yer boasted super-
iorness as a womern?

"But now, me, havin' did forty mile a day over that country yan, I need sustenance, an' I'm goin' to see ef ol' Cap'
Grant, the post trader, has ary bit o' Hundson Bay rum left.
Ef he has hit's mine, an' ef not, Jim Bridger's a liar, an'
that I say deliberate, I'm goin' to try to git inter normal
condition enough fer to remember a few plain, simple truths,
seein' as you all kain't. Way hit is, this train's in a hell of
a fix, an' hit couldn't be no worser."

Chapter XXXVIII

WHEN THE ROCKIES FELL

The news of Jim Bridger's arrival, and the swift rumor that he would serve as pilot for the train over the dangerous portion of the route ahead, spread an instantaneous feeling of relief throughout the hesitant encampment at this, the last touch with civilization east of the destination. He paused briefly at one or another wagon after he had made his own animals comfortable, laughing and jesting in his own independent way, *en route* to fulfill his promise to himself regarding the trader's rum.

In most ways the old scout's wide experience gave his dicta value. In one assertion, however, he was wide of the truth, or short of it. So far from things being as bad as they could be, the rapid events of that same morning proved that still more confusion was to ensue, and that speedily.

There came riding into the post from the westward a little party of old-time mountain men, driving their near-spent mounts and packs at a speed unusual even in that land of vast distances. They were headed by a man well known in that vicinity who, though he had removed to California since the fur days, made annual pilgrimage to meet the emigrant trains at Fort Hall in order to do proselyting for California, extolling the virtues of that land and picturing in direst fashion the horrors of the road thence to Oregon and the worthlessness of Oregon if ever attained. "Old Greenwood" was the only name by which he was known. He was an old, old man, past eighty then, some said, with a deep blue eye, long white hair, a long and unkempt beard and a tongue of unparalleled profanity. He came in now, shouting and singing, as did the men of the mountains making the Rendezvous in the old days.

"How, Greenwood! What brings ye here so late?" demanded his erstwhile crony, Jim Bridger, advancing, tin cup in hand, to meet him. "Light. Eat. Special, drink. How——to the old times!"

"Old times be damned!" exclaimed Old Greenwood. "These is new times."

He lifted from above the chafed hips of his trembling horse two sacks of something very heavy.

"How much is this worth to ye?" he demanded of Bridger and the trader. "Have ye any shovels? Have ye any picks? Have ye flour, meal, sugar—anything?"

"Gold!" exclaimed Jim Bridger. "Kit Carson did not lie! He never did!"

And they did not know how much this was worth. They had no scales for raw gold, nor any system of valuation for it. And they had no shovels and no pickaxes; and since the families had come they now had very little flour at Fort Hall.

But now they had the news! This was the greatest news that ever came to old Fort Hall—the greatest news America knew for many a year, or the world—the news of the great gold strikes in California.

Old Greenwood suddenly broke out, "Have we left the mines an' come this fur fer nothin'? I tell ye, we must have supplies! A hundred dollars fer a pick! A hundred dollars fer a shovel! A hundred dollars fer a pair o' blankets! An ounce fer a box of sardines, damn ye! An ounce fer half a pound o' butter! A half ounce fer a aig! Anything ye like fer anything that's green! Three hundred fer a gallon o' lik-

ker! A ounce for a box o' pills! Eight hundred fer a barrel
o' flour! Same fer pork, same fer sugar, same fer coffee!
Damn yer picayune hides, we'll show ye what prices is!
What's money to us? We can git the pure gold that money's
made out of, an' git it all we want! Hooray fer Californy!"

He broke into song. His comrades roared in Homeric chorus with him, passing from one to another of the current
ditties of the mines. They declared in unison, "Old Grimes
is dead, that good old man!" Then they swung off to yet
another classic ballad:

> *There was an old woman who had three sons—*
> *Joshua, James and John!*
> *Josh got shot, and Jim got drowned,*
> *And John got lost and never was found,*
> *And that was the end of the woman's three sons,*
> *Joshua, James and John.*

Having finished the obsequies of the three sons, not once
but many times, they went forward with yet another adap-
tation, following Old Greenwood, who stood with head
thrown back and sang with tones of Bashan:

> *Oh, then Susannah,*
> *Don't you cry fer me!*
> *I'm going to Californuah,*
> *With my wash pan on my*
> *knee.*

The news of the gold was out. Bridger forgot his cups,
forgot his friends, hurried to Molly Wingate's cart again.

"Hit's true, Miss Molly!" he cried—"truer'n true hitself!
Yan's men just in from Californy, an' they've got two
horseloads o' gold, an' they say hit's nothin'—they come
out fer supplies. They tried to stop Will Banion—they did
trade some with Woodhull. They're nigh to Humboldt by
now an' goin' hard. Miss Molly, gal, he's in ahead o' the
hull country, an' got six months by hisself! Lord give him
luck! Hit'll be winter afore the men back East kin know.

He's one year ahead—thanks ter yer lie ter me, an ter Kit, and Kit's ter his General.

"Gold! Ye kain't hide hit an' ye kain't find hit an' ye kain't dig hit up an' ye kain't keep hit down. Miss Molly, gal, I like ye, but how I do wish't ye was a man, so's you an' me could celerbrate this here fitten!"

"Listen!" said the girl. "Our bugle! That's Assembly!"

"Yes, they'll all be there. Come when ye kin. Hell's a-poppin' now!"

The emigrants, indeed, deserted their wagons, gathering in front of the stockade, group after group. There was a strange scene on the far-flung, unknown, fateful borderlands of the country Senator McDuffie but now had not valued at five dollars for the whole. All these now, half-way across, and with the ice and snow of winter cutting off pursuit for a year, had the great news which did not reach publication in the press of New York and Baltimore until September of 1848. It did not attain notice of the floor of Congress until December fifth of that year, although this was news that went to the very foundation of this republic; which, indeed, was to prove the means of the perpetuity of this republic.

The drunken hunters in their ragged wools, their stained skins, the emigrants in their motley garb—come this far they knew not why, since men will not admit of Destiny in nations—also knew not that they were joying over the death of slavery and the life of the Union. They did not know that now, in a flash, all the old arguments and citations over slavery and secession were ancient and of no avail. The wagoners of the Sangamon, in Illinois, gathered here, roistering, did not know that they were dancing on the martyr's grave of Lincoln, or weaving him his crown, or buying shot and shell for him to win his grievous ordeal, brother against brother. Yet all those things were settled then, beyond that range of the Rockies which senators had said they would not spend a dollar to remove, "were they no more than ten feet high."

Even then the Rockies fell. Even then the great trains of the covered wagons, driven by men who never heard of

Destiny, achieved their places on the unwritten scroll of Time.

The newcomers from beyond the Sierras, crazed with their easy fortune, and now inflamed yet further by the fumes of alcohol, even magnified the truth, as it then seemed. They spent their dust by the handful. They asked for skillets, cooking pans, that they could wash more gold. They wanted saws, nails, axes, hammers, picks. They said they would use the wagon boxes for Long Torns. They said if men would unite in companies to dam and divert the California rivers they would lay bare ledges of broken gold which would need only scooping up. The miners would pay anything for labor in iron and wood. They would buy any food and all there was of it at a dollar a pound. They wanted pack horses to cross the Humboldt Desert loaded. They would pay any price for men to handle horses for a fast and steady flight.

Because, they said, there was no longer any use in measuring life by the old standards of value. Wages at four bits a day, a dollar a day, two dollars, the old prices—why, no man would work for a half hour for such return when any minute he might lift twenty dollars in the hollow of an iron spoon. Old Greenwood had panned his five hundred in a day. Men had taken two thousand—three—in a week; in a week, men, not in a year! There could be no wage scale at all. Labor was a thing gone by. Wealth, success, ease, luxury was at hand for the taking. What a man had dreamed for himself he now could have. He could overleap all the confining limits of his life, and even if weak, witless, ignorant or in despair, throw all that aside in one vast bound into attainment and enjoyment.

Rich? Why should any man remain poor? Work? Why should work be known, save the labor of picking up pure gold—done, finished, delivered at hand to waiting and weary humanity? Human cravings could no longer exist. Human disappointment was a thing no more to be known. In California, just yonder, was gold, gold, gold! Do you mind—can you think of it, men? Gold, gold, gold! The sun had arisen at last on the millennial day! Now might man be happy and grieve no more forever!

Arguments such as these did not lack and were not needed with the emigrants. It took but a leap to the last conclusion. Go to California? Why should they not go? Had it not been foreordained that they should get the news here, before it was too late? Fifty miles more and they had lost it. A week earlier and they would not have known it for a year. Go to Oregon and plow? Why not go to California and dig in a day what a plow would earn in a year?

Call it stubbornness or steadfastness, at least Jesse Wingate's strength of resolution now became manifest. At first almost alone, he stayed the stampede by holding out for Oregon in the council with his captains.

They stood near the Wingate wagon, the same which had carried him into Indiana, thence into Illinois, now this far on the long way to Oregon. Old and gray was Mary Ann, as he called his wagon, by now, the paint ground from felly, spoke and hub, the sides dust covered, the tilt disfigured and discolored. He gazed at the time-worn, sturdy frame with something akin to affection. The spokes were wedged to hold them tight, the rims were bound with hide, worn away at the edges where the tire gave no covering, the tires had been reset again and again. He shook the nearest wheel to test it.

"Yes," said he, "we all show wear. But I see little use in changing a plan once made in a man's best sober judgment. For me, I don't think all the world has been changed overnight."

"Oh, well, now," demanded Kelsey, his nomad Kentucky blood dominant, "what use holding to any plan just for sake of doing it? If something better comes, why not take it? That stands to reason. We all came out here to better ourselves. These men have done in six months what you and I might not do in ten years in Oregon."

"They'd guide us through to California, too," he went on. "We've no guide to Oregon."

Even Caleb Price nodded.

"They all say that the part from here on is the worst—

drier and drier, and in places very rough. And the two fords of the Snake—well, I for one wish we were across them. That's a big river, and a bad one. And if we crossed the Blue Mountains all right, there's the Cascades, worse than the Blues, and no known trail for wagons."

"I may have to leave my wagons," said Jesse Wingate, "but if I do I aim to leave them as close to the Willamette Valley as I can. I came out to farm. I don't know California. How about you, Hall? What do your neighbors say?"

"Much as Price says. They're worn out and scared. They've been talking about the Snake crossings ever since we left the Soda Springs. Half want to switch for California. A good many others would like to go back home—if they thought they'd ever get there!"

"But we've got to decide," urged Wingate. "Can we count on thirty wagons to go through? Others have got through in a season, and so can we if we stick. Price?"

His hesitant glance at his staunch trail friend's face decided the latter.

"I'll stick for Oregon!" said Caleb Price. "I've got my wife and children along. I want my donation lands."

"You, Hall?"

"I'll go with you," said Hall, the third column leader, slowly. "Like to try a whirl in California, but if there's so much gold there next year'll do. I want my lands."

"Why, there's almost ten thousand people in Oregon by now, or will be next year," argued Wingate. "It may get to be a territory—maybe not a state, but anyways a territory, some time. And it's free! Not like Texas and all this new Mexican land just coming in by the treaty. What do you say, finally, Kelsey?"

The latter chewed tobacco for some time.

"You put it to me hard to answer," said he. "Any one of us'd like to try California. It will open faster the Oregon if all this gold news is true. Maybe ten thousand people will come out next year, for all we know."

"Yes, with picks and shovels," said Jesse Wingate. "Did ever you see pick or shovel build a country? Did ever you see steel traps make or hold one? Oregon's ours because we went out five years ago with wagons and plows—we all know that. No, friends, waterways never held a country. No path ever held on a river—that's for exploring, not for farming. To hold a country you need wheels, you need a plow. I'm for Oregon!"

"You put it strong," admitted Kelsey. "But the only thing that holds me back from California is the promise we four made to each other when we started. Our train's fallen apart little by little. I'm ole Kaintucky. We don't rue back, and we keep our word. We four said we'd go through. I'll stand by that, I'm a man of my word."

Imperiously as though he were Pizarro's self, he drew a line in the dust of the trail.

"Who's for Oregon?" he shouted; again demanded, as silence fell, "This side for Oregon!"

And Kelsey of Kentucky, man of his word, turned the stampede definitely.

Wingate, his three friends; a little group, augmenting, crossed for Oregon. The women and the children stood aloof—sunbonneted women, brown, some with new-born trail babes in arms, silent as they always stood. Across from the Oregon band stood almost as many men, for the most part unmarried, who had not given hostages to fortune, and were resolved for California. A cheer arose from these.

"Who wants my plow?" demanded a stalwart farmer from Indiana, more than fifteen hundred miles from his last home. "I brung her this fur into this damned desert. I'll trade her fer a shovel and make one more try fer my folks back home."

He loosed the wires which had bound the implement to the tail of his wagon all these weary miles. It fell to the ground and he left it there.

"Do some thinking, men, before you count your gold and drop your plow. Gold don't last, but the soil does. Ahead of you is the Humboldt Desert. There's no good wagon road over the mountains if you get that far. The road down Mary's River is a real gamble with death. Men can go through and make roads—yes; but where are the women and the children to stay? Think twice, men, and more than twice!" Wingate spoke solemnly.

"Roll out! Roll out!" mocked the man who had abandoned his plow. "This way for Californy!"

The council ended in turmoil, where hitherto had been no more than a sedate daily system. Routine, become custom, gave way to restless movement, excited argument. Of all these hundreds now encamped on the sandy sagebrush plain in the high desert there was not an individual who was not affected in one way or another by the news from California, and in most cases it required some sort of a personal decision, made practically upon the moment. Men argued with their wives heatedly; women gathered in groups, talking, weeping. The stoic calm of the trail was swept away in a sort of hysteria which seemed to upset all their world and all its old values.

Whether for Oregon or California, a revolution in prices was worked overnight for every purchase of supplies. Flour, horses, tools, everything merchantable, doubled and more than doubled. Some fifty wagons in all now formed train for California, which, in addition to the long line of pack animals, left the Sangamon caravan, so called, at best little more than half what it had been the day before. The men without families made up most of the California train.

The agents for California, by force of habit, still went among the wagons and urged the old arguments against Oregon—the savage tribes on ahead, the forbidding desolation of the land, the vast and dangerous rivers, the certainty of starvation on the way, the risk of arriving after winter had set in on the Cascade Range—all matters of which they themselves spoke by hearsay. All the great West was then unknown. Moreover, Fort Hall was a natural division point, as quite often a third of the wagons of a train might be bound for California even before the discovery of gold. But Wingate and his associates felt that the Oregon immigration for that year, even handicapped as now, ultimately would run into thousands.

It was mid-morning of the next blazing day when he beckoned his men to him.

"Lets pull out, he said. "Why wait for the Californians to move? Bridger will go with us across the Snake. 'Twill only be the worse the longer we lie here, and our wagons are two weeks late now."

The others agreed. But there was now little train organization. The old cheery call, "Catch up! Catch up!" was not heard. The group, the family, the individual now began to show again. True, after their leaders came, one after another, rattling, faded wagons, until the dusty trail that led out across the sage flats had a tenancy stretched out for over a half mile, with yet other vehicles falling in behind; but silent and grim were young and old now over this last defection.

"About that old man Greenwood," said Molly Wingate to her daughter as they sat on the same jolting seat, "I don't know about him. I've saw elders in the church with whiskers as long and white as his'n, but you'd better watch your hog pen. For me, I believe he's a liar. It like enough is true he used to live back in the Rockies in Injun times, and he may be eighty-five years old, as he says, and California may have a wonderful climate, the way he says; but some things I can't believe.

"He says, now, he knows a man out in California, a Spanish man, who was two hundred and fifty years old, and he had quite a lot of money, gold and silver, he'd dug out of the mountains. Greenwood says he's known of gold and silver for years, himself. Well, this Spanish man had relatives that wanted his property, and he'd made a will and left it to them; but he wouldn't die, the climate was so good. So his folks allowed maybe if they sent him to Spain on a journey he'd die and then they'd get the property legal. So he went, and he did die; but he left orders for his body to be sent back to California to be buried. So when his body came they buried him in California, the way he asked—so Greenwood says.

"But did they get his property? Not at all! The old Spanish man, almost as soon as he was buried in California dirt, he came to life again! He's alive today out there, and this man Greenwood says he's a neighbor of his and he knows him well! Of course, if that's true you can believe almost anything about what a wonderful country California is. But for one, I ain't right sure. Maybe not everybody who goes to California is going to find a mountain of gold, or live to be three hundred years old!

"But to think, Molly! Here you knew all this away back to Laramie! Well, if the hoorah had started there 'stead of here there'd be dead people now back of us more'n there is now. That old man Bridger told you—why? And how could you keep the secret?"

"It was for Will," said Molly simply. "I had given him up. I told him to go to California and forget me, and to live things down. Don't chide me any more. I tried to marry the man you wanted me to marry. I'm tired. I'm going to Oregon—to forget. I'll teach school. I'll never, never marry—that's settled at last."

"You got a letter from Sam Woodhull too."

"Yes, I did."

"Huh! Does he call that settled? Is he going to California to forget you and live things down?"

"He says not. I don't care what he says."

"He'll be back."

"Spare his journey! It will do him no good. The Indian did me a kindness, I tell you!"

"Well, anyways, they're both off on the same journey now, and who knows what or which? They both may be three hundred years old before they find a mountain of gold. But to think—I had your chunk of gold right in my own hands, but didn't know it! The same gold my mother's wedding ring was made of, that was mine. It's right thin now, child. You could of made a dozen out of that lump, like enough."

"I'll never need one, mother," said Molly Wingate.

The girl, weeping, threw her arms about her mother's neck. "You ask why I kept the secret, even then. He kissed me, mother—and he was a thief!"

"Yes, I know. A man he just steals a girl's heart out through her lips. Yore paw done that way with me once. Git up, Dan! You, Daisy!

"And from that time on," she added laughing, "I been trying to forget him and to live him down!"

Chapter XXXIX

THE CROSSING

Three days out from Fort Hall the vanguard of the remnant of the train, less than a fourth of the original number, saw leaning against a gnarled sagebrush a box lid which had scrawled upon it in straggling letters one word—"California." Here now were to part the pick and the plow.

Jim Bridger, sitting his gaunt horse, rifle across saddle horn, halted for the head of the train to pull even with him.

"This here's Cassia Creek," said he. "Yan's the trail down Raft River ter the Humboldt and acrost the Sierrys ter Californy. A long, dry jump hit is, by all accounts. The Oregon road goes on down the Snake. Hit's longer, if not so dry."

Small invitation offered in the physical aspect of either path. The journey had become interminable. The unspeakable monotony, whose only variant was peril, had smothered the spark of hope and interest. The allurement of mystery had wholly lost its charm.

The train halted for some hours. Once more discussion rose.

"Last chance for Californy, men," said old Jim Bridger

calmly. "Do-ee see the tracks? Here's Greenwood come in. Yan's where Woodhull's wagons left the road. Below that, one side, is the tracks o' Banion's mules."

"I wonder," he added, "why thar hain't ary letter left fer none o' us here at the forks o' the road."

He did not know that, left in a tin at the foot of the board sign certain days earlier, there had rested a letter addressed to Miss Molly Wingate. It never was to reach her. Sam Woodhull knew the reason why. Having opened it and read it, he had possessed himself of exacter knowledge than ever before of the relations of Banion and Molly Wingate. Bitter as had been his hatred before, it now was venomous. He lived thenceforth no more in hope of gold than of revenge.

The decision for or against California was something for serious weighing now at the last hour, and it affected the fortune and the future of every man, woman and child in all the train. Never a furrow was plowed in early Oregon but ran in bones and blood; and never a dollar was dug in gold in California—or ever gained in gold by any man—which did not cost two in something else but gold.

Twelve wagons pulled out of the trail silently, one after another, and took the winding trail that led to the left, to the west and south. Others watched them, tears in their eyes, for some were friends.

Alone on her cart seat, here at the fateful parting of the ways, Molly Wingate sat with a letter clasped in her hand, frank tears standing in her eyes. It was no new letter, but an old one. She pressed the pages to her heart, to her lips, held them out at arm's length before her in the direction of the far land which somewhere held its secrets.

"Oh, God keep you, Will!" she said in her heart, and almost audibly. "Oh, God give you fortune, Will, and bring you back to me!"

But the Oregon wagons closed up once more and held their way, the stop not being beyond one camp, for Bridger urged haste.

The caravan course now lay along the great valley of the Snake. The giant deeds of the river in its cañons they could only guess. They heard of tremendous falls, of gorges through which no boat could pass, vague rumors of days of earlier exploration; but they kept to the high plateaus, dipping down to the crossings of many sharp streams, which in the first month of their journey they would have called impassable. It all took time. They were averaging now not twenty miles daily, but no more than half that, and the season was advancing. It was fall. Back home the wheat would be in stack, the edges of the corn would be seared with frost.

The vast abundance of game they had found all along now lacked. Some rabbits, a few sage grouse, nightly coyotes— that made all. The savages who now hung on their flanks lacked the stature and the brave trappings of the buffalo plainsmen. They lived on horse meat and salmon, so the rumor came. Now their environment took hold of the Pacific. They had left the East wholly behind.

On the salmon run they could count on food, not so good as the buffalo, but better than bacon grown soft and rusty. Changing, accepting, adjusting, prevailing, the wagons went on, day after day, fifty miles, hundred, two hundred. But always a vague uneasiness pervaded. The crossing of the Snake lay on ahead. The moody river had cast upon them a feeling of awe. Around the sage fires at night the families talked of little else but the ford of the Snake, two days beyond the Salmon Falls.

It was morning when the wagons, well drawn together now, at last turned down the precipitous decline which took them from the high plateau to the water level. Here a halt was called. Bridger took full charge. The formidable enterprise confronting them was one of the real dangers of the road.

The strong green waters of the great river were divided at this ancient ford by two midstream islands, which accounted for the selection of the spot for the daring essay of a bridgeless and boatless crossing. There was something mockingly relentless in the strong rippling current, which cut off more than a guess at the actual depth. There was no ferry, no boat nor means of making one. It was not even possible to shore up the wagon beds so they might be dry.

One thing sure was that if ever a wagon was swept below the crossing there could be no hope for it.

But others had crossed here, and even now a certain rough chart existed, handed down from these. Time now for a leader, and men now were thankful for the presence of a man who had seen this crossing made.

The old scout held back the company leaders and rode into the stream alone, step by step, scanning the bottom. He found it firm. He saw wheel marks on the first island. His horse, ears ahead, saw them also, and staggeringly felt out the way. Belly-deep and passable—yes.

Bridger turned and moved a wide arm. The foremost wagons came on to the edge.

The men now mounted the wagon seats, two to each wagon. Flankers drove up the loose cattle, ready for their turn later. Men rode on each side the lead yoke of oxen to hold them steady on their footing, Wingate, Price, Kelsey and Hall, bold men and well mounted, taking this work on themselves.

The plunge once made, they got to the first island, all of them, without trouble. But a dizzying flood lay on ahead to the second wheel-marked island in the river. To look at the rapid surface was to lose all sense of direction. But again the gaunt horse of the scout fell out, the riders waded in, their devoted saddle animals trembling beneath them. Bridger, student of fast fords, followed the bar upstream, angling with it, till a deep channel offered between him and the island. Unable to evade this, he drove into it, and his gallant mount breasted up and held its feet all the way across.

The thing could be done! Jim Bridger calmly turned and waved to the wagons to come on from the first island.

"Keep them jest whar we was!" he called back to Hall and Kelsey, who had not passed the last stiff water. "Put the heavy cattle in fust! Hit maybe won't swim them. If the stuff gets wet we kain't help that. Tell the wimern hit's all right."

He saw his friends turn back, their horses, deep in the flood, plunging through water broken by their knees; saw the first wagons lead off and crawl out upstream, slowly and safely, till within reach of his voice. Molly now was in the main wagon, and her brother Jed was driving.

Between the lines of wading horsemen the draft oxen advanced, following the wagons, strung out, but all holding their footing in the green water that broke white on the upper side of the wagons. A vast murmuring roar came up from the water thus retarded.

They made their way to the edge of the deep channel, where the cattle stood, breasts submerged.

Bridger rose in his stirrups and shouted, "Git in thar! Come on through!"

They plunged, wallowed, staggered; but the lead yokes saw where the ford climbed the bank, made for it, caught footing, dragged the others through!

Wagon after wagon made it safe. It was desperate, but being done, these matter-of-fact folk wasted no time in imaginings of what might have happened. They were safe, and the ford thus far was established so that the others need not fear.

But on ahead lay what they all knew was the real danger—the last channel, three hundred yards of racing, heavy water which apparently no sane man ever would have faced. But there were wheel marks on the farther shore. Here ran the road to Oregon.

The dauntless old scout rode in again, alone, bending to study the water and the footing. A gravel bar led off for a couple of rods, flanked by deep potholes. Ten rods out the bar turned. He followed it up, foot by foot, for twenty rods, quartering. Then he struck out for the shore.

The bottom was hard, yes; but the bar was very crooked, with swimming water on either hand, with potholes ten feet deep and more all alongside. And worst of all, there was a vast sweep of heavy water below the ford, which meant destruction and death for any wagon carried down. Well had the crossing of the Snake earned its sinister reputation. Courage and care alone could give any man safe-conduct here.

The women and children, crying, sat in the wagons, watching Bridger retrace the ford. Once his stumbling horse swam, but caught footing. He joined them, very serious.

"Hit's fordin' men," said he, "but she's mean, she shore is mean. Double up all the teams, yoke in every loose ox an' put six yoke on each wagon, er they'll get swep' down, shore's hell. Some o' them will hold the others ef we have enough. I'll go ahead, an' I want riders all along the teams, above and below, ter hold them ter the line. Hit can be did—hit's wicked water, but hit can be did. Don't wait—always keep things movin'."

By this time the island was packed with the loose cattle, which had followed the wagons, much of the time swimming. They were lowing moaningly, in terror—a gruesome thing to hear.

The leader called to Price's oldest boy, driving Molly's cart, "Tie on behind the big wagon with a long rope, an' don't drive in tell you see the fust two yoke ahead holdin'. Then they'll drag you through anyhow. Hang onto the cart whatever happens, but if you do get in, keep upstream of any animile that's swimmin'."

"All set, men? Come ahead!"

He led off again at last, after the teams were doubled and the loads had been piled high as possible to keep them dry. Ten wagons were left behind, it being needful to drive back, over the roaring channel, some of the doubled heavy teams for them.

They made it well, foot by foot, the cattle sometimes swimming gently, confidently, as the line curved down under the heavy current, but always enough holding to keep the team safe. The horsemen rode alongside, exhorting, assuring. It was a vast relief when at the last gravel stretch they saw the wet backs of the oxen rise high once more.

"I'll go back, Jesse," said Kelsey, the man who had wanted to go to California. "I know her now."

"I'll go with you," added young Jed Wingate, climbing down from his wagon seat and demanding his saddle horse, which he mounted bare-backed.

It was they two who drove and led the spare yokes back to repeat the crossing with the remaining wagons. Those on the bank watched them anxiously, for they drove straighter across to save time, and were carried below the trail on the island. But they came out laughing, and the oxen were rounded up once more and doubled in, so that the last of the train was ready.

"That's a fine mare of Kelsey's," said Wingate to Caleb Price, who with him was watching the daring Kentuckian at his work on the downstream and more dangerous side of the linked teams. "She'll go anywhere."

Price nodded, anxiously regarding the laboring advance of the last wagons.

"Too light," said he. "I started with a ton and a half on the National Pike across Ohio and Indiana. I doubt if we average five hundred now. They ford light."

"Look!" he cried suddenly, and pointed.

They all ran to the brink. The horsemen were trying to stay the drift of the line of cattle. They had worked low and missed footing. Many were swimming—the wagons were afloat!

The tired lead cattle had not been able to withstand the pressure of the heavy water a second time. They were off the ford!

But the riders from the shore, led by Jim Bridger, got to them, caught a rope around a horn, dragged them into line, dragged the whole gaunt team to the edge and saved the day for the lead wagon. The others caught and held their footing, labored through.

But a shout arose. Persons ran down the bank, pointing. A hundred yards below the ford, in the full current of the Snake, the lean head of Kelsey's mare was flat, swimming hard and steadily, being swept downstream in a current which swung off shore below the ford.

"He's all right!" called Jed, wet to the neck, sitting his own wet mount, safe ashore at last. "He's swimming too. They'll make it, sure! Come on!"

He started off at a gallop downstream along the shore, his eyes fixed on the two black objects, now steadily losing distance out beyond. But old Jim Bridger put his hands across his eyes and turned away his face. He knew!

It was now plain to all that yonder a gallant man and a

gallant horse were making a fight for life. The grim river had them in its grip at last.

In a moment the tremendous power of the heavy water had swept Kelsey and his horse far below the ford. The current there was swifter, noisier, as though exultant in the success of the scheme the river, all along had proposed.

As to the victims, the tragic struggle went on in silence. If the man called, no one could hear him above the rush and roar of the waters. None long had any hope as they saw the white rollers bury the two heads, of the horse and the man, while the set of the current steadily carried them away from the shore. It was only a miracle that the two bobbing black dots again and again came into view.

They could see the mare's muzzle flat, extended toward the shore; back of it, upstream, the head of the man. Whichever brain had decided, it was evident that the animal was staking life to reach the shore from which it had been swept away.

Far out in midstream some conformation of the bottom turned the current once more in a long slant shoreward. A murmur, a sob of hundreds of observers packed along the shore broke out as the two dots came closer, far below. More than a quarter of a mile downstream a sand point made out, offering a sort of beach where for some space a landing might be made. Could the gallant mare make this point? Men clenched their hands. Women began to sob, to moan gently.

When with a shout Jed Wingate turned his horse and set off at top speed down the shore some followed him. The horses and oxen, left alone, fell into confusion, the wagons tangled. One or two teams made off at a run into the desert. But these things were nothing.

Those behind hoped Jed would not try any rescue in that flood. Molly stood wringing her hands. The boy's mother began praying audibly. The voice of Jim Bridger rose in an Indian chant. It was for the dead!

They saw the gallant mare plunge up, back and shoulders and body rising as her feet found bottom a few yards out from shore. She stood free of the water, safe on the bar;

stood still, looking back of her and down. But no man rose to his height beside her. There was only one figure on the bar.

They saw Jed fling off; saw him run and stoop, lifting something long and heavy from the water. Then the mare stumbled away. At length she lay down quietly. She never rose.

"She was standing right here," said Jed as the others came. "He had hold of the reins so tight I couldn't hardly open his hand. He must have been dead before the mare hit bottom. He was laying all under water, hanging to the reins, and that was all that kept him from washing on down."

They made some rude and unskilled attempt at resuscitation, but had neither knowledge nor confidence. Perhaps somewhere out yonder the strain had been too great; perhaps the sheer terror had broken the heart of both man and horse. The mare suddenly began to tremble as she lay, her nostrils shivering as though in fright. And she died, after bringing in the dead man whose hand still gripped her rein.

They buried Kelsey of Kentucky—few knew him otherwise—on a hillock by the road at the first fording place of the Snake. They broke out the top board of another tail gate, and with a hot iron burned in one more record of the road:

"Rob't. Kelsey, Ky. Drowned Sept. 7, 1848. A Brave Man."

The sand long ago cut out the lettering, and long ago the ford passed to a ferry. But there lay, for a long time known, Kelsey of Kentucky, a brave man, who kept his promise and did not rue back, but who never saw either California or Oregon.

"Catch up the stock, men," said Jesse Wingate dully, after a time. "Let's leave this place."

Loads were repacked, broken gear adjusted. Inside the hour the silent gray wagon train held on, leaving the waters to give shriving. The voice of the river rose and fell mournfully behind them in the changing airs.

"I knowed hit!" said old Jim Bridger, now falling back from the lead and breaking off his Indian dirge. "I knowed all along the Snake'd take somebody—she does every time.

This mornin' I seed two ravens that flew acrost the trail ahead. Yesterday I seed a rabbit settin' squar' in the trail. I thought hit was me the river wanted, but she's done took a younger an' a better man."

"Man, man," exclaimed stout-hearted Molly Wingate, "what for kind of a country have you brought us women to? One more thing like that and my nerve's gone. Tell me, is this the last bad river? And when will we get to Oregon?"

"Don't be a-skeered, ma'am," rejoined Bridger. "A accident kin happen anywheres. Hit's a month on ter Oregon, whar ye're headed. Some fords on ahead, yes; we got ter cross back ter the south side the Snake again."

"But you'll go on with us, won't you?" demanded young Molly Wingate.

They had halted to breathe the cattle at the foot of lava dust slope. Bridger looked at the young girl for a time in silence.

"I'm off my country, Miss Molly," said he. "Beyant the second ford, at Fort Boise, I ain't never been. I done aimed ter turn back here an' git back home afore the winter come. Ain't I did enough fer ye?"

But he hesitated. There was a kindly light on the worn old face, in the sunken blue eye.

"Ye want me ter go on, Miss Molly?"

"If you could it would be a comfort to me, a protection to us all."

"Is hit so! Miss Molly, ye kin talk a ol'-time man out'n his last pelt! But sence ye do want me, I'll sornter along a leetle ways furtherer with ye. Many a good fight is spoiled by wonderin' how hit's goin' to come out. An' many a long trail's lost by wonderin' whar hit runs. I hain't never yit been plumb to Californy er Oregon. But ef ye say I must, Miss Molly, why I must; an' ef I must, why here goes! I reckon my wimern kin keep my fire goin' ontel I git back next year."

Chapter XL

OREGON! OREGON!

The freakish resolves of the old-time trapper at least remained unchanged for many days, but at last one evening he came to Molly's wagon, his face grim and sad.

"Miss Molly," he said, "I'm come to say good-by now. Hit's for keeps."

"No? Then why? You are like an old friend to me. What don't I owe to you?"

"Ye don't owe nothin' ter me yit, Miss Molly. But I want ye ter think kindly o' old Jim Bridger when he's gone. I allow the kindest thing I kin do fer ye is ter bring Will Banion ter ye."

"You are a good man, James Bridger," said Molly Wingate. "But then?"

"Ye see, Miss Molly, I had six quarts o' rum I got at Boise. Some folks says rum is wrong. Hit ain't. I'll tell ye why. Last night I drinked up my lastest bottle o' that Hundson's Bay rum. Hit war right good rum, an ez I lay lookin' up at the stars, all ter oncet hit come ter me that I was jest exactly, no more an' no less, jest ter the ha'r, ez drunk I was on the leetle spree with Kit at Laramie. Warn't that fine? An' warn't hit useful? Nach'erl, bein' jest even up, I done thought o' everything I been fergettin'. Hit all come ter me ez plain ez a streak o' lightnin'. What it was Kit Carson told me I know now, but no one else shall know. No, not even you, Miss Molly. I kain't tell ye, so don't ask.

"Now I'm goin' on a long journey, an' a resky one; I kain't tell ye no more. I reckon I'll never see ye agin. So good-by."

With a swift grasp of his hand he caught the dusty edge of the white woman's skirt to his bearded lips.

"But, James—"

Suddenly she reached out a hand. He was gone.

* * *

One winter day, rattling over the icy fords of the road winding down the Sandy from the white Cascades, crossing the Clackamas, threading the intervening fringe of forest, there broke into the clearing at Oregon City the head of the wagon train of 1848. A fourth of the wagons abandoned and broken, a half of the horses and cattle gone since they had left the banks of the Columbia east of the mountains, the cattle leaning one against the other when they halted, the oxen stumbling and limping, the calluses of their necks torn, raw and bleeding from the swaying of the yokes on the rocky trail, their tongues out, their eyes glassy with the unspeakable toil they so long had undergone; the loose wheels wabbling, the thin hounds rattling, the canvas sagged and stained, the bucket under each wagon empty, the plow at each tail gate thumping in its lashings of rope and hide— the train of the covered wagons now had, indeed, won through. Now may the picture of our own Ark of Empire never perish from our minds.

On the front seat of the lead wagon sat stout Molly Wingate and her husband. Little Molly's cart came next. Alongside the Caleb Price wagon, wherein now sat on the seat— hugging a sore-footed dog whose rawhide boots had worn through—a long-legged, barefoot girl who had walked twelve hundred miles since spring, trudged Jed Wingate, now grown from a tousled boy into a lean, self-reliant young man. His long whip was used in baseless threatenings now, for any driver must spare cattle such as these, gaunt and hollow-eyed. Tobacco protuberant in cheek, his feet half bare, his trousers ragged and fringed to the knee, his sleeves rolled up over brown and brawny arms, Jed Wingate now was enrolled on the list of men.

"Gee-whoa-haw! You Buck an' Star, git along there, damn ye!" So rose his voice, automatically but affectionately.

Certain French Canadians, old-time *engagés* of the fur posts, now become *habitants*, landowners, on their way home from Sunday chapel, hastened to summon others.

"The families have come!" they called at the Falls, as they had at Portland town.

But now, though safely enlarged at last of the confinement and the penalties of the wagon train, the emigrants, many of them almost destitute, none of them of great means, needed to cast about them at once for their locations and to determine what their occupations were to be. They scattered, each seeking his place, like new trout in a stream.

Chapter XLI

THE SECRETS OF THE SIERRAS

Sam Woodhull carried in his pocket the letter which Will Banion had left for Molly Wingate at Cassia Creek in the Snake Valley, where the Oregon road forked for California. There was no post office there, yet Banion felt sure that his letter would find its way, and it had done so, save for the treachery of this one man. Naught had been sacred to him. He had read the letter without an instant's hesitation, feeling that anything was fair in his love for this woman, in his war with this man. Woodhull resolved that they should not both live.

He was by nature not so much a coward as a man without principle or scruple. He did not expect to be killed by Banion. He intended to use such means as would give Banion no chance. In this he thought himself fully justified, as a criminal always does.

But hurry as he might, his overdriven teams were no match for the tireless desert horse, the wiry mountain mount and the hardy mules of the tidy little pack train of Banion and his companion Jackson. These could go on steadily where wagons must wait. Their trail grew fainter as they gained.

At last, at the edge of a waterless march of whose duration they could not guess, Woodhull and his party were obliged to halt. Here by great good fortune they were overtaken by the swift pack train of Greenwood and his men, hurrying back with fresh animals on their return march to California. The two companies joined forces. Woodhull now had a guide. Accordingly when, after such dangers and hardships as then must be inevitable to men covering the gruesome trail between the Snake and the Sacramento, he found himself late that fall arrived west of the Sierras and in the gentler climate of the central valley, he looked about him with a feeling of exultation. Now, surely, fate would give his enemy into his hand.

Men were spilling south into the valley of the San Joaquin, coming north with proofs of the Stanislaus, the Tuolumne, the Merced. Greenwood insisted on working north into the country where he had found gold, along all the tributaries of the Sacramento. Even then, too, before the great year of '49 had dawned, prospectors were pushing to the head of the creeks making into the American Fork, the Feather River, all the larger and lesser streams heading on the west slopes of the Sierras; and Greenwood even heard of a band of men who had stolen away from the lower diggings and broken off to the north and east—some said, heading far up for the Trinity, though that was all unproved country so far as most knew.

And now the hatred in Woodhull's sullen heart grew hotter still, for he heard that not fifty miles ahead there had passed a quiet dark young man, riding a black Spanish horse; with him a bearded man who drove a little band of loaded mules! Their progress, so came the story, was up a valley whose head was impassable. The trail could not be obliterated back of them. They were in a trap of their own choosing. All that he needed was patience and caution.

Ships and wagon trains came in on the Willamette from the East. They met the coast news of gold. Men of Oregon also left in a mad stampede for California. News came that all the world now was in the mines of California. All over the East, as the later ships also brought in reiterated news, the mad craze of '49 even then was spreading.

But the men of '48 were in ahead. From them, scattering like driven game among the broken country over hundreds of miles of forest, plain, bench land and valley lands, no word could come out to the waiting world. None might know the countless triumphs, the unnumbered tragedies— none ever did know.

There, beyond the law, one man might trail another with murder stronger than avarice in his heart, and none ever be the wiser. To hide secrets such as these the unfathomed mountains reached out their shadowy arms.

*   *   *

Now the winter wore on with such calendar as altitude, latitude, longitude gave it, and the spring of '49 came, East and West, in Washington and New York; at Independence on the Missouri; at Deseret by the Great Salt Lake; in California; in Oregon.

Above the land of the early Willamette settlements forty or fifty miles up the Yamhill Valley, so a letter from Mrs. Caleb Price to her relatives in Ohio said, the Wingates, leaders of the train, had a beautiful farm, near by the Cale Price Mill, as it was known. They had up a good house of five rooms, and their cattle were increasing now. They had forty acres in wheat, with what help the neighbors had given in housing and planting; and wheat would run fifty bushels to the acre there. They had bought young trees for an orchard. Her mother had planted roses; they now were fine. She believed they were as good as those she planted in Portland, when first she went through there—cuttings she had carried with her seed wheat in the bureau drawer, all the way across from the Saganon. Yes, Jesse Wingate and his wife had done well. Molly, their daughter, was still living with them and still unmarried, she believed.

There were many things which Mrs. Caleb Price believed; also many things she did not mention.

She said nothing, for she knew nothing, of a little scene between these two as they sat on their little sawn-board porch before their door one evening, looking out over the beautiful and varied landscape that lay spread before them. Their wheat was in the green now. Their hogs reveled in their little clover field.

"We've done well, Jesse," at length said portly Molly Wingate. "Look at our place! A mile square, for nothing! We've done well, Jesse, I'll admit it."

"For what?" answered Jesse Wingate. "What's it for? What has it come to? What's it all about?"

He did not have any reply. When he turned he saw his wife wiping tears from her hard, lined face.

"It's Molly," said she.

Chapter XLII

KIT CARSON RIDES

Following the recession of the snow, men began to push westward up the Platte in the great spring gold rush of 1849. In the fore-front of these, outpacing them in his tireless fashion, now passed westward the greatest traveler of his day, the hunter and scout, Kit Carson. The new post of Fort Kearny on the Platte; the old one, Fort Laramie in the foothills of the Rockies—he touched them soon as the grass was green; and as the sun warmed the bunch grass slopes of the North Platte and the Sweet-water, so that his horses could paw out a living, he crowded on westward. He was a month ahead of the date for the wagon trains at Fort Bridger.

"How, Chardon!" said he as he drove in his two light packs, riding alone as was his usual way, evading Indian eyes as he of all men best knew how.

"How, Kit! You're early. Why?" The trader's chief clerk turned to send a boy for Vasquez, Bridger's partner. "Light, Kit, and eat."

"Where's Bridger?" demanded Carson. "I've come out of my country to see him. I have government mail—for Oregon."

"For Oregon? *Mon Dieu!* But Jeem"—he spread out his hands—"Jeem, he's dead, we'll think. We do not known. Now we know the gold news. Maybe-so we know why Jeem he's gone!"

"Gone? When?"

"Las' H'august-Settemb. H'all of an' at once he'll took the trail h'after the h'emigrant train las' year. He'll caught him h'on Fort Hall; we'll heard. But then he go h'on with those h'emigrant beyon' Hall, beyon' the fork for Califor'n'. He'll not come back. No one know what has become of Jeem. He'll been dead, maybe-so."

"Yes? Maybe-so not! That old rat knows his way through the mountains, and he'll take his own time. You think he did not go on to California?"

"We'll know he'll didn't."

Carson stood and thought for a time.

"Well, its bad for you, Chardon!"

"How you mean, M'sieu Kit?"

"Eat your last square meal. Saddle your best horse. Drive four packs and two saddle mounts along."

"*Oui?* And where?"

"To Oregon!"

"To Oregon? *Sacre 'Fan!'* What you mean?"

"By authority of the Government, I command you to carry this packet on to Oregon this season, as fast as safety may allow. Take a man with you—two; pick up any help you need. But go through.

"I cannot go further west myself, for I must get back to Laramie. I had counted on Jim, and Jim's post must see me through. Make your own plans to start tomorrow morning. I'll arrange all that with Vasquez."

"But, M'sieu Kit, I cannot!"

"But you shall, you must, you will! If I had a better man I'd send him, but you are to do what Jim wants done."

"*Mais, oui*, of course."

"Yes. And you'll do what the President of the United States commands."

"*Bon Dieu*, Kit!"

"That packet is over the seal of the United States of

America, Chardon. It carries the signature of the President. It was given to the Army to deliver. The Army has given it to me. I give it to you, and you must go. It is for Jim. He would know. It must be placed in the hands of the Circuit Judge acting under the laws of Oregon, whoever he may be, and wherever. Find him in the Willamette country. Your pay will be more than you think, Chardon. Jim would know. Dead or alive, you do this for him.

"You can do thirty miles a day. I know you as a mountain man. Ride! Tomorrow I start east to Laramie—and you start west for Oregon!"

And in the morning following two riders left Bridger's for the trail. They parted, each waving a hand to the other.

Chapter XLIII

THE KILLER KILLED

A rough low cabin of logs, hastily thrown together, housed through the winter months of the Sierra foothills the two men who now, in the warm days of early June, sat by the primitive fireplace cooking a midday meal. The older man, thin, bearded, who now spun a side of venison ribs on a cord in front of the open fire, was the mountain man, Bill Jackson, as anyone might tell who ever had seen him, for he had changed but little.

That his companion, younger, bearded, dressed also in buckskins, was Will Banion it would have taken closer scrutiny even of a friend to determine, so much had the passing of these few months altered him in appearance and in manner. Once light of mien, now he smiled never at all. For hours he would seem to go about his duties as an automaton. He spoke at last to his ancient and faithful friend, kindly as ever, and with his own alertness and decision.

"Let's make it our last meal on the Trinity, Bill. What do you say?"

"Why? What's eatin' ye, boy? Gittin' restless again?"

"Yes, I want to move."

"Most does."

"We've got enough, Bill. The last month has been a crime. The spring snows uncovered a fortune for us, and you know it!"

"Oh, yes, eight hundred in one day ain't bad for two men that never had saw a gold pan a year ago. But she ain't petered yit. With what we've learned, an' what we know, we kin stay in here an' git so rich that hit shore makes me cry ter think o' trappin' beaver, even before 1836, when the beaver market busted. Why, rich? Will, hit's like you say, plumb wrong—we done hit so damned easy! I lay awake nights plannin' how ter spend my share o' this pile. We must have fifty-sixty thousand dollars o' dust buried under the floor, don't ye think?"

"Yes, more. But if you'll agree, I'll sell this claim to the company below us and let them have the rest. They offer fifty thousand flat, and it's enough—more than enough. I want two things—to get Jim Bridger his share safe and sound; and I want to go to Oregon."

The old man paused in the act of splitting off a deer rib from his roast.

"Ye're one awful damn fool, ain't ye, Will? I did hope ter finish up here, a-brilin' my meat in a yaller-gold fireplace; but no matter how plain an' simple a man's tastes is, allus somethin' comes along ter bust 'em up."

"Well, go on and finish your meal in this plain fireplace of ours, Bill. It has done us very well. I think I'll go down to the sluice a while."

Banion rose and left the cabin, stooping at the low door. Moodily he walked along the side of the steep ravine to which the little structure clung. Below him lay the ripped-open slope where the little stream had been diverted. Below again lay the bared bed of the exploited water course, floored with bowlders set in deep gravel, at times with seamy dams of flat rock lying under and across the gravel stretches; the bed rock, ages old, holding in its hidden fingers the rich secrets of immemorial time.

Here he and his partner had in a few months of strenuous

labor taken from the narrow and unimportant rivulet more wealth than most could save in a lifetime of patient and thrifty toil. Yes, fortune had been kind. And it all had been so easy, so simple, so unagitating, so matter-of-fact! The hillside now looked like any other hillside, innocent as a woman's eyes, yet covering how much! Banion could not realize that now, young though he was, he was a rich man.

He climbed down the side of the ravine, the little stones rattling under his feet, until he stood on the bared floor of the bed rock which had proved so unbelievably prolific in coarse gold.

There was a sharp bend in the ravine, and here the unpaid toil of the little waterway had, ages long, carried and left especially deep strata of gold-shot gravel. As he stood, half musing, Will Banion heard, on the ravine side around the bend, the tinkle of a falling stone, lazily rolling from one impediment to another. It might be some deer or other animal, he thought. He hastened to get view of the cause, whatever it might be.

And then fate, chance, the goddess of fortune which some men say does not exist, but which all wilderness-goers know does exist, for one instant paused, with Will Banion's life and wealth and happiness lightly a-balance in cold, disdainful fingers.

He turned the corner. Almost level with his own, he looked into the eyes of a crawling man who—stooped, one hand steadying himself against the slant of the ravine, the other below, carrying a rifle—was peering frowningly ahead.

It was an evil face, bearded, aquiline, not unhandsome; but evil in its plain meaning now. The eyes were narrowed, the full lips drawn close, as though some tense emotion now approached its climax. The appearance was that of strain, of nerves stretched in some purpose long sustained.

And why not? When a man would do murder, when that has been his steady and premeditated purpose for a year, waiting only for opportunity to serve his purpose, that purpose itself changes his very lineaments, alters his whole cast of countenance. Other men avoid him, knowing unconsciously what is in his soul, because of what is written on his face.

For months most men had avoided Woodhull. It was known that he was on a man hunt. His questions, his movements, his changes of locality showed that; and Woodhull was one of those who cannot avoid asseverance, needing it for their courage sake. Now morose and brooding, now loudly profane, now laughing or now aloof, his errand in these unknown hills was plain. Well, he was not along among men whose depths were loosed. Some time his hour might come.

It had come! He stared now full into the face of his enemy! He at last had found him. Here stood his enemy, unarmed, delivered into his hands.

For one instant the two stood, staring into one another's eyes. Banion's advance had been silent. Woodhull was taken as much unawares as he.

It had been Woodhull's purpose to get a stand above the sluices, hidden by the angle, where he could command the reach of the stream bed where Banion and Jackson last had been working. He had studied the place before, and meant to take no chances. His shot must be sure.

But now, in his climbing on the steep hillside, his rifle was in his left hand, downhill, and his footing, caught as he was with one foot half raised, was insecure. At no time these last four hours had his opportunity been so close—or so poor—as precisely now!

He saw Will Banion's eyes, suddenly startled, quickly estimating, looking into his own. He knew that behind his own eyes his whole foul soul lay bared—the soul of a murderer.

Woodhull made a swift spring down the hill, scrambling, half erect, and caught some sort of stance for the work which now was his to do. He snarled, for he saw Banion stoop, unarmed. It would do his victim no good to run. There was time even to exult, and that was much better in a long-deferred matter such as this.

"Now, damn you, I've got you!"

He gave Banion that much chance to see that he was now to die.

Half leaning, he raised the long rifle to its line and touched the trigger.

The report came; and Banion fell. But even as he wheeled and fell, stumbling down the hillside, his flung arm apparently had gained a weapon. It was not more than the piece of rotten quartz he had picked up and planned to examine later. He flung it straight at Woodhull's face—an act of chance, of instinct. By a hair it saved him.

Firing and missing at a distance of fifty feet, Woodhull remained not yet a murderer in deed. In a flash Banion gathered and sprang toward him as he stood in a half second of consternation at seeing his victim fall and rise again. The rifle carried but the one shot. He flung it down, reached for his heavy knife, raising an arm against the second piece of rock which Banion flung as he closed. He felt his wrist caught in an iron grip, felt the blood gush where his temple was cut by the last missile. And then once more, on the narrow bared floor that but now was patterned in parquetry traced in yellow, and soon must turn to red, it came to man and man between them—and it was free!

They fell and stumbled so that neither could much damage the other at first. Banion knew he must keep the impounded hand back from the knife sheath or he was done. Thus close, he could make no escape. He fought fast and furiously, striving to throw, to bend, to beat back the body of a man almost as strong as himself, and now a maniac in rage and fear.

The sound of the rifle shot rang through the little defile. To Jackson, shaving off bits of sweet meat between thumb and knife blade, it meant the presence of a stranger, friend or foe, for he knew Banion had carried no weapon with him. His own long rifle he snatched from its pegs. At a long, easy lope he ran along the path which carried across the face of the ravine. His moccasined feet made no sound. He saw no one in the creek bed or at the long turn. But now there came a loud, wordless cry which he knew was meant for him. It was Will Banion's voice.

The two struggling men grappled below him had no notion of how long they had fought. It seemed an age, and the dénouement yet another age deferred. But to them came the sound of a voice:

"Git away, Will! Stand back!"

It was Jackson.

They both, still gripped, looked up the bank. The long barrel of a rifle, foreshortened to a black point, above it a cold eye, fronted and followed them as they swayed. The crooked arm of the rifleman was motionless, save as it just moved that deadly circle an inch this way, an inch back again.

Banion knew that this was murder, too, but he knew that naught on earth could stay it now. To guard as much as he could against a last desperate knife thrust even of a dying man, he broke free and sprang back as far as he could, falling prostrate on his back as he did so, tripped by an unseen stone. But Sam Woodhull was not upon him now, was not willing to lose his own life in order to kill. For just one instant he looked up at the death staring down on him, then turned to run.

There was no place where he could run. The voice of the man above him called out sharp and hard.

"Halt! Sam Woodhull, look at me!"

He did turn, in horror, in fascination at sight of the Bright Angel. The rifle barrel to his last gaze became a small, round circle, large as a bottle top, and around it shone a fringed aura of red and purple light. That might have been the eye.

Steadily as when he had held his friend's life in his hand, sighting five inches above his eyes, the old hunter drew now above the eyes of his enemy. When the dry report cut the confined air of the valley, the body of Sam Woodhull started forward. The small blue hole an inch above the eyes showed the murderer's man hunt done.

Chapter XLIV

YET IF LOVE LACK

Winding down out of the hills into the grassy valley of
the Upper Sacramento, the little pack train of Banion
and Jackson, six hardy mules beside the black horse and
Jackson's mountain pony, picked its way along a gashed and
trampled creek bed. The kyacks which swung heavy on the
strongest two mules might hold salt or lead or gold. It all
was one to any who might have seen, and the two silent
men, the younger ahead, the older behind, obviously were
men able to hold their counsel or to defend their property.

The smoke of a distant encampment caught the keen eye
of Jackson as he rode, humming, care-free, the burden of a
song.

"Oh, then, Susannah!" admonished the old mountain man,
and bade the said Susannah to be as free of care as he himself then and there was.

"More men comin' in," said he presently. "Wonder who
them people is, an' ef hit's peace er war."

"Three men. A horse band. Two Indians. Go in easy,
Bill."

Banion slowed down his own gait. His companion had tied the six mules together, nose and tail, with the halter of the lead mule wrapped on his own saddle horn. Each man now drew his rifle from the swing loop. But they advanced with the appearance of confidence, for it was evident that they had been discovered by the men of the encampment.

Apparently they were identified as well as discovered. A tall man in leggings and moccasions, a flat felt hat over his long gray hair, stood gazing at them, his rifle butt resting on the ground. Suddenly he emitted an unearthly yell, whether of defiance or of greeting, and springing to his own horse's picket pin gathered in the lariat, and mounting bareback came on, his rifle high above his head, and repeating again and again his war cry or salutation.

Jackson rose in his stirrups, dropped his lead line and forsook more than a hundred and fifty thousand dollars some two mule-pack loads of gold. His own yell rose high in answer.

"I told ye all the world'd be here!" he shouted back over his shoulder. "Do-ee see that old thief Jim Bridger? Him I left drunk an' happy last summer? Now what in hell brung him here?"

The two old mountain men flung off and stood hand in hand before Banion had rescued the precious lead line and brought on the little train.

Bridger threw his hat on the ground, flung down his rifle and cast his stoic calm aside. Both his hands caught Banion's and his face beamed, breaking into a thousand lines.

"Boy, hit's you, then! I knowed yer hoss—he has no like in these parts. I've traced ye by him this hundred miles below an' up agin, but I've had no word this two weeks. Mostly I've seed that, when ye ain't lookin' fer a b'ar, thar he is. Well, here we air, fine an' fitten, an' me with two bottles left o' somethin' they call coggnac down in Yerba Buena. Come on in an' we'll make medicine."

They dismounted. The two Indians, short, deep-chested, bow-legged men, went to the packs. They gruntled as they unloaded the two larger mules.

The kyacks were lined up and the mantas spread over

them, the animals led away for feed and water. Bridger produced a ham of venison, some beans, a bannock and some coffee—not to mention his two bottles of fiery fluid—before any word was passed regarding future plans or past events.

"Come here, Jim," said Jackson after a time, tin cup in hand. The other followed him, likewise equipped.

"Heft this pannier, Jim."

"Uh-huh? Well, what of hit? What's inter hit?"

"Not much, Jim. Jest three-four hundred pounds o' gold settin' there in them four packs. Hit hain't much, but hit'll help some."

Bridger stooped and uncovered the kyacks, unbuckled the cover straps.

"Hit's a true fack!" he exclaimed. "Gold! Ef hit hain't, I'm a putrified liar, an' that's all I got to say!"

Now, little by little, they told, each to other, the story of the months since they had met, Bridger first explaining his own movements.

"I left the Malheur at Boise, an' brung along yan two boys. Ye needn't be a-skeered they'll touch the cargo. The gold means nothin' ter 'em, but horses does. We've got a good band ter drive north now. Some we bought an' most they stole, but no rancher cares fer horses here an' now.

"We come through the Klamaths, ye see, an' on south— the old horse trail up from the Spanish country, which only the Injuns knows. My boys say they kin take us ter the head o' the Willamette.

"So ye did get the gold! Eh, sir?" said Bridger, his eyes narrowing. "The tip the gal give ye was a good one?"

"Yes," rejoined Banion. "But we came near losing it and more. It was Woodhull, Jim. He followed us in."

"Yes, I know. His wagons was not fur behind ye on the Humboldt. He left right atter ye did. He made trouble, huh? He'll make no more? Is that hit, huh?"

Bill Jackson slapped the stock of his rifle in silence. Bridger nodded. He had been close to tragedies all his life. They told him now of this one. He nodded again, close lipped.

"An' ye want courts an' the settlements, boys?" said he. "Fer me, when I kill a rattler, that's enough. Ef ye're touchy an' want yer ree-cord clean, why, we kin go below an' fix hit. Only thing is, I don't want ter waste no more time'n I kin help, fer some o' them horses has a ree-cord that ain't maybe so plumb clean their own selves. Ye ain't goin' out east—ye're goin' north. Hit's easier, an' a month er two closter, with plenty o' feed an' water—the old Cayuse trail, huh?

"So Sam Woodhull got what he's been lookin' fer so long!" he added presently. "Well, that simples up things some."

"He'd o' got hit long ago, on the Platte, ef my partner hadn't been a damned fool," confirmed Jackson. "He was where we could a' buried him nach'erl, in the sands. I told Will then that Woodhull'd murder him the fust chancet he got. Well, he did—er ef he didn't hit wasn't no credit ter either one o' them two."

"What differ does hit make, Bill?" remarked Bridger indifferently. "Let bygones be bygones, huh? That's the pleasantest way, sence he's dead.

"Now here we air, with all the gold there ever was molded, an' a hull two bottles o' coggnac left, which takes holt e'enamost better'n Hundson's Bay rum. Ain't it a perty leetle ol' world to play with, all with nice pink stripes er-roun' hit?"

He filled his tin and broke into a roaring song:

> There was a ol' widder which had three sons—
>   Joshiway, James an' John.
> An' one got shot, an' one got drowned,
> An' th' last un got losted an' never was found—

"Ain't hit funny, son," said he, turning to Banion with cup uplifted, "how stiff likker allus makes me remember what I done fergot? Now Kit told me, thar at Laramie—"

"Fer I'm goin' out to Oregon, with my wash pan on my knee!" chanted Bill Jackson, now solemnly oblivious of most of his surroundings and hence not consciously discourteous to his friends; "Susannah, don't ye cry!"

They sat, the central figures of a scene wild enough, in a world still primitive and young. Only one of the three remained sober and silent, wondering, if one thing lacked, why the world was made.

Chapter XLV

THE LIGHT OF THE WHOLE WORLD

At the new farm of Jesse Wingate on the Yamhill the wheat was in stack and ready for the flail, his deer-skin sacks made ready to carry it to market after the threshing. His grim and weather-beaten wagon stood, now unused, at the barnyard fence of rails.

It was evening. Wingate and his wife again sat on their little stoop, gazing down the path that led to the valley road. A mounted man was opening the gate, someone they did not recognize.

"Maybe from below," said Molly Wingate. "Jed's maybe sent up another letter. Leave it to him, he's going to marry the most wonderful girl! Well, I'll call it true, she's a wonderful walker. All the Prices was."

"Or maybe it's for Molly," she added. "Ef she's ever heard a word from either Sam Woodhull or—"

"Hush! I do not want to hear that name!" broke in her husband. "Trouble enough he has made for us!"

His wife made no comment for a moment, still watching the stranger, who was now riding up the long approach, little noted by Wingate as he sat, moody and distrait.

"Jess," said she, "let's be fair and shame the devil. Maybe we don't know all the truth about Will Banion. You go in the house. I'll tend to this man, whoever he may be."

But she did not. With one more look at the advancing figure, she herself rose and followed her husband. As she passed she cast a swift glance at her daughter, who had not joined them for the twilight hour. Hers was the look of the mother—maternal, solicitious, yet wise and resolved withal; woman understanding woman. And now was the hour for her ewe lamb to be alone.

Molly Wingate sat in her own little room, looking through her window at the far forest and the mountain peaks in their evening dress of many colors. She was no longer the tattered emigrant girl in fringed frock and mended moccasins. Ships from the world's great ports served the new market of the Columbia Valley. It was a trim and trig young woman in the habiliments of sophisticated lands who sat here now, her heavy hair, piled high, lighted warmly in the illumination of the window. Her skin, clear white, had lost its sunburn in the moister climate between the two ranges of mountains. Quiet, reticent, reserved—cold, some said; but all said Molly Wingate, teacher at the mission school, was beautiful, the most beautiful young woman in all the great Willamette settlements. Her hands were in her lap now, and her face as usual was grave. A sad young woman, her Oregon lovers all said of her. They did not know why she should be sad, so fit for love was she.

She heard now a knock at the front door, to which, from her position, she could not have seen anyone approach. She called out, "Come!" but did not turn her head.

A horse stamped, neighed near her door. Her face changed expression. Her eyes grew wide in some strange association of memories suddenly revived.

She heard a footfall on the gallery floor, then on the floor of the hall. It stopped. Her heart almost stopped with it. Some undiscovered sense warned her, cried aloud to her. She faced the door, wide-eyed, as it was flung open.

"Molly!"

Will Banion's deep-toned voice told her all the rest. In terror, her hands to her face, she stood an instant, then sprang toward him, her voice almost a wail in its incredulous joy.

"Will! Will! Oh, Will! Oh! Oh!"

"Molly!"

They both paused.

"It can't be! Oh, you frightened me, Will! It can't be you!"

But he had her in his arms now. At first he could only push back her hair, stroke her cheek, until at last the rush of life and youth came back to them both, and their lips met in the sealing kiss of years. Then both were young again. She put up a hand to caress his brown cheek. Tenderly he pushed back her hair.

"Will! Oh, Will! It can't be!" she whispered again and again.

"But it is! It had to be! Now I'm paid! Now I've found my fortune!"

"And I've had my year to think it over, Will. As though the fortune mattered!"

"Not so much as that one other thing that kept you and me apart. Now I must tell you—"

"No, no, let be! Tell me nothing! Will, aren't you here?"

"But I must! You must hear me! I've waited two years for this!"

"Long, Will! You've let me get old!"

"You old?" He kissed her in contempt of time. "But now wait, dear, for I must tell you.

"You see, coming up the valley I met the Clerk of the Court of Oregon City, and he knew I was headed up for the Yamhill. He asked me to serve as his messenger. 'I've been sending up through all the valley settlements in search of one William Banion,' he said to me. Then I told him who I was. He gave me this."

"What is it?" She turned to her lover. He held in his hands a long package, enfolded in an otter skin. "Is it a court summons for Will Banion? They can't have you, Will!"

He smiled, her head held between his two hands.

" 'I have a very important document for Colonel William Banion,' the clerk said to me. 'It has been for some time in our charge, for delivery to him at once should he come into the Oregon settlements. It is from His Excellency, the President of the United States. Such messages do not wait. Seeing it of such importance, and knowing it to be military, Judge Lane opened it, since we could not trace the addressee. If you like—if you are, indeed, Colonel William Banion'—that was what he said."

He broke off, choking.

"Ah, Molly, at last and indeed I am again William Banion!"

He took from the otter skin—which Chardon once had placed over the oilskin used by Carson to protect it—the long and formal envelope of heavy linen. His finger pointed—"On the Service of the United States."

"Why, Will!"

He caught the envelope swiftly to his lips, holding it there an instant before he could speak.

"My pardon! From the President! Not guilty—oh, not guilty! And I never was!"

"Oh, Will, Will! That makes you happy?"

"Doesn't it you?"

"Why, yes, yes! But I knew that always! And I know now that I'd have followed you to the gallows if that had had to be."

"Though I were a thief?"

"Yes! But I'd not believe it! I didn't! I never did! I could not!"

"You'd take my word against all the world—just my word, if I told you it wasn't true? You'd want no proof at all? Will you always believe in me in that way? No proof?"

"I want none now. You do tell me that? No, no! I'm afraid you'd give me proofs! I want none! I want to love you for what you are, for what we both are, Will! I'm afraid!"

He put his hands on her shoulders, held her away arms' length, looked straight into her eyes.

"Dear girl," said he, "you need never be afraid any more."

She put her head down contentedly against his shoulder,

her face nestling sidewise, her eyes closed, her arms again quite around his neck.

"I don't care, Will," said she. "No, no, don't talk of things!"

He did not talk. In the sweetness of the silence he kissed her tenderly again and again.

And now the sun might sink. The light of the whole world by no means died with it.

Available by mail from

TOR
FORGE

1812 • David Nevin
The War of 1812 would either make America a global power sweeping to the pacific or break it into small pieces bound to mighty England. Only the courage of James Madison, Andrew Jackson, and their wives could determine the nation's fate.

PRIDE OF LIONS • Morgan Llywelyn
Pride of Lions, the sequel to the immensely popular *Lion of Ireland,* is a stunningly realistic novel of the dreams and bloodshed, passion and treachery, of eleventh-century Ireland and its lusty people.

WALTZING IN RAGTIME • Eileen Charbonneau
The daughter of a lumber baron is struggling to make it as a journalist in turn-of-the-century San Francisco when she meets ranger Matthew Hart, whose passion for nature challenges her deepest held beliefs.

BUFFALO SOLDIERS • Tom Willard
Former slaves had proven they could fight valiantly for their freedom, but in the West they were to fight for the freedom and security of the white settlers who often despised them.

THIN MOON AND COLD MIST • Kathleen O'Neal Gear
Robin Heatherton, a spy for the Confederacy, flees with her son to the Colorado Territory, hoping to escape from Union Army Major Corley, obsessed with her ever since her espionage work led to the death of his brother.

SEMINOLE SONG • Vella Munn
"As the U.S. Army surrounds their reservation in the Florida Everglades, a Seminole warrior chief clings to the slave girl who once saved his life after fleeing from her master, a wife-murderer who is out for blood." —*Hot Picks*

THE OVERLAND TRAIL • Wendi Lee
Based on the authentic diaries of the women who crossed the country in the late 1840s. America, a widowed pioneer, and Dancing Feather, a young Paiute, set out to recover America's kidnapped infant daughter—and to forge a bridge between their two worlds.